SECOND CHANCE

GREGORY BYRNE

ISBN 978-1-954345-98-0 (paperback)
ISBN 978-1-954345-99-7 (digital)

This is a work of fiction. All of the characters, organizations, places, locations in this novel are either products of the author's imagination or are used fictionally

Rushmore Press LLC
1 800 460 9188
www.rushmorepress.com

Printed in the United States of America

CHAPTER 1

He checks himself one last time in the bathroom vanity. He blinks several times, not recognizing the man looking back at him. The wavy, collar-length black wig completes the transformation. With the wig, his favorite polarized sunglasses, and a baseball hat, he's virtually unrecognizable. Even an observer with a trained eye would not recognize him. That's vitally important because he's in it for the long haul—or, as those idiotic motivational speakers would say, he's in it to win it. The game has proven to be everything he hoped it would be, which makes sense. He created it, makes all the rules, dictates who the players are, and, most importantly, dictates who the targets are.

He walks over to the perfect little bar setup the maître d' prepared for him when he checked into the room. That is one of the many reasons he always stays at the Peninsula when visiting New York City, although it doesn't hurt that the hotel bar downstairs attracts some of New York's finest, most highly prized escorts. His $2,500 choice last night was worth every penny: as limber as a gymnast and an aficionado of the *Kama Sutra*. He behaved himself, albeit reluctantly, because today is too important, too integral to the overall plan.

Still, it was fun.

Licking his lips and letting out a huge sigh, he snaps back to the present.

After pouring three fingers of Jameson, he takes a seat in front of the TV. Sure, it's only 8:45 in the morning, but the task before him is formidable, and alcohol calms him and helps him focus. It doesn't have the same effects on him as it does on other people. In fact, he relies on alcohol to quiet the demons that torment his mind to a greater and greater degree each day.

The burn in the back of his throat is soothing and familiar, and the taste, as far as he's concerned, is the nectar of the gods.

He has to be down at Thirty-Second and Second in a little more than an hour. Today's movie of choice is *The Seventh Son*. It's not something he'd normally choose, but the time frame ensures a nearly empty theater, and the mature content increases the likelihood of potential captive victims. It has to. He has invested too much time in scouting the area, the theater especially, for it to fail. He has taken a few days off work at a time when his supervisor's foot is knee deep in his ass over his workload. The bureaucratic moron is really starting to get on his nerves. In fact, all the people he works with are morons.

It's time for a quick accessory check. He taps his ankle holster, where the .38 snub nose resides, its presence calming and reassuring. He would rather have his Glock, but concealment is too important today. He can't afford to go naked, though.

He takes some time to admire his outfit. The pin-striped Armani suit is expertly tailored, the off-pink French-cuff Turnbull and Asser shirt is stunning, and the Brioni tie makes the whole package pop.

Damn. Even disguised, I'm an incredible specimen.

He gets up to pour another small one. Why not? He has time, and rushing isn't his style. No, not at all. Moments like this need to be savored, placed in the memory bank, just as a fantastic sexual encounter should be. He likes to take his time to prolong the experience. It makes reliving it much easier and much more vivid.

That thought prompts him to reflect on Albany, his last theater experience.

Albany was great—no doubt about it—but it had its fair share of mishaps. Certainly, it was not the success that Philly had been. First of all, choosing a children's movie was stupid and over the top.

He just wasn't able to resist. The thought of hot nannies, mommies, and babysitters—whatever—was too enticing.

His execution was less than stellar. It was downright poor—amateurish. Circumstances played a huge role in that, but even so, he had always been a perfectionist, and he knew the business inside and out.

He arrived late. The theater was fairly crowded, and he was forced to make a choice that turned out to be unfortunate. Actually, it was the only option, but looking back, that didn't make it any better. He never would have gotten a chance to execute the plan if the little girl hadn't made the nanny take her to the bathroom thirty minutes into the movie. Yeah, it was dumb luck that the hot mommy had five minutes all to herself.

Well, not all to herself.

The memory makes him laugh out loud.

In Albany, the pressure of time forced him to act much more quickly than he would have liked. He barely got to savor that last gasp, the choking gurgle of desperation, the eye-bugging glimpse of the end. Sexual gratification during the act itself was not possible, given the time constraints and the effects of all his other mistakes.

Still, Albany was a necessary part of his evolution, a coming-of-age transformation that had been years in the making. Today will be different—incredible. Kips Bay is going to put him on the map. It will be his coming-out party, guaranteeing him center stage—a place he has long been destined to occupy—via all major media outlets.

More importantly, Kips Bay will give him a prominent place in the annals of horror.

He gets up quickly, excited to get the show underway, the bulge in his pants noticeable as he walks by the mirror. He opts to walk to the theater rather than take a cab—an easy decision, really. He has more time to prepare and less chance to fail. He's on autopilot now, with excitement coursing through his veins. He can't wait for the aftermath—the notoriety, the respect, and, most importantly, the fear.

The Movie Theater Killer has arrived.

+ + + + + +

He is careful, even while walking the sidewalk south on Second Avenue. Cameras are everywhere today, and he's incredibly proficient at identifying them—as he should be. He has made this exact walk no fewer than ten times in the last two days alone. If he is to be the best, nothing can be left to chance. The smallest, most minute detail can make the difference between success and failure. Sure, it helps that he is smarter than everyone else. Shit, he is a Harvard graduate, and he didn't even have to apply himself to achieve that. But there are no guarantees, especially in this business.

He glances from side to side, noting landmarks he can pinpoint with his eyes closed: the Empire Deli, New York Sports Club, Starbucks, Dunkin' Donuts, Chipotle, the Coffee Bean and Tealeaf, TD Bank, Profit, and the Waterfront Ale House. If all goes well, he will have a Jameson and a Sierra Nevada at the Waterfront before celebrating at Dock's Seafood and Oyster Bar nearby on Third.

The Kips Bay Loews Cineplex has been a neighborhood attraction for as long as he's been coming to New York. It offers a far more user-friendly experience than some of Manhattan's other behemoth theaters. He feels comfortable here, at home, even though home is some 175 miles away.

He buys his ticket from one of the self-serve kiosks to avoid human interaction. He's diligent about averting his face from the cameras; at least he swerves any direct shot. The cameras are everywhere, so this takes constant focus, but he's used to that.

His movie is showing in theater eight, so he rides the escalator up to the second floor. He smiles amiably at the pimple-faced moron who takes his ticket, knowing this jackass won't remember him five minutes from now anyway. With his head down, he walks directly to the men's room. This is a risky move, a stupid move even, but he is compelled to take one last look at himself. He just can't help it.

Damn, I look good.

He enters theater eight, taking care to avert his gaze from the security camera above the entrance. The advertising for coming attractions is about to begin.

He is a coming attraction. He is going to be famous. Soon he will be someone everybody knows and fears.

When he rounds the corner to the floor-level seating, he glances up to the left.

There is no need to go any farther.

A lone female is sitting way up on the left, all by herself, in the second-to-last row. She looks youngish and attractive—exactly what he looks for. If the scenario would not present itself, he would move on to another movie.

He heads up the steep staircase. Why would someone choose to sit so far back? Chuckling, he goes all the way to the last row and takes a seat, not directly behind her but two seats down on the right.

She's wearing scrubs, so she's probably a nurse or doctor at the liberal, left-wing NYU Medical Center right around the corner.

Perfect. Just perfect.

She spends most of the first twenty minutes of the movie firing off texts on her cell phone. When she finally settles into the movie, he gives it another few minutes and then makes his move.

He has already readied the hypodermic needle. He crawls a short distance to the left to position himself directly behind her. With catlike agility and speed, he plunges the hypodermic needle filled with succinylcholine—sux for short—exactly where it needs to go. Then his hand is around her mouth, and once it becomes evident the paralytic has taken effect, he quietly makes his way to the seat on her right.

The fun is just beginning.

CHAPTER 2

It's November 2, 2019, a day I've been looking forward to for some time. Today is the day I leave rehab.

I've been holed up for the last thirty-one days at Caron Rehabilitation and Addiction Treatment Center in Wernersville, Pennsylvania, but now I, Declan "Deke" O'Brien, FBI special agent extraordinaire, am being put among the general population. Wow. It feels as if I've been here for a year, and it feels incredible to be heading home.

Home is Washington, DC—tony Georgetown, to be precise. I love the vitality and history of the neighborhood, and it's only about forty miles from where I work, which is the National Center for the Analysis of Violent Crimes (NCAVC), at the FBI Academy in Quantico, Virginia. NCVAC gets to the root of the motivations that drive crime. Our work supports high-profile federal, state, local, and international law enforcement agencies that are investigating repetitive violent crimes, threats of violence, terrorism, and a variety of other cruel acts. It comprises five Behavioral Analysis Units (BAUs). I'm in the second, BAU-2, which focuses on unusual criminal offenses, such as mass murders, serial rape cases, and kidnapping. I've spent the last eleven years there, although it feels like a lifetime.

I've seen far more horrors and evil than any individual should have to endure. I've profiled and apprehended some of America's most memorable and notorious serial killers. Unlike the rest of my unit, who collaborate with FBI special agents across the nation on research and training at the National Academy and are not involved operationally in cases, my partner and I have been given the unique opportunity to get down and dirty in the field. I love my job—I can't imagine another job I'd rather have—but its daily stresses can take a huge toll on one's well-being. It's these very stresses, however, that get my blood pumping and my ass out of bed every morning. To be good at the job—and I am—you need to make it your life without completely making it your life, as confusing as that may sound. It's like walking a tightrope: if you lean too far one way or the other, you fall.

It was my alcoholism that finally got me placed on indefinite administrative leave from work. The powers that be strongly recommended I seek in-patient treatment for my issues with drink, and the myriad other issues I was obviously dealing with, if I were to have any hope of returning to active duty. To be honest, had it not been for my ability to get inside the minds of serial killers and eventually catch them, which was celebrated across the nation, my job would have been taken away long ago.

Will I be allowed to return to active duty with the FBI? I don't know. Thinking about it causes crippling stress, so I try not to. I'm scheduled to meet with my supervisor in fourteen days to discuss my return. The thought of losing my job is downright terrifying. It's what I do and all I know. God gave me this uncanny ability to get inside the mind of a serial killer. I wouldn't wish this gift on anyone, but sometimes I feel that using it is the only thing I've done right in this life, the sole reason I was put here. If that sounds egotistical, it's not meant to; it's just what I believe.

My journey to Caron began thirty-one days ago, when family and friends staged an intervention that saved my life. Together with work's not-so-subtle suggestion—it was more of a demand, really— their joint action sealed my fate.

That fate had been several hard, often painful years in the making. Some might even argue it had been building for a lifetime, despite my growing up with perfect parents and five equally perfect siblings, having two beautiful kids, and enjoying every possible advantage one could hope for. Yet when I look to pinpoint causes, reasons, or justifications, a long list of possibilities comes to mind.

A little more than four years ago, my son, Patrick, suffered a traumatic brain injury. He was pushed—well, thrown, really—off a slide by another child at a playground in our neighborhood. I was there when it happened. Patrick was my responsibility, and I failed him in the worst way imaginable. I'm not sure I'll ever be able to forgive myself. Patrick suffered profound, permanent brain impairment on that day, so he'll never be able to live on his own and will always need round-the-clock care.

To say that event turned my life upside down is insulting in its understatement. It changed my life. How could it not have? But to describe in words how it changed me isn't possible, at least not yet. Many people, my loved ones included, have identified that event as the cataclysmic spark that prompted my downward spiral.

But saying that wouldn't be fair to Patrick, and to be honest, it wouldn't be true. Patrick is a beautiful, wonderful little boy today, and I can't imagine my life without him. His infectious smile, happy approach to every day, and purity of heart defy any attempt to describe them in words. Going away for a bit helped me to realize this and to be forever grateful for what God has so graciously given me.

In truth, my life had been on a steady downward spiral for more than five years leading up to my entering rehab. If it hadn't been for my work—profiling at the FBI, a job I love deeply—that spiral would have come to an abrupt end long ago.

But the day-to-day stresses of the job and the unspeakable horrors I have witnessed over the years have taken their toll. How could they not?

I have encountered evil personified. I find it hard to banish the memories of the killers I've hunted down, however much I try to force them back to the deep, dark depths of my mind where they belong, even when I close my eyes, hold my children, and try to find peace. Alcohol became an escape from the horrors—a temporary one, but I came to rely on it.

My wife—I mean my ex-wife—Catherine, and I divorced almost two years ago. Our marriage, however, was over way before that. I spent years drinking away the day's stresses, but there were too many stresses to wash down, most of them job-related, and I drank five times as much vodka and whiskey—anything I could get my hands on, to be honest—after Patrick's diagnosis. I went from having a lifelong love affair with alcohol to being completely out of control and impossible to be around. Unless I was at least mildly inebriated, I couldn't face my wife or my kids. Even Patrick's physical therapy on Saturday mornings became too much to handle sober. I never attended the music lessons of my daughter, Sean, without a covered thermos of vodka tonic disguised as coffee.

I didn't contest the divorce. I was ashamed of my reaction to Patrick's condition—really damn ashamed. Now I know that God truly blessed me by putting Patrick in my life.

I agreed to take care of my kids financially for the rest of their lives and gave Catherine our beautiful home in Chevy Chase, Maryland. She declined alimony, being an incredibly successful orthopedic surgeon in her own right. She didn't deserve any of the grief I gave her. I want the best for her. I really do. She's the most incredible person I've ever met and ever had the luxury of falling in love with.

A matter less important to my life's overall scheme is the fact that I'm the author of a highly successful series of murder-mystery books starring FBI special agent Sean Patrick. This success has afforded me luxuries I could only have dreamed of otherwise, as well as the ability to help others, even if only financially. Let's be clear, though: writing is a hobby, a welcome distraction from my life. It is not a job and remains a relatively unimportant matter in the grand scheme of things.

I can't argue with those who tell me I look and feel better today. I have my athletic and toned six-foot-two body back. Gone are the beer bloat and despair. I'm rested, healthy, and maybe even happy.

I feel guilty for feeling this way.

———— ✦✦✦✦✦ ————

I snap awake in the Lincoln Town Car that is taking me home from Caron Rehabilitation Center just as we are pulling into the driveway of my three-bedroom townhouse on Q Street in Georgetown. The stunning Georgetown gem is a short walk from Congress and Union Station and a quick cab ride to the Metro.

It feels surreal to be home. It seems like ages since I've been alone.

After unpacking, or at least attempting to unpack, I call my work partner, Louise D'Antoni, on her cell, craving any possible link to the job I love. As I expected, the call goes straight to voice mail.

"Louise, it's Deke. It's been a long time, girl. They took my cell phone away at the loony bin, and I was under strict instructions to follow the program—their program—whether I wanted to or not. Listen, I'm scheduled to meet with O'Shaughnessy in two weeks, but I guess you already know that. Hopefully I still have a job. I certainly don't deserve one, and I don't expect O'Shaughnessy to do me any favors. Anyway, give me a call when you get a chance. See ya."

CHAPTER 3

While I'm washing the dishes after my first home-cooked meal in a while, the phone rings, and I make no attempt to grab it or even look at it. I fear it could be Bridget, an SEC bigwig I've been seeing off and on for the last fourteen months. Lately, it's been significantly more off than on. I didn't even tell her I was checking into rehab. I also chickened out on calling her during my stay.

Fuck it.

She's a gorgeous five-foot-ten redhead, and I've had a lot of fun with her. She shares many of my interests, including golf, tennis, running, and, of course, sex. She's pretty decent in the sack, but something is definitely missing. Her rudeness to service staff in restaurants has always rubbed me the wrong way. Hell, come to think of it, she's rude to everyone.

So there's that—and the fact that she's just not Catherine. The heart wants what the heart can't have.

I check my work email for the first time in a month. The volume is low, which makes sense because everyone in my unit knows of my absence and the reason for it. There's a perfunctory note from my supervisor, Special Agent O'Shaughnessy, reminding me we're scheduled to meet in two weeks to discuss my potential return to work—*potential* being the operative word.

There's also an email from D'Antoni detailing what she's been working on for the last month. One of her investigations piques my curiosity.

She was pulled into a murder investigation ten days ago, an investigation into a possible serial killer who might be responsible for a murder spree conducted at movie theaters in Boston, Philadelphia, and Albany over the last eleven months. The investigation is ongoing, but little to no progress has been made in finding the killer.

That is why D'Antoni was brought in. Her profiling skills and experience with serial killers over the past decade rival mine.

Together we closed the Resort Killer investigation the month before I entered Caron. We profiled and helped to apprehend a truly psychopathic serial killer, Jeremiah Williams, who had murdered guests at resorts in upstate New York, Maine, New Hampshire, Massachusetts, and West Virginia over a period of almost twenty years.

Each of his victims was disemboweled, and their mutilated bodies were displayed on the beds in their rooms. The killer's rage further manifested itself in drawings inked in the victim's blood and scrawled on the walls. The liver and heart were always taken as macabre trophies. It was suggested yet never proved there had been an element of cannibalism to the murders.

In that case, a series of horrific events preceded the killer's transformation into a monster. He was raped and sodomized as a sixteen-year-old busboy at the Greenbrier Resort in West Virginia by one of the resort's well-heeled guests. Williams served drinks and lunch poolside on the weekends. His attacker lured him back to his suite with the promise of a generous tip for his services over the previous two days. Instead, a vicious attack ensued, and the boy was left forever mentally scarred.

The attacker was never prosecuted; instead, he paid Williams's family $20,000 to make the problem go away. The victim's family— destitute, downtrodden, and addiction-afflicted—were willing to accept financial reparation at the cost of their son's sanity. The attacker's good fortune was short-lived. He was himself murdered at the Greenbrier the very next summer—disemboweled and then laid out upon the king-sized bed in his room. It was among the most grisly murders in West Virginia's history. Williams, while questioned shortly after the murder in light of his employment at the Greenbrier, was not considered a viable suspect.

Mr. Williams was able to evade capture for twenty years thanks to his grifter lifestyle. He lived day to day on the periphery of society. He rarely held jobs that made him accountable to anyone other than himself. He never stayed in one place long enough to gain the attention of the authorities.

His fatal mistake was in performing some electrical work on the books for the Whiteface Inn Resort in Lake Placid, New York, in 2014, the same year a gruesome murder occurred at the resort. Having identified several damning pieces of evidence, D'Antoni and I were able to tie him back to the Greenbrier murder and some of the other resort murders via similar electrical work he'd done. He fit our profile perfectly: a white male aged between thirty-five and forty-five who likely was a loner and worked menial jobs. The individual had experienced significant physical and emotional abuse in his past.

CHAPTER 4

Sitting in my favorite leather recliner in front of the fireplace with a lukewarm cup of coffee and a pint of Ben and Jerry's Coffee Toffee Crunch within reach, I sift through emails before coming to one sent by D'Antoni.

In the email, D'Antoni has included a few details about the potential serial killer now under investigation:

> The latest killing occurred at the Regal Cinemas movie theater in Albany, New York. The victim was injected with a powerful paralytic and sexually assaulted. The MO in all the murders is the exact same. Immediately prior to death, each victim was texting during the movie. A forensic check of the phone records verifies this.
>
> Saliva and/or semen were recovered from crime scenes two, three, and four. The victim of the first murder had been sexually assaulted, but DNA wasn't recovered.

D'Antoni has closed the email with the following:

> I know you are still suspended, but I would appreciate your immediate input and assistance with the case. Call me tomorrow, jackass.

By the time I lie down in my king-sized bed, it's nearly midnight. It feels good to be back on my own schedule. I flip by an episode of *Criminal Minds*. Joe Mantegna is one of my favorite actors, but the show and reality are many miles apart. BAU-2 agents, with the unique exception of my partner and me, do not work operationally but, rather, assist special agents in the FBI's fifty-six field offices around the country as well as state and local police.

The next thing I know, the alarm is trilling, and it's six o'clock in the morning. I roll out of bed, throw on some sweats, lace up my aqua-blue Hoka running shoes, and head out for a jog.

It feels good to be able to run when I want to. That was not the case in rehab. Caron was pretty confining—downright claustrophobic, actually. A set schedule determined every day's activities, including workouts.

The five-mile run is exhilarating. I find that exercise sharpens both mind and body, and I use the time on the pavement or treadmill to reflect on cases I'm working on or plots and scenarios for my current book. Forty minutes later, I'm back at the townhouse, eager to commence the day.

After a steamy, long shower, I throw on a pair of my favorite Lucky jeans, a white button-down, and a pair of Bruno Mali loafers. My phone rings. I check the number ID and pick up the call on the third ring.

"D'Antoni, it's been a while. You miss me?"

"Fuck off, Deke. You didn't think to call once. I had to get weekly updates from your mother. That woman can talk and talk and talk. You deflower any rich, pill-addicted socialite on your little vacation?"

"You jealous? I miss you too. The facility took my cell phone, and I was given ten minutes a day on a landline, which I had to sign up in advance to use. What's up? You do realize I'm still suspended, right? Maybe permanently."

"O'Shaughnessy is not going to let you off that easily. It's a real boost to his morale to have a famous crime writer on his team. Meet me at the Froggy Bottom pub at seven. We can grab a burger and a beer—well, maybe not a beer—and catch up on the movie theater investigation. That work for you and your busy schedule?"

"See you there, dipshit."

I spend the remainder of the morning and all afternoon screwing around on the computer. Around four o'clock, I make the dreaded call to my publisher. I'm three months late with the latest installment of the Special Agent Sean Patrick series. I received a $750,000 advance almost a year ago. To say that my publisher, Connor Watson, is angry is the understatement of the year.

Connor picks up on the first ring. "Deke, please tell me you finished the book while you were away."

"Connor, I'm feeling great—thanks for asking. How are the wife and kids?"

"Cut the bullshit, Deke. My bosses are getting antsy. We expected the book months ago. It better be in good shape when our editors get a hold of it. When can we realistically expect it?"

"I should have a draft in four to six weeks."

"Two weeks it is then. Don't let me down, Deke. We'll never give you an advance again."

"I'll do my best."

Click. The line goes dead.

I arrive at the pub early and ask the waitress for a table at the rear. I sit with my back to the wall and enjoy a perfect view of the entire bar. The raucous buzz of the patrons and the smell of hot wings, burgers, and fries are all too familiar. I feel anxious, and my palms are sweaty.

Why the fuck do I feel like this?

I survey each shelf of booze in turn, spending the most time on the high-end stuff. Ketel One, Belvedere, Grey Goose, Johnnie Walker Blue, Oban, Macallan eighteen-year—these all used to be my friends. I know each of them intimately, and I miss them. The bottles beckon me, captivate me, and overflow with false promises.

I order a Diet Coke from the waitress, when what's really on the tip of my tongue is "A double Johnnie Black, neat, with a Guinness chaser." *Fuck, why can't I just be normal?* I must always look back to my last bender, a twenty-five-day booze fest spent locked in a shitty motel, hiding from the world. I had hit the lowest of lows.

D'Antoni walks in fifteen minutes later. I've been told I'm the ruggedly handsome sort. D'Antoni, however, is a dark-haired, olive-skinned Italian knockout. She's five feet eleven, and when she wears heels, which she doesn't do often, she's almost as tall as I am.

We hug. "Sorry I'm late. Traffic was a bitch."

"You mean your ninety-second walk was a bitch?"

She ignores the barbed comment. "So you cured?" she asks, looking around the bar. "Maybe this wasn't the smartest place to meet."

"To answer your first question, no, I'm still insane, but I now have the tools to deal with my insanity should I choose to do so. Secondly, this place is fine. They do make a hell of a cheeseburger. You getting laid these days, or is your vibrator still working overtime?"

"Never mind, you cretin. I never thought these words would come out of my mouth, but I've missed you."

"Oh, D'Antoni, it's touching to know you care."

We both order cheeseburgers medium rare and enjoy them in near silence. Having finished my last french fry, I get down to business.

"Tell me about the investigation."

She sighs. "I've only been on the case for a little over a week. It took these morons a long time to figure out that we may be dealing with a serial killer. We're dealing with one sick son of a bitch here, Deke. I mean sick. I want you just to listen without interrupting until I'm finished, okay? You can ask anything you want after you get the full picture."

I nod.

She opens a file and thumbs through it for about a minute. "The first murder happened twelve months ago in Boston, at a cinema near Fenway Park. The victim was a nineteen-year-old female, a Boston University theater student. She loved to go to the movies by herself. She attended a morning showing of *Halloween* on October 28, 2018.

"She texted a friend continuously for nearly twenty-five minutes straight after the movie started, talking about how predictable and stupid the movie was. The texting abruptly stopped, and she didn't resume for approximately twenty minutes. The only other text, the last one, says, 'This movie is the best I've ever seen. I'm touching myself. So wet.'

"We know that the victim was injected with a powerful paralytic, succinylcholine. It paralyzes all the muscles of the body, including those used for breathing. It works incredibly fast, often within seconds. Without ventilatory support, anyone administered a proper dose of the drug will die of asphyxia. Horribly, the victim was wide awake until she died, because sux causes muscular paralysis but has no sedative effects. In the medical community, it's used for anesthesia. Because it paralyzes the muscular system, it makes passing the endotracheal tube much easier. She could have been awake for as long as three minutes or more before losing consciousness and dying.

"She was completely defenseless, wide awake, and unable to call out for help. I cannot even imagine what must have been going through her head. Her fear must have been all-consuming, and the perp took full advantage of her helplessness. Her blouse and bra were ripped open, exposing her left breast. Her left nipple had been virtually bitten off.

"The second murder also occurred in Boston, on January 14, 2019. The victim was a middle-aged housewife. She attended a late-morning showing of *Glass*. The victim started texting a friend about fifteen minutes into the movie. The texting continued pretty regularly for the next thirty minutes. She tells her buddy that the movie is terrific and completely exceeding her expectations. There are no texts for almost twenty-five minutes. Then this last text is sent: 'I love her Brazilian wax job. Ha-ha!'

"She too was injected with sux in the upper right side of her neck."

D'Antoni sighs. "As with the first murder, the killer sexually assaulted the victim. The scumbag removed her panties and hiked her skirt up. Saliva was found on her face."

"What a sicko," I say.

"The third murder occurred in Philadelphia, on June 15, 2019. The victim went to a 10:40 a.m. showing of *Hustle*. Only three other patrons attended the movie, and all were seated in the front portion of the theater. The victim was seated toward the rear.

"She was injected with sux on the right side of her neck. The victim was sexually assaulted. Her pants and panties were pulled down, and the scumbag jerked off on her inner thigh. The DNA recovered matched the DNA from the second Boston murder and the Philly murder."

"The last murder occurred in Albany, New York, on October 28, 2019. The victim was a twenty-nine-year-old mother. She attended an early showing of the animated movie *Abominable* with her three-year-old daughter and the babysitter. There were very few additional patrons.

"Twenty minutes into the movie, the babysitter and daughter left the theater to use the restroom. It's assumed that at about the same time, the victim started texting her housekeeper. The text reads as follows: 'Nancy, please make sure to wash the linens in the master. Wash them real good because me and slugger fucked like bunnies last night.'

"The babysitter and daughter returned five minutes later to a horrific scene. The babysitter puked all over the body. Can you imagine a three-year-old coming back to that? Fucking animal.

"The victim was injected with sux on the right side of her neck and was sexually assaulted. Her pants and panties were removed, and saliva was found on her vaginal area. No matches to the DNA were found in VICAP, CODIS, or any database, for that matter, but the DNA was a ten-point match for the second and third murders.

D'Antoni's right. This isn't the perp's first go-around. He probably started his career as a Peeping Tom and matured into the demented sexual sadist we find today. Now he's comfortable carrying out his twisted fantasies in public in the middle of the day. And he's not afraid to leave his DNA behind. This is a highly confident, evolved killer.

"There's surveillance footage of the perp at all four theaters. The best footage was retrieved from the first Boston murder."

D'Antoni rifles through her notes. "Surveillance at the theaters shows a tall, athletic-looking adult male with wavy dark hair to the collar, nicely attired in a navy suit and tie. He's also wearing a ball cap and sunglasses at each scene, and he does a terrific job of hiding his face from the cameras. My guess is he scouted each location well in advance.

"Interestingly, the perp is only caught on surveillance entering the theaters—never leaving. In Albany, he was also caught entering the mall where the theater was located and at various points on his walk to the theater. At some point, though, he simply disappeared like a ghost. Nothing was left to chance."

She takes a sip of her soda. "This guy moved like a pro. He scouted these locations in advance. He knew where surveillance was located. He's not nervous—just the opposite. He appears confident and carefree. We know from DNA that the same person committed the second Boston, Philly and Albany murders. Per surveillance, it seems likely the same person committed all four murders."

D'Antoni sighs. "Thanks for not interrupting. Your thoughts, though rarely helpful, would be appreciated."

I clear my throat. "Sux used to be known as the world's most discreet and perfect murder weapon because it fully metabolizes into its by-products incredibly fast. Depending on the dose, it can be fully metabolized within ten minutes and is not present in the body on autopsy. It can be given via IV or as an intramuscular injection. Within seconds, the victim has trouble moving the eyes and fingers, followed shortly by the arms and legs. Loss of the ability to breathe soon follows. The victim is in a state of utter waking terror."

D'Antoni checks her notes. "No one knows when sux was first used as a murder weapon, but the first high-profile killings occurred in 1966 and 1967. The murders were committed by a Dr. Carl Coppolino, an anesthesiologist, who killed both his mistress's husband and his own wife using sux. If his mistress had not confessed to the police, Dr. Coppolino would most likely have walked at trial."

I interject. "Sux is broken down in the body extremely quickly. This makes it very difficult for crime labs. By the time they autopsy the body, there is no six left to test, and testing for it will prove negative. However, testing for the metabolite by-products of sux, like succinylmonocholine and choline acid, has proven successful. This testing was instrumental in attaining convictions in the Genene Jones, Kathy Augustine and Chaz Higgs cases. And let's not forget the case of Hamas operative Mahmoud al-Mabhouh, who was injected with sux before being tortured to death."

"I assume the ME in all the cases saw the injection marks on the victims' necks and tested for the metabolite by-products?" I say.

"Yes."

"How much information from the first murder reached the public?"

D'Antoni checks her notes. "A lot. The surveillance photos were shown on every major network both in Massachusetts and nationally, and the fact that sux was used was also broadcast by all the networks."

I crack my shoulder blades and then continue. "At the very least, we could be dealing with a primary killer and a copycat. However, surveillance certainly suggests one perp. Nothing else is jumping out at me other than that you might be dealing with a medical professional, possibly a doctor, because sux is not available on the street."

I rub my temple, thinking. "It's not crazy to imagine the killer's comfort level escalating with each murder. You need to spend some time with the witnesses in the fourth case. Our perp was seen. He must have been. When are you going to Albany?"

"Tomorrow first thing."

I nod. "The matter of witness identification is huge. Might be all you need to break it. It's rarely that easy, but who knows? Wish I was joining you." I mean that more than I can say.

"Bullshit. I know you haven't done dick on your new book. You need every bit of the next two weeks to write while the rest of us hump it working real jobs." She smiles. "I'll fill you in on what I learn when I get back to DC. I made you a copy of my file."

"Sounds good. Chow is on me. Try not to enjoy working solo too much. Maybe we would already have this guy if I was on the case with you."

"Yeah," D'Antoni says. "Something like that."

+ + + ♦ + + +

I take my time in walking back to my townhouse. I feel good—invigorated. My brain is firing again, and I have that triple-shot-of-espresso feeling. In the past, I used booze to even out that very feeling, but I don't want to even it out anymore. I like the electrical charge the job gives me. Writing doesn't give me the same jolt.

I enjoy writing, and I love my job with the FBI.

I flip through emails, and my heart skips a beat when I see one from my ex-wife, Catherine. She directs me to a video on her Facebook page. I open the video, and my whole world tilts on its axis.

My son Patrick is at school, with many other children with similar issues, and he's standing in front of his class. He is presenting a picture he has sketched from memory. It is a picture of the view from my back porch in Lake Placid, looking out toward the rear of Whiteface Mountain. It is stunningly realistic and has clearly been created by someone with talent—an artist. Patrick talks the class through virtually every detail of the breathtaking landscape, and when he finishes, the entire class stands and erupts into deafening applause. Patrick's wearing an ear-to-ear grin, beaming. He's as happy—and surprised—as I've ever seen him.

I watch the video over and over again. The next thing I know, my eyes are soaked with tears. I get down on my knees and thank God.

CHAPTER 5

At five thirty the next morning, I make a cup of coffee and settle before the kitchen table with the case file. I focus my attention on the first murder and turn first to the responding detective's account of the slaughter. It has been written by Detective William Slaughter.

> On October 28, 2018, at 1:40 p.m., my partner, Detective Tom Bronstein, and I were dispatched to the Regal Cinema Fenway 13 at 201 Brookline Avenue, Boston, Massachusetts. Upon arrival, I met with Officer William Clark, the first officer on the scene, who told me that an apparent homicide had occurred inside theater five. He indicated that no murder weapon was left at the scene. Officer Clark told me that he had sealed the entire perimeter of the crime scene with crime-scene tape and had called the coroner and emergency personnel. He also stated that Officer John Hart was posted at the front door of the cinema and was maintaining the crime-scene logbook.
>
> At twenty-five past twelve, Officer Hart handed over control of the crime scene. Detective Bronstein and I entered theater five through the front entrance. Officer Hart had both of us sign the log-in book before entering, so I scribbled my initials and badge number. The only name before mine in the logbook is the coroner's.
>
> The body of a female, Kathleen Higgins, was found seated in seat thirteen, row twenty-five, which is close to

the rear of the theater. Her lifeless body had been spotted after the movie ended by one of the other moviegoers, who reported it to theater personnel immediately. Officer Clark had retrieved her driver's license from her purse, which sat in her lap. I shone a flashlight on the body. Her head was tilted to the left; her face was bluish in color. Her eyes were open, staring.

The victim's shirt had been torn open, leaving her left breast exposed. Deep bite marks were visible on the left breast and nipple. A dark brown-colored liquid covered the ground around the body, and a plastic cup and several ice cubes lay in the liquid, which was likely soda. Popcorn was strewn everywhere, and there was a cell phone in the cup holder.

The theater was large and modern. The victim had been attending a 10:05 a.m. showing of *Halloween*. Only five people, including the victim, bought tickets to that showing. Three of the patrons were identified and interviewed at the scene by the responding officers. Each had taken a seat near the front of the theater. The other patron, the only male to attend, could not be found. He was described by the ticket taker as being white, tall, and athletic looking, with wavy, medium-length dark hair. He wore a suit and tie, ball cap, and sunglasses. We decided that theater surveillance would need to be looked at and that my partner and I would interview each of the witnesses again at headquarters.

Dr. Margot Brown, coroner of the City of Boston, confirmed that the victim was deceased and informally suggested there were no outward signs pointing to cause of death. Possibly the victim suffered a heart attack or some other pulmonary event. Dr. Brown stated that an autopsy would be performed to determine the actual cause of death.

Even though I knew she was dead, I placed a gloved finger to the victim's throat where her pulse would have been. Her flesh was still relatively warm to the touch, and I could just smell her perfume. The deceased was approximately five feet seven inches tall and well presented and I think had been attractive when alive. She had red hair to a length just below her shoulders. The coroner's attendants waited until I had finished my examination and then loaded the body onto a gurney for transportation to the morgue. Dr. Brown advised me that she would notify the family.

Detective William Slaughter
Badge number 145

The report is detailed and well written. I review the witness reports next; there is nothing terribly revealing. Only two of the other three attendees interviewed recall seeing anyone of interest.

In summary, the report indicates that Mary Shelby, a twenty-four-year-old nanny from Brookline, Massachusetts, attended the October 28 screening of *Halloween* with her friend Kristine Carbo. Both recall seeing a middle-aged man in a suit and tie enter the theater and take a seat near the back. Neither noticed him leave during the movie, nor did they see him after it ended. Even when pressed, neither could give any distinguishing characteristics. They were not even sure of the man's hair color because he was wearing a ball cap, and the lighting in the theater was dim.

I make a mental note that these witnesses should be reinterviewed. Pertinent facts are often uncovered upon later reflection.

Next, I move on to the coroner's report. I read through the detail, paying close attention to the coroner's summary and the time and cause of death.

Summary of Findings

Body temperature, rigor, livor mortis, and stomach contents indicate approximate time of death between 10:45 a.m. and 12:45 a.m. on October 28, 2018.

An injection mark was noted on the right side of victim's neck.

Also noted:

Scattered cutaneous petechiae

Bulbar and palpebrate subconjunctival petechial hemorrhage indicative of apnea

Severe pulmonary edema with pleural effusions

Multifocal petechial hemorrhage of the heart and lungs

Bite marks on left breast and nipple

Immediate cause of death: asphyxia due to introduction of a paralytic, succinylcholine, into victim's system via intramuscular injection.

Toxicology screen positive for high levels of succinylmonocholine and choline.

Manner of death: homicide.

I take time to digest the report and its implications. The use of sux, a drug used in the intubation process, is nothing new. The first reported cases were in 1966 and 1967. More recently, two tourists were killed in August 2014 with sux at a resort in Longboat Key, Florida.

In this case, the victim was injected with a lethal dose of succinylcholine. This would have caused paralysis of the muscles, including those used for breathing. Horribly, the victim was wide awake while the killer sexually assaulted her and did God knows what else, with no ability to scream or defend herself. She must have been utterly terrified and in great pain.

There was obviously a sexual element to the crime. The victim's left breast was exposed, her shirt having been ripped open, and there were clear bite marks around her nipple.

He's lucky there were so few other patrons in the theater and that the victim was seated way in the back. Still, this was a brazen act by the killer.

I continue to thumb through the file, taking notes as I go. The next document that catches my attention is an inventory of personal items recovered at the crime scene.

A cell phone was found in a cup holder next to the victim. Several texts were retrieved from it by the Boston Police Department's crime-scene techs, including nine that were sent and received by the victim between 10:05 and 11:08 on the morning of the murder. All were exchanged with Beverly Adams, a friend of the victim. I read through the victim's conversation with Beverly.

> 10:05: Hey, I took ur recommendation. I'm going to see *Halloween.*
>
> 10:08: Cool.
>
> 10:13: Movie is starting. I'm one of only a few people in the theater. Are you sure the movie is good?
>
> 10:18: Relax. U will love it.
>
> 10:25: What did u get me into?
>
> 10:29: What do u mean?
>
> 10:31: This is way too ridiculous for me.
>
> 10:34: God forbid u see something other than a romantic comedy.
>
> 10:56: The movie is making me wet. I'm touching myself.

Twenty-two minutes elapsed between the victim's last two texts. Before that, she was consistently texting approximately every five minutes. Her last text is way out of context. I've seen *Halloween*; it isn't a sexy movie. Scary? Yes. Sexy? No way.

A call to Detective Slaughter revealed that he interviewed Beverly Adams on March 11. She stated that she and the victim had been best friends since childhood. They saw each other, or communicated via phone or text, almost every day. She described Karen as being prim and proper and said there was no way Karen had drafted that final text.

I sit back down at the table with my salad and look at my notes.

The assailant must have been sitting behind the victim. He must have fled the scene shortly after the murder. No one recalls seeing a man in a suit and tie exit the theater. Maybe he snuck out through an emergency exit. Again, though, you'd think someone would have noticed. Maybe they were too engrossed in the movie.

I turn to the surveillance report in the file. My cell phone rings, causing me to jump.

The number is familiar: it's Supervisory Special Agent O'Shaughnessy.

I answer on the third ring. "O'Brien."

"Deke, it's O'Shaughnessy." I neglect to tell him I knew that. "I need to see you ASAP. Pack an overnight bag."

"Boss, am I missing something? I thought we were scheduled to meet in two weeks to discuss my job status."

"Something has come up—something big. Get here as quick as you can."

With that, he ends the call. O'Shaughnessy is a man of few words.

CHAPTER 6

Arriving back on the Quantico campus feels strange. Three security clearances later, I walk into my work area, a sea of cubes as far as the eye can see. O'Shaughnessy has an all-glass inner office that affords him a 360-degree view. I make a pit stop at my workstation, which is really just a glorified cubicle, to drop off my briefcase and laptop. I lock eyes with O'Shaughnessy, and he waves me in.

He's on the phone. He rolls his eyes and sighs. "Just get back here as soon as you can. Deke just walked in. This is such a clusterfuck. I want you and Deke tires up ASAP. Yeah. Just hustle!"

Click.

"Deke, you look a lot better than the last time I saw you." O'Shaughnessy smiles. "Take a seat. We need to talk."

"It's good to see you too, boss."

"Enough small talk, dipshit," O'Shaughnessy says. "I've got a real problem here. I need you to end your vacation, effective immediately, and come back to work. I hope you realize how lucky you are to still have a job."

"I know, boss. I—"

"Just listen," O'Shaughnessy says. "I've got some things to say, and you need to fucking listen. If the higher-ups had their way, you'd be on a permanent vacation. I really stuck my neck out for you. If you were a cat, you'd be on life number ten. I'm being serious here. No bullshit. You don't have any more chances. If you like your job, keep your nose clean. Have I made myself clear?"

"Yes, I really appreciate you going to bat for me."

"Just don't make me look stupid, Deke."

"I won't."

"We've got a real shit storm brewing here. There's been another movie theater killing. This one's even sicker than the others."

"Where?" I ask. "Do we know the same perpetrator is involved?"

"New York. Right in Kips Bay," O'Shaughnessy says. "There's an injection site on the right side of the victim's neck. He also left his calling card in her mouth. We should know soon if there's a match to the DNA recovered at the second, third and fourth murders, but the MO is the same. Granted, it could be a copycat, but I don't think so."

O'Shaughnessy stands, hands flailing, eyes blazing. "I just can't figure out how he goes unnoticed. It's a movie theater, for God's sake! Granted, there were only eight other people in the theater this time, and the victim was all by herself near the back, but still. There was real sickness demonstrated here. How the fuck does he pull it off?"

I pause before speaking, waiting to see if O'Shaughnessy is done. The coast is clear, so I add my two cents' worth. "He's obviously careful to a fault. He cases these joints well in advance. Looks for an isolated woman. He's a planner, motivated but patient. He's particular about the movies and theaters he chooses, and his DNA isn't on file. Also, sux acts incredibly fast, often within seconds. She would have been unable to utter a sound or defend herself. That being said, there's no way he wasn't seen by someone or captured on surveillance at the theaters. He's getting bolder and more confident with each killing. He feels a very personal connection with the victims; his choice of sux as a murder weapon clearly indicates this. He is free to do anything he wishes to the victims. The torture itself is his sexual release, his motivation to keep killing. He will not stop until he's caught." I pause. "Do you know—was the victim texting during the movie?"

"I don't know the details," O'Shaughnessy says. "All I know is the victim is a white thirty-five-year-old female. She apparently went to the movie alone, but who the fuck knows? Maybe she went with the perp."

O'Shaughnessy reflexively taps his chin, thinking. "You need to pay extra attention to any surveillance footage taken at the scene. He was captured in Boston, Philly and Albany. Not that it did any good. Pay careful attention to height, eye and hair color, what he's wearing, and his overall demeanor. All we know now is that he's tall, white, and well dressed. This guy is smart. He knows there are surveillance cameras—maybe even where they're sited. He probably staked out these theaters long before the killings. Whether we're dealing with a serial or copycat is irrelevant. We need to work up a profile ASAP. The media sharks are running 24-7."

"Boss, you chose me for a reason," I say. "D'Antoni and I will catch this sicko. We just need a little time."

O'Shaughnessy sits back down. "Time is a luxury we don't have. There's a great deal of public fear here, given the apparent random and motiveless nature of the crimes. People's lives are at stake, Deke. We need a profile of this son of a bitch. I don't need to tell you the pressure being placed on our unit from up high. Have D'Antoni update you on the other murders while you're on the plane."

"Yes, sir. She already gave me the executive summary." I stare intently at O'Shaughnessy. "This is what we do, boss. We'll get this guy."

"D'Antoni will be here in roughly ninety minutes," O'Shaughnessy says. "Use the time to go through the file. I need you to give me one hundred and ten percent here. Good luck. I want updates."

I get up to leave, and as I'm heading out the door, O'Shaughnessy stops me.

"Deke, it's good to have you back. The team needs you. Don't let us down. You're going to have to put your other career on hold for a while. Okay?"

"Yes, sir, and thanks again."

I grab a cup of crappy coffee in the lounge and head to my workstation, where I turn my attention to the surveillance photos from the first murder.

Eight men entered the main doors of the Cineplex between nine and ten thirty that morning. The only man to enter the theater showing *Halloween* was wearing a suit and tie. He was also wearing a ball cap and sunglasses. Even with the hat on, it's apparent he has wavy, medium-to-medium-long dark hair. He took care to avert his face from the camera.

The man is tall and athletic looking. Little else can be determined. There's no security footage of the man after he enters the theater.

While we likely have the perp on tape, I don't see how helpful the images will be.

The surveillance photos are grainy. That is definitely not helpful. The guy shown could be any tall guy in a nice suit, ball cap, and sunglasses. Like O'Shaughnessy said, it's obvious he knows there are surveillance cameras, and he's careful not to show too much of himself. I need to view the actual footage myself, but even so, I'm not optimistic.

D'Antoni and I will need to sit down with the two people who noticed the man in the theater. Maybe they saw something— anything—that's not evident on the security footage.

I take another pass through Detective Slaughter's report, amazed by the reckless, diseased actions this perp took without being perceived. Catching up with Slaughter in person is a priority. The file can only answer so many questions on its own.

I turn my attention to the second murder just as D'Antoni walks into the room. I give her a big smile. "Where's your overnight bag?"

She laughs sarcastically. "A road trip wasn't part of the plan this morning. I was told to get back here ASAP so I could brief you on all the cases on the flight to New York."

We're sitting in leather recliners toward the rear of the jet, facing each other. I thumb through the file.

"I've spent some time with the first murder. Can you brief me on the second, third and fourth murders? I think we're both on the same page with New York City. We don't know a lot."

D'Antoni flips through her file. "I'll do my best. Keep in mind I was only recently invited to the party. I know more about the third murder because I spent time on the ground in Albany, but I'll give you what I've got.

"The second murder also occurred in Boston, at the AMC Loews 19, Boston Common, at the United Artists Riverview Plaza, on January 14, 2018. The victim was a forty-year-old housewife from Brighton. She went to a 10:20 a.m. showing of *Glass*.

"Toxicology shows high levels of succinylmonocholine and choline, metabolites of sux, in the victim's bloodstream. The injection site was on the right side of the victim's neck, meaning our killer is likely right-handed and approached from behind.

"A forensic check of the victim's cell phone revealed that she texted one person, a friend, continuously from 10:40 to 11:15. In those texts, she says the movie is awesome. Then the texting stops. A final text is sent to the friend at 11:50, stating, 'I definitely shouldn't have cum alone. Ha-ha!'

"Surveillance footage only caught one man entering the theater. He did so approximately ten minutes after the movie started. He's tall and athletic looking. He's nicely attired in an expensive-looking suit and tie. He does a great job of averting his face from the surveillance camera. It appears he knew exactly where the cameras were. Just like the first Boston murder, there's no surveillance footage of him leaving the theater.

"Unlike Fenway, the killer left his DNA on the victim this time. Saliva was found all over the victim's face. Best guess is that this psychopath was licking the victim's face while she sat there helpless, or he did it postmortem."

I clear my throat. "The killer is escalating; he's getting more comfortable. Sure, he's taking more risks—he has to. He's a slave to his prurient desires."

"I know, I know," she says.

"Anything taken?" I ask.

"Nothing obvious. Her purse, cell phone, wallet, credit cards, cash, and jewelry were all accounted for."

"These guys usually take some sort of trophy so they can relive the experience."

"We should check with the husband."

"Agreed."

"The third murder occurred in Philadelphia, at the PFS Roxy Theater near Rittenhouse Square.

"She was injected with sux on the right upper side of her neck and was sexually assaulted. Her pants and panties were removed, and semen was found on her inner thigh. The scumbag jerked off on her. No matches to the DNA were found in VICAP, CODIS, or any database, for that matter, but the DNA was a ten-point match for the second murder.

"The babysitter may have gotten a good look at him. He took a seat directly behind her. The theater employee who took his ticket also provided a description, as did several other patrons. Unfortunately, they're all vague; none are particularly useful.

"He must have stuck out like a sore thumb. An adult male attending a little kids' movie alone is creepy, right?"

I stand up and stretch. "Very. We only have fifteen minutes till touchdown, so let's move on to Albany."

"The fourth murder occurred in Albany, New York, at the Criterion Cineplex at the Crossgates Mall. I know you are very familiar with the area."

"Yeah," I say. "When I went to Albany Law School, we went to a movie at that theater almost every Thursday night."

"The victim was injected with sux on the right side of her neck. She was sexually assaulted like the others. Her pants and panties were pulled down, and saliva was found on the vaginal area. The DNA recovered matched the DNA from the second Boston murder and the Philly murder."

"Toxicology showed large amounts of succinylmonocholine and choline acid in the victim's bloodstream. She would've been totally incapacitated."

D'Antoni glances out the window momentarily. The sun burns brightly, almost blindingly, and the clouds resemble big, fluffy white pillows that the plane balances upon. "This is the part that really gets to me. This sicko wasn't content merely killing these young woman, who were innocently sitting at the movies, minding her own business. Nope, he wasn't done having fun yet. He had to dominate, humiliate them, in the worst possible way. She turns away from the window, once more facing me. "And no fucking DNA matches."

✦✦✦✦✦✦

His mind drifts in and out of the present. He's back at Rayburn House, a group home for adolescents aged fourteen to eighteen. He lived there for a little more than three years. The home was supposed to prepare misguided youths for return to their families, foster care, or independent living. In reality, the home gave him much more.

Services at Rayburn House were supposed to include individual, group, and family psychotherapy and health-care advice. What a joke. The only service he got from the home in his first two years was the experience of being bullied, beaten, and sexually assaulted. The third year, though—now, that was a year to remember.

Initially, he was the smallest boy in the home. He was five feet four and slight until he was seventeen. In the summer of that year, which would turn out to be his last summer at Rayburn, he grew eight inches and filled out. Physically, he had been unable to defend himself from the beatings, humiliation, and sexual assaults. He wasn't completely helpless, though. Far from it.

He was the brightest adolescent in the home, and he knew it. He spent the majority of his waking hours thinking of ways to embarrass, humiliate, and torment his housemates or the people or things they loved. He was damn good at it.

He remembers every single day he spent in that home. One day in particular stands out more than the others. It still gives him nightmares, frequently jarring him awake to find the sheets soaked with sweat, his eyes wide with terror. It was August 18, 1996, his first summer at Rayburn, a hot day, ninety-six degrees and humid.

One of the house counselors, Jimmy Collins, a useless excuse for a human life if there ever was one, volunteered to take all of the residents to a public pool within walking distance of the home. He jumped at the chance, even though he didn't know how to swim. The house had no air-conditioning, and the thought of seeing cute girls in bikinis was too enticing to miss.

He spent the first couple hours splashing around in the shallow end of the pool. Mostly, he leered at the scantily clad girls and women. He felt on top of the world.

The feeling was short-lived. Toward the end of the day, he and a group of other kids from the home congregated near some chairs next to the deep end of the pool. There was a lot of pushing, shoving, and horsing around. He joined right in.

He forcibly shoved one of the girls from the home. She nearly fell into the pool but managed to regain her balance at the last second. Her name was Jane Martin; she was seventeen and attractive, with a real wild side. He pushed her from the front, his hands lingering on her small but perfect breasts. The feeling was incredible.

It was also gone in an instant.

She grabbed him with both hands, lifted him off the ground, and flung him into the deep end of the pool. Then she walked away and never looked back.

He sank like a rock. He tried to hold his breath, confident someone would save him. The seconds ticked by, and his terror grew, the pressure in his head building.

The pounding in his head grew in a crescendo. He began thrashing back and forth, his eyes bugging out of his head. When the pain became unbearable, he opened his mouth to scream. Water filled his lungs. His chest felt as though it would explode.

Then, mercifully, everything went dark.

When he came to, he had no idea where he was. He was in a drab, plain, medicinal-smelling room. A small TV was suspended from the wall. Electronics and machines hummed and beeped all around him. Some kind of tube was stuck in his throat; it was huge and prevented him from talking or screaming. The machine the tube was attached to beeped at two-second intervals. His eyes darted from side to side, and he clutched the apparatus attached to his throat, debating whether to tear it out. He felt as if he would choke to death.

Just then, a woman dressed entirely in white walked into the room. She inserted something into a tube attached to his arm. Within seconds, a warm haze enveloped him, and everything went dark once more. When he next awoke, his throat felt raw and sore. He tried to speak and found his voice was hoarse and raspy, barely a whisper.

"Where am I?"

Thankfully, the tube in his throat was gone. A man in a white coat with his name inscribed on the top pocket, obviously a doctor, and a pudgy gray-haired nurse with an open, caring face were standing to the left of his bed. They stared at him intently. The women held his hand.

"Welcome back, dear. You've slept for nearly two days. You must be very hungry." Her voice was calm and soothing. No one had ever spoken to him that way before, and it made him feel strange. The nurse continued. "I'm sure your throat is sore from being intubated, but I can get you something that won't irritate it any further. I'll be right back. What would you like to drink?"

"Juice, please," he managed to squeak out. She nodded and left the room.

The doctor then turned to him. "How do you feel?"

"Okay, I guess," he squeaked.

"You're extremely lucky. Another minute under water, and we wouldn't be having this conversation. What were you thinking of, jumping into the deep end, knowing you can't swim?"

"I didn't fucking jum—"

He never got to finish that sentence. The doctor had already left.

CHAPTER 7

Just before four o'clock in the afternoon, we touch down at Teterboro, where a black Suburban is waiting on the runway to rush us into Midtown. The sun is almost completely down; there are maybe twenty minutes of daylight left.

For those lucky enough not to have to fly commercial, Teterboro is an awesome alternative to the hustle and bustle, maddeningly long waits, and overall agitation of LaGuardia and JFK. There are no security lines or long walks; you simply exit your plane and get in your car.

In the backseat of the Suburban is Christopher Griffith, the head of the New York field office and my best friend. He's also close with D'Antoni. In fact, I'm fairly certain they've been more than friends at some point, but neither is the kiss-and-tell type.

I've not seen or talked to Griff since heading to rehab. We clap each other on the back and catch up for a few minutes. He's too good a friend to pry into the catastrophe that's been my life recently.

After a few minutes of small talk, Griff gets down to business. "I know you guys are running point on this, and I can't think of anyone better to head up the investigation, but I would really appreciate it if you could keep me informed at all points and let me have a seat in the inner circle."

His eyes dart nervously, first to D'Antoni and then to me. "I know I didn't even have to ask; it's just that I'm under an enormous amount of pressure. The city's in an uproar. People are afraid. Every major national network has set up shop outside the Kips Bay Loews."

"Of course," we say in near unison.

He lets out an audible sigh. "I'm giving a press conference tonight at seven. I've no idea what I'm gonna say."

D'Antoni interjects. "I made a copy of our case file on the other three murders for you. As far as the press conference is concerned, I would limit the discussion to the fact that you have a dedicated team on the ground, working the case 24-7, and the odds favor our catching him."

"I agree," I say. "I would deflect any questions about potential suspects—for obvious reasons."

"Thanks, guys. Would you like to be a part of the press conference?"

I laugh. "As much as I like to see myself on TV, we need to process the scene and conduct interviews. I don't see us getting a lot of sleep tonight, so I'm afraid you're on your own, cowboy." I pause. "What can you tell us about this one?"

"I probably don't know much more than you do. The victim is a thirty-five-year-old female named Anne Richards. She attended the 10:45 a.m. showing of *Knives Out* alone. Security footage confirms this. The responding officers are still at the scene and will be able to provide you with far more detail than I can."

The car, lights blazing, barely slows down as we sail through the toll plaza at the George Washington Bridge. Fifteen minutes later, we're idling curbside by the Kips Bay Loews Cineplex.

A wave of nostalgia hits me; I lived in this neighborhood with Catherine for nearly five years, and we frequented the Kips Bay theater on a regular basis. We both loved catching a matinee on a rainy Saturday or Sunday.

We were truly happy then. We had bought our first house, a vacation home in Lake Placid. We made the five-hour drive most weekends when free and spent our vacation time fly-fishing and hiking the Adirondacks. Everyone thought we were crazy to buy a weekend getaway place before we bought a primary residence. We didn't care. We were happy and in love.

Around that time, I got my first book in the Sean Patrick series published. Financial security came quickly, and I dreamed of moving to Lake Placid with Catherine to live there full-time while we were still young.

Instead, we exchanged New York City for the stuffy confines of Chevy Chase, Maryland; life in suburbia on steroids; and my new role as a profiler with the BAU. Catherine was happy about the move; she felt that New York City was no place to raise children. I didn't necessarily agree, but I was willing to do anything to make Catherine happy.

The shame, guilt, and pain I feel over choices I made then will probably be with me forever. I don't deserve forgiveness, and I certainly don't deserve to have Catherine, Sean, or Patrick back in my day-to-day life.

I snap out of my walk down shitty memory lane just as we approach the Cineplex entrance. I've taken this walk more times than I could ever count. Crime-scene tape seals the entire perimeter, and an NYPD officer is stationed at the entrance.

We flash our badges. "I'm Supervisory Special Agent O'Brien of the FBI, and these are Supervisory Special Agents D'Antoni and Griffith. We've been called in to assist the investigation."

"I'm Officer Lisa Raymond of the Seventeenth Precinct," she says. "We were told to expect you. Go on in. Detective Frank Mullaney is heading up the investigation."

As I walk through the front doors, memories flood my mind and are quickly replaced by a sharp and sudden sadness. I was happy when I lived here. Truly happy.

We have a murder to investigate. My focus needs to be on that.

We walk past a throng of police officers and theater workers on the main floor, take the escalator to the second floor, and pass the concession stand, which smells of popcorn and hot dogs. Crime-scene techs and two plainclothes detectives block the entrance to theater eight.

I recognize one of the detectives immediately—D'Antoni and I worked a serial rape case with homicide detective Joe Flynn four years ago. After working together closely for more than two months, we apprehended the perp, who had raped thirteen women in New York City. Joe's a great detective, and I'm glad to be working with him again.

A broad smile plays across Joe's face as he approaches us with his hand outstretched. "Look what the cat dragged in! Are you guys sticking your big noses into another one of my cases?" He laughs and claps me on the back. "Good to see you, Deke." Then he hugs D'Antoni—and holds on for just a little too long, in my opinion. Joe and Griff go way back, and they simply nod to each other.

"Did you miss me?" I ask. "You're working this one?"

"Yup. Me and my partner, Frank Mullaney, are running lead. Let me introduce you." He turns and calls out, "Hey, Frankie, get your bony ass over here!"

Flynn introduces Frank to each of us, and we exchange pleasantries. Frank is tall and razor thin. I've heard about him. He's widely recognized as one of the NYPD's finest homicide detectives, and I look forward to working with him and Flynn—guys of this class don't get their tail feathers ruffled by having to work with the FBI. They realize we're there to help and that we bring tremendous resources to the table.

I address both Joe and Frank. "Why don't you walk us through what happened?"

Joe nods and jumps right in. "The deceased, Anne Richards, was a thirty-five-year-old RN at NYU Hospital. She lived up on Forty-Fourth and Second, across the street from the UN. Her wallet, driver's license, credit cards and work ID were all found in her purse, which was left on her lap. Nothing is obviously missing from the purse. Her cell phone was found in the cup holder to her right."

"Any texts found on the phone?" D'Antoni asks.

"Crime-scene techs are running it now," Frank says.

Joe continues. "Cause of death is unknown. The coroner said that there is an injection site on the upper right side of the victim's neck. She is aware of the other movie theater killings and is having toxicology run as we speak. We should get the toxicology results back quickly. I'll take you to view the body whenever you're ready."

Frank shakes his head, his face twisted in disgust. "The coroner found what she thought was semen on the victim's lips and inside her mouth. He jerked off in her mouth, for God's sake. We're dealing with a true sicko, a fucking animal that needs to be put down."

"I hear you," I say. "Can we see the crime scene? Have you viewed any of the surveillance footage?"

"Still waiting on surveillance," Joe says. "The victim wasn't found until thirty-five minutes after the movie ended. Scared the daylights out of the cleanup crew."

"Were you able to interview any potential witnesses?" I ask.

Joe nods. "The ticket taker recalls two men presenting him tickets for the ten forty-five showing of *Knives Out*. One of the men appeared to be in his late sixties or seventies and walked with a cane. The other man was described as late twenties or early thirties, dressed nicely, with longish dark hair, wearing a suit and tie, a ball cap, and sunglasses. That's all the little pothead was able to provide, even after some encouragement from Frank. There were only five additional moviegoers, all women, and none of them were interviewed, given the amount of time that elapsed between the end of the movie and the body being found. Another theater employee working the concession stand recalls seeing a man in a suit and tie enter the theater. That's it, however, as far as witnesses are concerned. Hopefully the surveillance footage will be more helpful."

D'Antoni turns and makes her way toward the entrance to theater eight. "Might as well take a look." The rest of us follow.

Yellow crime-scene tape blocks the entrance, and an officer stands next to it. Frank barks something to the uniformed cop, and after signing the logbook, we duck under the tape and enter the theater.

How many movies have I seen in this exact theater? Dozens probably.

Joe points to the back left of the theater. "She was seated in the second-to-last row, on the left side. That would put the killer in the very last row."

"You'd think she would've been suspicious. Uncomfortable," D'Antoni says. "He has to have taken a seat directly behind her."

We walk up the steeply inclined stairs to the back of the theater. Crime-scene tape cordons off the victim's seat and the surrounding area. The first thing I notice upon approaching the area is the strong scent of urine. The seat she sat in is wet, and a small amount of liquid has pooled beneath it.

Frank notices me studying the chair. "Yeah, she wet herself. I can't even imagine how terrified she was."

It's obvious the techs have dusted for prints all around the area. *Pointless*, I think.

Something catches my eye on the floor—something flashy and mostly hidden under a seat in the last row, about fifteen feet from the victim's chair. I slap on a pair of latex gloves, bend down, and pick up the object. It's a pen—a fancy pen at that. I realize it's a Montblanc, the same make and model as my own lucky pen, which retails for several hundred dollars. The initials WAS are inscribed on one side. Then I catch a glimpse of something small and white wadded up on the floor underneath the seat. Bending over, I pick up a small scrap of paper. Something is written on it. I take out my flashlight.

Scribbled in black ink is a cryptic message: "You missed me. I already came and left." It was signed "The Movie Theater Killer."

How had the crime-scene techs missed these items?

I tell Joe, Frank, Griff, and D'Antoni what I've found; read the note aloud to them; and then put everything into an evidence bag. Nothing else catches my eye.

When D'Antoni and Griff have finished giving the scene the once-over, we head back outside the theater. I feel as though it was just yesterday I was here, standing in line and then ordering a bucket of popcorn and a large Diet Coke with Catherine by my side. I glance around, noticing that the walls are still adorned with movie posters touting movies from my childhood rather than new releases, which is something I haven't seen at other theaters.

I turn to Joe and Frank and ask if they think there would be any benefit in re-interviewing the ticket taker or the concession stand employee.

Frank shakes his head. "They're both stoners—clueless morons. We should have the surveillance footage in a moment, though."

I laugh. "Well then, let's go see the body."

* * *

The chief medical examiner's office is on First and Twenty-Sixth, and it takes less than five minutes to get there. Morgues—anything autopsy-related—make me uncomfortable, despite the fact that my job requires me to confront death on a regular basis. I guess it's the meat locker–like smell and grisly atmosphere of the autopsy room that does it. I can't comprehend how someone would voluntarily go through the hell that is medical school only to work on the dead.

Not that the life of an FBI profiler is glamorous. My failed marriage, pathetic attempts at parenting, alcoholism, and nightmares that mar my sleep every night can all attest to that. I would give anything for dreamless sleep.

We make our way through the maze that is one of the largest morgues in the world to Dr. Kristin Connor's office.

A thought pops into my mind. "Hey, Joe and Frank, we should get someone canvassing every store in the city that sells Montblanc pens. See if anyone remembers customizing that make of Montblanc with the initials WAS."

"Way ahead of you, buddy," Joe says. "I made a call to home base, and we've a team mobilized and doing exactly that."

D'Antoni and I have met Dr. Connor on several occasions. She's the most competent medical examiner I know and a knockout to boot—tall, blonde, and athletic. She smiles warmly as we enter the office.

"Wow, looks like we've got the A team assembled," she says. Connor has also worked with Frank, Joe, and Griff. We catch up briefly before heading into autopsy room A. The room is plain, drab, and gray, like a stainless-steel sink.

Connor clears her throat and glances at each of us in turn. "I've had very little time with the body, but I'll be performing the autopsy myself later today. Toxicology is already underway."

Connor gently pulls open the first drawer on her left. Anne Richards is a cute, petite blonde with short hair. She looks much younger than thirty-five. Her eyes stare up at the ceiling, seeing nothing. Red pinpricks dot the whites—a telltale sign of asphyxiation. She wears a horrific mask of surprise.

The next thing I notice is the damage to her right breast. The nipple has been completely bitten off.

Connor continues. "Cause of death has yet to be determined. The only noticeable trauma to the exterior body is an injection mark about two inches below her right ear, on the upper right side of her neck. The damage to the right breast occurred postmortem, as evidenced by the lack of a large amount of blood and bruising. If this is the same MO as the other murders and the killer used sux, the victim suffered terribly. She must have been in a heightened state of panic and terror."

Frank closes his eyes and shakes his head. "Why didn't she scream?"

"Well, if the killer used sux, the victim would have been unable to scream or move. As little as forty milligrams is deadly when injected intramuscularly," Connor says. "Semen—at least we're fairly certain it's semen—was found on the victim's lips and in her mouth.

Swabs were taken, and we should know shortly if there's a match with one of your other cases."

Connor looks at me. "Deke, tell me what you can about your other cases. Are we dealing with one killer here?"

I nod. "Kristin, I'll tell you what I can. We're investigating four other killings that have occurred in movie theaters on the East Coast over the past eleven months. Two occurred in Boston, one in Philadelphia, and one in Albany. The MO in each case has been similar. Each victim was injected with sux. The dosage varied, but each victim was incapacitated and died of asphyxia. Thankfully, the coroner in Boston looked for the metabolites of sux. Recent homicides in which sux was used probably prompted the search for the presence of succinylmonocholine and choline, which were found in high concentrations. DNA was left on the bodies in the second Boston murder, Philadelphia, and Albany, and we've matched that to the same individual. Unfortunately, he's not in CODIS—or any other database, for that matter."

Kristin interjects. "What about the first Boston murder?"

"No DNA was recovered from the scene, but the MO is identical," I say.

She nods. "I've already heard from the mayor about the case before us now. This case is top priority, but that goes without saying. I'll coordinate with the medical examiners on your other cases, and you let me know if you need anything from me. DNA matching and toxicology will be done today. I really hope you catch this sicko quickly."

"You and me both, Kristin," I say. "Thanks for taking the time to meet with us. Can you have your executive assistant email me and the team the DNA and toxicology findings? I'll leave our contact information with her on the way out."

"Absolutely," she says.

I shake my head and rub my temples. "Perhaps just once, one day, maybe we can meet under different circumstances, Kristin."

As the three of us leave the building and head to Starbucks, my phone beeps, and I answer it.

"Special Agent O'Brien?" asks a voice I don't recognize.

"Last time I checked," I reply dryly.

"Detective Greg Taylor from the Seventeenth. I just sent you the Kips Bay surveillance footage. Also, we're doing a city-wide comb of all stores that sell Montblanc pens. Nothing to report on that yet. We retrieved several texts both sent and received while the victim was in the theater. I'll forward them when we have finished speaking."

Another thought floods my mind. "Can you coordinate with my Quantico team to see if any of the other victims may have owned the pen?"

"Will do."

The Starbucks on Thirty-First and Second is relatively empty, and we're able to commandeer a large table at the back. As everyone sits down with his or her drink, I pull up the surveillance footage on my phone so the entire team can view it.

I pause and replay the thirty seconds of footage several times.

I clear my throat. "I could be wrong, but it looks like the same guy from Boston, Philly, and Albany. Look at the height, hair, and jawline. I am almost one hundred percent certain."

D'Antoni nods. "I agree."

"We ought to be checking with the New York Sports Club, the Coffee Bean, TD Bank, and any other establishments bordering the theater for additional surveillance."

Joe laughs. "What? You think you're dealing with the Mayberry police here. We have boots on the ground doing that as we speak!"

"I knew I liked working with you for some reason," I say. "Back to the footage. What do you see? The smallest thing could be important."

D'Antoni jumps in first. "White male, twenty-eight to thirty-five, approximately six feet two to six feet four. Wavy, medium-length dark hair. Athletic looking. The suit and the rest of his attire look expensive to me, but what do I know? It certainly looks like he knows where the cameras are, because we never get a direct look at his face."

"I think he looks thirty to thirty-five," Frank says. "I concur with D'Antoni on height and build. While we never get a direct look at his face, I swear he's smirking. Please play it again."

I do.

"Stop," Frank says. "Right there. See? Notice the lips. Am I crazy?"

"No," Griffith says. "He's definitely smirking. The sanctimonious prick!"

Joe jumps in. "Play it from the beginning one more time."

About halfway through, Joe says, "Stop. Look at his right hand. What's he holding?"

"He's twirling something. Looks like a black pen," I say. "We should hear back from Kristin's team on the DNA, but that's the same guy as in Philly and Albany. No doubt about it."

CHAPTER 8

He's lying in his bed with a slight alcohol buzz calming him. His mind wanders again. He thinks back to one of his mother's former boyfriends. His name was Joe. He was the worst of the worst. Joe was especially fond of forcibly sodomizing him. His initial refusals, objections, and threats to tell his mom were dealt with swiftly and brutally. His injuries included a severe concussion, broken arm, broken eye socket, and dislocated jaw. Mom didn't seem even to notice. She certainly didn't care.

He visited Joe some five years ago to have a little heart-to-heart. Late one Friday night, Joe arrived at his decrepit trailer outside of Worcester, Massachusetts, around two thirty in the morning, shit-faced and belligerent—par for the course for Joe. He parked his fat ass in the only piece of furniture in the main room: a ratty, well-worn easy chair. He flipped on the surprisingly large TV, popped a beer, and lit a cigarette.

Before Joe managed a single puff, he slipped a syringe filled with pentobarbital, a strong sedative, into his bulbous neck.

It was his first experiment with the drug, and it didn't disappoint. It did take longer than he thought, though, to subdue the obese slob. Joe kept trying to stand up, but well-placed kicks kept him seated. Joe was rendered helpless after a minute or so. Still, Joe was aware of his surroundings and what was going on. His research had paid off. The dosage he'd chosen did what it was supposed to.

It was going to be a great night. He had complete control.

He feels himself get hard as he relives the moment.

He made sure Joe knew exactly who he was, as he looked nothing like the frail little boy Joe had preyed upon. He joined Joe in a beer and tried to make him feel comfortable. He told him that he forgave him and that he was only there to help him find God, to save his soul. He laughs out loud, thinking of how much Joe wanted to believe him. Joe's eyes were the size of saucers, practically popping out of his head.

The moment he thought Joe might slip into unconsciousness, he went into the other room and retrieved the garden shovel. He had spent a solid fifteen minutes sharpening the blade earlier that night. It was sharp enough to shave with.

He showed it to Joe, switching it from one hand to the other. He touched the blade of the shovel to Joe's cheek, gently caressing the flesh with metal. Tears streamed down Joe's face. He moved the shovel to Joe's mouth, prodding him to open it, but Joe refused to comply. That was all right. He was getting bored, and the smell of spoiled food, cigarettes, and dirty socks inside the pigsty was starting to sicken him.

He forced the entire blade of the shovel into Joe's mouth with one push. There was a sickening popping sound, and blood sprayed everywhere. Joe's mouth was completely ripped open on both sides, extending to almost three times its original size. Joe tried—unsuccessfully—to scream.

He smiled at Joe, admiring his handiwork. Joe stared back in horror. He spoke to him, his tone mocking and condescending. "Too bad it's not Halloween. You would scare the crap out of the little kiddies. Unfortunately for you, it's not Halloween. It's your worst nightmare, and it's one you get to experience right now.

"Joe, I want you to listen to me. This is important. Everyone eventually pays for their sins, their misdeeds. Some just pay a hell of a lot more than others. Ha-ha!"

With that, he took a couple steps back. He hefted the shovel above his head, howled like a crazed animal, and then rushed the helpless man, smashing out every last one of his now completely exposed teeth.

Next—and he really wants to savor this memory—he grabbed the ax he had taken from Joe's shed and lopped his head off. It took several strikes of the ax to complete the job. He has to hand it to Joe: he hung in there as long as he could.

He has no idea how many times he's relived those precious moments. The rush, the excitement—even now the feeling motivates him, adrenalizing him to push his achievements to ever loftier heights.

CHAPTER 9

Just as Griff, D'Antoni, and I finish up dinner at PJ Clarke's on Fifty-Third and Third, my cell phone vibrates.

The message is from the medical examiner's office. As expected, the DNA matches that of the perp from the second murder in Boston, Philadelphia, and Albany. My heart rate quickens, firing on all cylinders. I'm electrified, eager to get back to the chase and ultimately catch this sick, perverted psychopath before more lives are lost.

I bring D'Antoni and Griff up to speed on what I've learned, and then a thought hits me. While no DNA evidence was found in the first Boston homicide, bite marks were observed—deep marks. Maybe a forensic dentist could analyze both sets and see if they came from the same person. I share this thought with D'Antoni and Griff, who vigorously nod their assent.

D'Antoni immediately calls members of our team back at Quantico to get the ball rolling on this analysis. I've worked with forensic dentists, also known as forensic odontologists, in the past. The technology they use is amazing.

Back at the station, D'Antoni and I agree to meet Griff in his office in an hour, and then the two of us walk around the block for a pit stop at Starbucks. My large espresso roast coffee with an inch and a half of steamed milk gets me even more focused and amped up. I live for this feeling. It allows me to block out my past failures, my depression, and all the other defects that plague me.

Given the late hour, D'Antoni and I are able to commandeer a plain, drab conference room on the seventeenth floor. The 9/11 Memorial and Museum and the full expanse of downtown are visible from the window. We put in a call to O'Shaughnessy and spend the next twenty minutes updating the team.

O'Shaughnessy informs us that a forensic odontologist on retainer with the FBI has already been brought on board. Unfortunately, the effort to locate any store that has sold a Montblanc pen with the initials WAS engraved has failed so far. D'Antoni suggests doing the same search in Boston, Philadelphia, and Albany. The team agrees to get right on it.

O'Shaughnessy sighs audibly. "I want you guys to wrap up there tomorrow unless something important pops and then get to Boston. A helicopter is on call and at your disposal. I want an update in the morning, in the afternoon, and at the end of the day. I want a profile within the next forty-eight hours—the sooner the better."

It's time to catch up with Griff's team in New York. Yeah, it's late, but the city is in an uproar, and Griff's team will be working around the clock. We hop into the elevator and head up to the nineteenth floor. We head directly to the office of Griff's number-one field agent, a woman named Maeve O'Shea. She's a red-haired, freckled Irish beauty.

She walks around her desk and warmly embraces us both.

"How have you guys been?" she asks.

"No complaints, Maeve," I answer. D'Antoni echoes my sentiment.

"How are the kids?" I ask.

"Driving their daddy batshit fucking crazy."

D'Antoni and I both laugh. "It's about time Jim has to work for a living," I say.

"You got that right. I see you guys opted for Starbucks over the sludge we brew here. Smart move. I've a conference room reserved right down the hall. My team is already in there, so let's head down."

The conference room is large and spacious. Seven agents—five men and two women—sit around the table in the center of the room. A huge dry-erase whiteboard takes up an entire wall at the front of the room. Stickies, notes, and newspaper clippings cover almost the entire board. Maeve makes introductions, and we take our seats at the head of the table.

We spend the next thirty minutes getting the lowdown on what the New York City field team has learned today. Most importantly, we learn that toxicology results have just come in, and they confirm the presence of a large amount of succinylmonocholine and choline in the victim's blood.

We're also informed that five texts were retrieved from the victim's phone, and one of the agents reads them.

> 11:08: Hey, Nancy. At the movies. Rough day in the office. Just needed to get away.
>
> 11:15: Good for you, kiddo.
>
> 11:29: Movie sucks but better than work.
>
> 11:38: Have a wonderful Thanksgiving.
>
> 11:57: Gobble gobble to you too. I started early.

A picture is attached to the message, and a blowup of that picture is circulated to everyone at the table. While the image is grainy and dark, there's little doubt as to what it shows: the perp thrusting himself into the victim's mouth. Her face is contorted, her eyes staring blankly ahead.

The room is eerily quiet.

D'Antoni clears her throat. "Okay, first things first. We need to try to clean this up as much as possible. The perp's face is not in the picture, so I doubt it'll be of much use, but we have to try."

"The crime-scene techs are already working on it," New York agent Tom Ramone says.

"Good," D'Antoni replies. "I can't fathom how he did this unnoticed. I know the theater was almost empty, but still. Everyone who was in that theater must be reinterviewed."

"The reinterview process is already underway," Ramone says.

Next, D'Antoni and I take turns bringing the team up to speed on the murders in Boston, Philadelphia, and Albany.

We spend a while discussing the significance of the note and pen found at the crime scene. D'Antoni and I both feel strongly that it reflects a pivotal change in the killer's mind-set—that is, assuming a note wasn't missed at the other crime scenes. The perp is enjoying the public paranoia that his sick actions are eliciting. He craves fame and exposure.

Hopefully, this will ultimately lead to his downfall.

It's after ten by the time we make it to Griff's office. We give him a condensed version of everything we've learned and agree to meet back at his office at seven in the morning.

D'Antoni and I hail a cab and head to the hotel on Central Park South. We agree to meet at six for breakfast. I'm too amped up at this point to consider sleep. After a workout on the third floor and a shower, I sit on the bed and check my iPad for emails.

My heart skips a beat when I see a message from Catherine. I hurriedly open it only to be deflated by its contents. She tells me I can't see or talk to the kids until I have two months of documented sobriety outside of rehab. *Fuck! What does she mean by* documented?

I have two scathing emails from Bridget. I man up and send a reply. I apologize profusely for not getting back to her sooner. I let her know I'm out of town, working around the clock on a big case, and would like us to get together when I'm back in town. I could have taken the easy route and just told her that things aren't working, but that's not how a responsible, sober individual acts. She deserves to hear what I have to say—in person.

My phone beeps, grabbing my attention. A long series of text messages, all from a number I don't recognize, pops up. I can scarcely breathe as I read it:

Hey, Deke. I can't tell you how happy I am that you were chosen to work my case. It is truly humbling to get to work with the best. Tell D'Antoni that I said hello as well. I anticipate a truly epic chess match, with me ultimately emerging victorious. I know everything about you—what makes you tick and keeps you up at night. By the way, how was Caron? Do you still crave the drink? Do you white-knuckle it, counting your days sober?

Do you view it as a great accomplishment? I doubt it, Deke. We both know alcoholism is a moral weakness, not a disease. It's truly pathetic how the weak are coddled and allowed to continue in their pathetic existences. Don't you think?

How the fuck did he get my number? He comes across as pompous and overconfident. He also comes across as intelligent and articulate. The string of texts continues:

How are the kids? Oh, I'm sorry. You haven't seen them in a while, have you? You still tapping that hot redhead? Oh, the things I would like to do to her. Mmm. Maybe I should show her what it's like to be with a real man.

Losing Catherine must be the toughest part of it all, though. She's a keeper. No one else will ever hold a candle to her. She gives so much love—love you can't find in your own heart—to your kids. I commend her for that.

Leaving you was the smartest thing she's ever done. You couldn't be trusted around the little retard—always drunk, caring only for yourself. Deep down, you're ashamed of him, Deke. You know it. I know it. At least the slobbering little moron has his mommy and that ridiculously expensive school you send him to. Not that he's capable of appreciating it.

Well, enough about you, and on to me. I've been busy—busier by the minute. This last gal was such a treat. She pissed herself she was so frightened. The smell excited me to the point that I practically came without even touching myself. No one is safe at the movies anymore.

Do you know how orgasmically awesome it is to literally suck the breath and life out of someone? It's an incredible out-of-body experience—a gift, really. The bulging eyes and face etched with terror. Being the last person they will ever see. Godlike.

Also, I learned a thing or two this go-around. Who knew a dead bitch could give such a memorable blow job? Blew me away, if you know what I mean.

I bet you wasted a lot of time forensically. I'm not in CODIS or any other federal, state, or international database. I'm a ghost. Boo!

You're going to have to catch me with good old-fashioned detective work. Are you up to the challenge? Take a nip of the Johnnie Walker bottle, and get some liquid courage going. You're going to need it.

The whole world will know me and fear me. My legacy will live on well after your death. And trust me, this game ends only one way: with your death. Get on your knees, and say your prayers—not that it will do any good. The prayers of soulless cowards are never answered.

By the way, I didn't do the first Boston murder. I certainly admired the killer's actions, though. Broad daylight! Absolutely incredible! When I learned that the killer used sux, I knew it had to be a medical professional, most likely an anesthesiologist. I took this knowledge as well as a halfway decent picture of the perp from surveillance photos that were all over the TV and set out to find the guy. It took me almost five days, but find him I did.

I jumped him in his parking garage, quickly subdued him, bound his ankles and wrists, threw him into my trunk, and took him to an abandoned building on Highland Avenue in Somerville. I spent hours with him, and he proved very forthcoming as to dosing. One hundred milligrams injected intramuscularly is fatal. He also explained how to gain access to sux on the black web. When I could no longer bear his screaming and begging, I drove a screwdriver through his right eye socket, all the way to the brain stem. I wanted to take more time with him but felt I owed him for everything he taught me. You'll find the body in the basement.

My hand is shaking so hard I'm having trouble continuing. I close my eyes, take a deep breath, exhale slowly, and then proceed, less shaky but still enraged.

Just to let you know and to make the game more interesting, we've met before, and we will meet again in the near future. Got you thinking? I can't wait to meet D'Antoni. She's fucking gorgeous. Does she like movies? Hey, pal, one last thing, and this is as certain as death: I'll drive you to drink again. That's what every good drunk wants, right? Johnny Walker Black forever, baby! The Movie Theater Killer.

I read the texts over and over again. Numbness and fear give way to cold, hard anger. What he says about Patrick goes way beyond cruelty.

How the fuck does this sicko know so much about my life? Assuming the text really is from the killer. Who am I kidding? Of course it is. He knows things about the crime scene that haven't been revealed to the public. The moniker Movie Theater Killer hasn't been released either.

I quickly forward the texts to O'Shaughnessy and D'Antoni, suggesting we catch up first thing in the morning. I also forward the message to the techies back at Quantico and ask them to find out where it originated and who might have sent it—a fruitless exercise to be sure. He's too careful.

I turn off the lights and climb into bed, fully expecting sleep to elude me. Around two thirty, I drift off, but I sleep—if you can call it that—fitfully. Vivid dreams of people I've met at conferences, at crime scenes, at book signings, and in everyday life flash through my mind like a movie. I wake up soaked in sweat and exhausted.

CHAPTER 10

He has the four newly purchased fifty-inch TVs tuned into four different networks. NBC has his attention now. He's watching a replay of the nightly news with Lester Holt.

His return flight and eight-hour shift made him miss the live feed. He likes Lester Holt because the American public loves Lester Holt. The lead story is about the movie theater killings in Boston, Philadelphia, Albany, and New York City.

Of course it is. He's famous.

Lester doesn't disappoint and makes no attempt to allay the public's fear. There's no point. The public has every right to be terrified.

Holt opens by stating that interviews with reliable sources point to one killer, a serial killer. "Well, Lester, you're mostly right," he says out loud. He glances toward the mirror above the fireplace and sees that he's smiling widely. This is so fucking perfect. He couldn't have imagined it working out any better.

NBC goes to a commercial break. He turns his focus to other networks, including ABC, CBS, Fox, and CNN. A pandemic of fear flashes across all of the screens. The same story, or a version of it, is being unveiled nationwide. The fear is real, palpable, piercing political partisanship and religious ideology. He's center stage for the first time in his life. Truth be told, he's never felt better.

NBC returns with Holt conducting interviews on the streets of New York City. The first interview is with a twenty-one-year-old female NYU student. Lester asks her what the mood is like on the NYU campus. She shudders noticeably before replying. "Everybody is terrified. I can't even imagine what those last moments were like for the victims. I'm not sure I can ever go to the movies again."

His last victim was an NYU nurse. He hates the liberal pansies who make up a huge percentage of the NYU community. They know nothing about reality. They live in their little rich bubbles, casting aspersions on those who think differently. *Well, guess what? I'm reality.* They can't ignore him.

He watches one more Holt interview, this one with a middle-aged Wall Street type. The bozo is all bravado, confidently proclaiming the killer to be a weak, attention-seeking lunatic who will be apprehended shortly.

He smiles at this and wonders how different the moron's response would've been if one of his loved ones had suffered the fate of the victims.

His planning has been too precise, too well thought out, and too utterly brilliant for him even to consider the possibility of getting caught. A feeling of omnipotence overwhelms him. Remote in hand, he switches off the TVs.

He walks into his bedroom and stops to admire his walls. They are adorned with newspaper and web articles about the murders in Boston, Philly, and Albany. He's going to thoroughly enjoy adding coverage of New York City tomorrow night.

He climbs into his four-poster bed, fully satiated, anxious to dream about his next adventures. He relives the events of this morning. The fear he saw in her eyes, the unmitigated power he held over her, sends an electrical current through his synapses. He notices a swelling between his legs. He grabs it with both hands, unable to help himself. He will sleep like a baby tonight, especially knowing that Deke O'Brien will not.

CHAPTER 11

Just before six in the morning, I step out of the hotel elevator and almost bump headfirst into D'Antoni. She wastes no time in ripping into me.

"Why the fuck didn't you answer your phone last night? You don't spring something like that on me and then disappear."

I laugh softly. "Calm down. Take a breath, would you? I was exhausted and needed to get a little bit of shut-eye. We can talk about it now over coffee."

Lots of coffee, I think.

Given the early hour, we have our choice of tables in the elegant white-table-clothed dining room. Mozart is being played softly in the background. As usual, I pick a table at the back that affords a view of the entire room and sit facing the entrance. D'Antoni and I both opt for vegetarian omelets, fresh fruit, and a large pot of coffee.

"Assuming it's him, how'd he get your unlisted phone number?" she asks. "And how does he know so much about your personal life? Shit, he knows more about your personal life than I do. Did you forward everything to our forensic techies?"

I shrug. "Your guess is as good as mine. It's pretty creepy. That being said, I'm not surprised. It's not unusual for these psychos to reach out to the lead detectives. When I reply to his message, I intend to let him know exactly that."

"How are you acting so calm? Aren't you furious?"

"Yeah, you have no idea, but it doesn't help. I need to stay focused, rely on my experience, and rely on my partner. If I do that, we'll catch him."

D'Antoni likes my answer, and a small smile escapes her lips. "Do me a favor: get O'Shaughnessy's blessing before sending any response. We don't want to inflame him anymore."

I nod. "It won't do any good to respond. But at some point, I need to correspond with this guy. This scumbag likes the back-and-forth. He equates what's going on to a chess match, and it's my move. I intend to make an educated move, one that doesn't let him know he's gotten under my skin in even the slightest way. It's a giant lie but one I'm confident I can pull off. I intend to take some of the wind out of his sails."

"Just be careful," she says.

* * * * * * * *

When we get to 26 Federal, which is now a bustling nightmare compared to last night, I jump right in and tell Griff about the message. I pull up the text I assume came from the killer and then hand my cell phone to Griff to let him read it.

After a while, Griff looks up, clearly shaken.

"I don't see how this could have come from anyone other than the killer—or his proxy," I say. "He knows too much about the crime scene, too much about me, and too much about the case in general. I have our techies at Quantico on it to see if they can find out where the text was sent from and any information about the sender. I don't expect them to find anything useful, but you're free to have your forensic team sink their teeth into it as well. More importantly, I have our Boston guys looking for an abandoned building in Somerville with a dead body in the basement.

"I haven't replied to the text—yet. I'll not do so until we get feedback from forensics, from Boston, and from you and O'Shaughnessy. Louise and I already discussed everything over breakfast, and I'll do nothing until she and I are on the same page. Thoughts?"

Griff clears his throat. "It appears the killer has been interested in you for a long time. If we believe him, you have met him before. More disturbing is that he knows intimate details about your life—details that only those closest to you would know. That really bothers me. You're well known. You've been all over the news the last ten years because of your involvement in dozens of high-profile cases; plus, you're a writer with devoted fans across the globe.

"I don't know. The only thing I'm certain of is that we haven't heard the last from this guy. We need him to make a mistake. He's an overconfident narcissist, and such people do eventually make mistakes. I guess we might as well give O'Shaughnessy a call."

Griff and I nod in agreement, and we head back up to Griff's office.

O'Shaughnessy picks up on the first ring and wastes no time in commandeering the conversation. "Deke, you should've called me last night. I tried you a dozen times. What the fuck?"

I interrupt O'Shaughnessy and speak assertively. "I told you we'd catch up in the morning. I was burning the midnight oil and needed to get a couple hours of sleep to be sharp today. Nothing would have been accomplished last night."

"Whatever," he says. "Don't turn your phone off. Let's move on. Deke, I assume you haven't responded to the text yet."

"Of course not."

"Good," he says. "We should discuss what we're going to do. Opening a dialogue with this psycho is probably not a bad idea. We'll know soon where the text originated from geographically because he sent it from a cell phone. I'm sure it's a burner, but in any case, I expect to hear back from our forensic guys this morning. So what do you people think should be our next move?"

D'Antoni dives in. "I think engaging him on a personal level is critical. We need to make him feel comfortable communicating with us. That being said, the whole point of opening a line of communication is to produce results. If he's as smart as I think he is, this will be an uphill battle, but obtaining any more information than we have now is a win."

"This is all a big game to him," I say. "He'll see through any mental jockeying immediately. I think we need to speed things up. Let's put together a preliminary profile no later than tomorrow. This will help me get inside his head. Right now, he's in the driver's seat, and we need to stop that."

"I think getting the profile done as soon as possible is critical," O'Shaughnessy says. "Take some more time to consider how we can begin communication with this sicko, and let's regroup at four. Deke and Louise, I want you guys in Boston this afternoon unless something pops there. Homicide detective Bill Slaughter of the Boston PD is expecting your call."

The line goes dead.

✦✦✦✦✦✦✦

"Do you have Slaughter's direct dial?" I ask D'Antoni. "We should try to meet with him and his partner before the end of the day."

"Yeah, I have his number. I think we should tentatively schedule something for four o' clock. I'd like some time tonight and tomorrow to finalize our investigation there and to hammer out a preliminary profile. I have a lot of thoughts on it already."

"Agreed. We can spend our time on the flight to Boston discussing it. Why don't you reach out to Slaughter now, unless we need to discuss anything first?"

She shakes her head, pulls out her iPhone, and scrolls through her contact list for Slaughter's number.

Slaughter picks up on the third ring. He agrees to meet us at Boston FBI headquarters at half past four.

Meanwhile, I call Special Agent Brian Barnes and arrange transportation from Logan Airport to our Boston office. Brian is the agent in charge in Boston and is heading up the investigation of the Boston murder.

D'Antoni and I have fifteen minutes to kill before meeting with Griff's team, and we use the time to check emails. In my work email is a note from our IT forensic team explaining that the email I received originated from a coffee shop called Java Girl on East Sixty-Sixth Street.

I look at another message. *Oh joy!* Bridget has responded to my email. She's glad I'm okay, and she can't wait to catch up when my case wraps. It's not the answer I was looking for; I really wanted the easy way out.

D'Antoni taps me on the shoulder. "We need to get going."

✦ ✦ ✦ ✦ ✦

In the conference room, Griff's lead special agent, Maeve O'Shea, takes the floor. "Unfortunately, there isn't a lot to update you on. Our forensics team triangulated the text to the Upper East Side. As expected, it's a burner, so we have not been able to uncover anything about the sender himself.

"Nothing new to report on the Montblanc pen search. I have surveillance pictures from the movie theater for you guys to take a look at. To be honest, it looks like he's wearing the exact same getup the perp wore in Boston, Philly, and Albany. I've seen the text the killer sent you last night and realize it's highly probable the Fenway perp is not our killer, bolstered by the fact that the Somerville police and members of our Boston team have just found a body in an abandoned building in Somerville. The victim, Mark Raymond, was an anesthesiologist at Massachusetts General Hospital, according to his driver's license and work ID.

"We're still sifting through surveillance from other businesses near the theater to see if our suspect was captured on those, but nothing yet."

68

We spend the next several minutes perusing the still footage taken by the surveillance cameras. A tall man in an expensive-looking suit, wearing a ball cap and sunglasses, appears in each of the photos. His head is always tilted downward, obscuring his face. It's obvious he has scouted the theater in advance and identified exactly where the cameras are. It is cold, calculated preparation. I look up from the photos. "We need to go back two weeks on the surveillance. Coordinate with Boston, Philly, and Albany. This guy did a lot of prep in advance."

"We're already on it, Deke," Maeve says. "We actually requested three weeks of footage from Kips Bay and asked for the same in Boston, Philly, and Albany. We will be through the Kips Bay footage today. Can I request a daily update call?"

"Of course, Maeve," D'Antoni replies.

There is a gap in the conversation, and I use it as a chance to grab the floor. "D'Antoni and I will have a preliminary profile to you guys by tomorrow night. Give us a few minutes now to let you know where we're at.

"We're dealing with a smart, organized, methodical, and sadistic killer. A sexual sadist and a serial killer. History is full of them. Our killer appears to be intelligent and likely holds down a skilled professional job. It's possible, maybe even likely, that he is a medical professional. Sux is not readily available on the street.

"I'm sure Griff has brought you up to speed on the text the perp sent to me last night. It was written by an educated, determined, and well-prepared individual. He knew a lot of things about my personal life. Things that date back years. Things I've not shared with anyone. The text shows that he loves head games. This won't be the last we hear from him, not by a long shot. The spotlight beckons, and he will continue to heed its call. The psychological gymnastics get him off as much as the murders do. This game is a giant intellectual mind fuck to this guy. And because he revels in the psychological gameplay, he'll be drawn to any media coverage of the case. This is his one real shot at fame."

D'Antoni takes a deep breath. "Men who commit sexual murder generally crave and fantasize about violent sexual acts. Murders that appear motiveless are actually driven by sexual fantasy and the anticipated gratification. It's common for sexual serial killers to asphyxiate their victims almost to the point of death and then release the pressure just as the victim's about to die, because it allows them to prolong the sexual experience. In the Boston, Philly, Albany, and New York City killings, the killer had up to three minutes to watch the life drain out of the victim's eyes."

I jump in. "Many of our most famous, most prolific serial killers were fond of asphyxiation. John Wayne Gacy is a prime example.

"History shows us that asphyxiation is the MO in over sixty percent of sexually charged homicides, almost always via manual or ligature strangulation, which makes our killer different, an outlier. Ted Bundy is worth mentioning. Let's not forget Gary Leon Ridgway, the Green River Killer, who may have strangled over a hundred women. Anthony Sowell, the Cleveland Strangler, is another example, as is Jeffrey Dahmer. The sexual sadist gets off on hurting people, looking into the victims' eyes, savoring their terror.

"Our creep is extremely proud of himself. He wears it on his chest like a war medal. He exudes cockiness, and his ego might bring about his downfall. I don't know how this guy evolved into what he is today; I'll find out, but I need your help to do it. This killer has done nothing new or original. Yet he wants us to know how smart and creative he is. He wants to be famous.

"Let me tell you something: he's smart in terms of planning and in the educational sense, but his endeavors when it comes to his more prurient interests don't impress me at all. Everything he does has been done before. Even the use of sux as the murder weapon. He borrowed that from Dr. Raymond. He'll never be famous compared to the most infamous serial killers of all time. He'll never be anything other than an afterthought, a copycat in the annals of the sick and sadistic. Everything he's doing has been done before.

"Even the postmortem sexual mutilation we saw in Boston and New York is nothing original. Sick but not novel. We see sexual mutilation in a substantial number of sexually motivated murders. Most of these scumbags have been sexually abused themselves. This abuse carries on into their own sick exploits later in life."

I clear my throat to get everyone's attention. "It's highly likely our perp was abused sexually as a child and likely into late adolescence. Studies have shown that almost three-quarters of sexual sadists suffered some form of sexual abuse in adolescence. He may have been emotionally and physically abused as well. Research has shown that more than eighty percent of all serial killers suffered systematic abuse in childhood. Ed Gein, Ted Bundy, Jeffrey Dahmer, Ted Ridgway, John Wayne Gacy, Bobby Joe Long, and Henry Lee did not employ the same killing methods, but each admitted to highly traumatic childhood experiences that led to emotional, physical, psychological, and sexual scarring that lasted for the rest of their lives.

"Gein was born to a weak alcoholic father and a domineering, deeply religious mother who taught her children the evil of women and discouraged all sexual desires. Gein was very attached to his mother, likely sexually, and this caused jealousy among his siblings. When his mother died, he started living out his dark fantasies, performing macabre experiments on dead bodies before moving on to live specimens.

"Dahmer was a happy kid. He played and socialized with other children. Not until he was sexually abused by a neighborhood boy and his parents went through a highly acrimonious divorce did Dahmer's plunge into sadistic darkness begin.

"Gacy suffered extreme psychological and physical abuse at the hands of his alcoholic father. His dad called him a sissy and a queer and beat him savagely. He actually beat him unconscious with a broomstick, likely causing neurological damage to Gacy's frontal lobe and limbic system, which controls emotion, motivation, and self-control. Scans of the brains of over a hundred serial killers showed that the majority of them have little to no activity in their frontal lobe and limbic system. Interestingly, the individual who performed these studies, Dr. John Fallon, also scanned his own brain, and he too showed almost no activity in the frontal-lobe area of his brain, matching the serial killers' brain patterns, leading the majority of scientists today to agree that brain pattern alone does not create a serial killer. Clearly, not all people with neurological damage become serial killers.

"Many serial killers have suffered head injuries, including Leonard Lake, David Berkowitz, Kenneth Bianchi, Carl Panzram, and Bobby Joe Long. Berkowitz was involved in a motorcycle accident that damaged his frontal lobe and the limbic system of his brain. After the accident, he became far more aggressive, and his prurient sexual desires soared.

"Henry Lee was beaten by a prostitute mother with broom handles for years and forced to watch her have sex with clients.

"Bobby Joe Long was abused by his prostitute mother and sexually abused by her male clients."

I stretch and clear my throat. "Sound research shows that sexually abused serial killers are much more likely to mutilate their victims than those who were not sexually abused. Our killer is following a script used dozens of times before.

"This abuse may have come at the hands of anyone in the perp's life. It's possible there's a caregiver, a past cohabitant, or a total stranger out there who was instrumental in creating, molding, and defining this monster.

"While a huge long shot, it is at least possible the killer's home life was fine, and he was born with neurological damage leading to blunted emotions, impulsive inclinations, and an overall inability to feel remorse or guilt. David Berkowitz's adoptive parents raised him in a loving, trusting, nurturing environment. They provided him with everything he needed and treated him with love. But Berkowitz suffered from deep psychosis, saying he killed to keep the demons at bay."

I stand up, stretch, and walk over to the water carafe, more to release tension than because I am thirsty. I gather my thoughts and recommence.

"My gut tells me that our perp may have grown up in foster, or state-sponsored, care. His keen focus on my family life, my ex-wife and my children, shows a potential fascination with the family dynamic, albeit a sick one. I doubt very much there was or is much love in his life. He's probably not super close to anyone. Perhaps he has friends, and maybe family, he keeps in touch with, but these people are on the periphery of his life."

I take a sip of the water I have just drawn from the carafe. Adrenaline courses through me, generating a thrill that is both electrifying and inexplicable. It feels good to be back, doing what I do best.

"I'm talking about a monster, but that's nothing new. It doesn't mean he's not personable. He is. He's smart and socially engaging, and this helps him to manipulate people and situations to get what he wants. Like a chameleon, he can change his colors to adapt, fit in, and protect himself when necessary.

"He likely had a very troubled childhood. He fought a lot, stole solely for the sake of stealing, and, most notably, engaged in acts of cruelty and lewdness that increased in frequency and severity over time. Neither you nor your pets wanted this kid as a neighbor, and trust me, his neighbors still remember him. We find one of these people, and we catch this sicko."

"Let me interrupt, or we could be here all day," D'Antoni says. "I agree with almost everything Deke has said so far. Experience and history make it impossible not to. That being said, there are several important facts that need to be addressed. These point to a killer who is not, in fact, wholly predictable and unoriginal."

I roll my eyes and sigh. "She always has to steal my thunder."

D'Antoni makes her way to the whiteboard, grabbing a dry-erase marker along the way. "I want to record some key factors to be considered here." She pulls the cap from the marker and addresses the room. "First, let's talk about the locations of the murders." She writes *LOCATION* in caps in the top left corner. "He's murdering women in very open public spaces. Theaters usually have decent surveillance. Plus, he interacts with the ticket sellers and takers. He's been seen by other theater patrons who've provided a general description of him, even if it hasn't been terribly helpful. Most sexual murders are committed outdoors, in the victim's or perp's vehicle, or in the victim's home. In each situation, the murder occurs out of public view. Our perp, however, gets off on the public nature of his acts. The brazenness and danger of the act is part of his arousal. It's his way of telling us how much smarter he is than us."

D'Antoni smiles. "He differs significantly from some of our most famous serial sexual murderers. Take, for instance, Gary Ridgway, Ted Bundy, Antonio Rodriguez, John Wayne Gacy, and Anthony Sowell. All of these men were more prolific killers than our perp, but they killed almost entirely out of the public eye. Our killer sees them as having taken the easy route. The unoriginal route, as Deke is so fond of calling it. But it is just this confidence, cockiness, or whatever you call it that will ultimately lead to his downfall. I know it will!"

She pauses and then continues. "Secondly, we must look closely at the victims themselves." She writes *VICTIMOLOGY* in caps on the board. "Most notably, he's not targeting vulnerable victims. He's not killing prostitutes, drug users, or street people. He's killing normal everyday people. These are people who will be missed immediately.

"Many sexual murderers prey on prostitutes, drug addicts, and others among society's unfortunates. Just look at the Green River Killer, Gary Ridgway. He was convicted of killing forty-seven prostitutes and drug addicts, admitted to killing seventy-one, and is widely believed to have killed over a hundred of society's forgotten. No one missed those girls. He got away with these murders for more than thirty years. And just like Ridgway, Sowell, Rodriguez, Gacy, and Dahmer all preyed on victims who were particularly vulnerable.

"What makes Ridgway's story even more incredible is that he was dumber than a box of rocks. Most organized serial killers tend to be educated. Even those without advanced education degrees tend to possess excessive astuteness and resourcefulness. He was left back in grammar school twice. Just goes to show you that no one gives a flying fuck about a dead prostitute or drug addict.

"Our perp, in contrast, is highly intelligent. He's good looking and articulate. In these ways, he's similar to Bundy. He's killing normal people out in the open in the middle of the day. He thinks he's invincible."

I jump in. "Okay, maybe this guy isn't completely unoriginal. Doesn't matter. We'll catch him." I turn to face the room in general. "We should have a preliminary profile to you by tomorrow night or next day at the latest. Profiles don't catch these guys, though. A profile is an investigative tool only. Sharing information, hard work, and experience will put this guy away."

I point out that the time between murders is decreasing, and we all agree that this decrease is likely to continue. We also spend quite a bit of time discussing the Kips Bay crime scene.

This crime scene clearly shows the killer's escalating egotism. The note and the pen epitomize that. He craves attention, whether it be our attention, the media's, or that of the public at large. It's what fuels his lust. It also increases his risk of getting caught.

✦ ✦ ✦◆✦ ✦ ✦

I'm shocked to realize that almost four hours have passed. We need to get a ride to Boston ASAP. D'Antoni and I thank the group members for their assistance, promise to keep everyone in the loop, and request a quick word with Maeve.

"Maeve, we need to hit the road now," D'Antoni says. "Can we plan on regrouping tonight?"

"Sounds good, Louise. Safe travels, you two."

✦ ✦ ✦◆✦ ✦ ✦

The MD 530 Little Bird is ready and waiting. D'Antoni and I get settled into the small, hard seats; buckle up; put on headsets and sunglasses; and prepare for takeoff. We're airborne moments later, with Boston a scenic seventy-five minutes away.

I glance out the window, taking in the congestion of Midtown, the vastness of Central Park, the elegant prewar townhouses of the Upper East Side, and the splendors of the city that are only visible from the air.

I'm sifting through work emails, when I suddenly catch my breath. Catherine has sent an email to my work address. She never does that. Never. Hands trembling, I open the email on my phone.

I almost fall off my seat. Patrick had a mild to moderate seizure at school today. This isn't his first; seizures are another awful repercussion of the accident. He's fine, according to the doctor, although the seizures can be dangerous, and he might have to go on medication to prevent them in the future. The medication has a long list of harmful side effects.

What the fuck is "mild to moderate"? I strain against the seat belt, instinctively wanting to pace.

D'Antoni stops typing on her cell. "Deke, what is it?"

"Patrick had another seizure. Catherine says he's fine, but I don't know why she didn't call me."

"Calm down. Everything's going to be fine." She rests her hand on my knee, her eyes locked on mine.

"I have to call her—now."

D'Antoni, aware I'm in no condition to deal with IT-related complexities, plugs the CellSet's cable into the headset jack on my phone.

Catherine doesn't answer, of course. I leave a frantic, somewhat terse voice mail imploring her to call me back as soon as she gets the message. My heart is racing, my blood is burning, and a mixture of fear and anger courses through my body.

D'Antoni knows me well, better even than Catherine. She has not lifted her hand from my knee. She maintains eye contact. "Deke, it's going to be okay. You know that, right?"

"I sure hope—"

"You know I'm right," she says, interrupting.

Most of the fear and rage subsides. She would've made one heck of a psychiatrist. I'm ready to get back to work.

D'Antoni sees the change come over my face. She taps my knee twice. "You good, pal?"

I smile at her. "I'm good. And thanks."

She clears her throat. "Why don't I write up a first draft of the profile?"

"You don't have to ask me that twice."

"Good. Let's discuss it and then plan our meeting with Slaughter."

"Sounds good."

D'Antoni nods. "Between the both of us, I think we hit every major point this morning, but let's recap anyway. He wasn't a well-behaved, well-adjusted kid. There's probably a lengthy history of acting out, vandalism, and cruelty. He may have spent time in the juvenile system, in foster care, or even on the street. He didn't wake up one day and start strangling and sexually abusing women. A lot of planning, preparation, and dedication went into making the monster we see today. My guess is at least ten to fifteen years." She looks at me intently. "One thing we've yet to discuss is demographics. Thoughts?"

"He's almost certainly East Coast. It's possible he could be required to travel on the East Coast for business, but again, my gut tells me he lives here and is probably a medical professional, maybe a doctor. It wouldn't surprise me if he lives in Boston or the suburbs nearby, since the second murder occurred there. It would make sense that he committed his first murder, at least the first murder we are aware of, where he's most comfortable, most familiar with surroundings. Then he spread his web to deflect attention. What do you think?"

She chews on that for a few seconds. "I think that makes perfect sense. We should probably have our team comb through passenger flight manifestos from Boston into Philly for the two days prior to the Philly murder to see if anything pops. The same going back to Boston. New York as well."

"Good idea."

D'Antoni has an investigative high going. She looks ready to jump out of her seat. "The time between the murders is decreasing. That'll continue. You agree?"

"Yes, no doubt," I say. "He's more comfortable killing now; he's getting cocky. That's why he left the note and pen at the crime scene. He craves attention and personal interaction, which is why he sent me the text. This personal interaction will likely continue. Also, something we haven't discussed, and I'm not sure how important it is: the killer almost certainly abuses alcohol, drugs, or both, especially at or around the time of the killings. Studies tell us it's, like, more than ninety percent likely.

"Just as an aside, we need to discuss potential conversations with the killer. He has a hard-on for me, and I'm just waiting for the phone to ring. I've been going over and over in my head what I'll say to this creep. I know exactly what I want to say, but O'Shaughnessy will never go for it."

D'Antoni's eyebrows rise, and she smiles. "Tell me."

"I want to tell him what a giant fucking pussy he is for picking on innocent, unsuspecting women in the dark. I want to tell him how unoriginal, uncreative, and utterly boring he is. That he doesn't need to pass along the horrors he suffered at the hands of some very sick people."

Just saying it out loud makes me feel better, but none of it is helpful.

"Why don't we spend a couple minutes working through how I deal with this psycho if he does call me or finds some other way to communicate? We both know damn well he's going to eventually. I know what I want to say, but it won't be constructive and will likely set him off. Fuck. I'm just having a really tough time blocking out what he said about Patrick."

"Okay," she responds. "You need to engage him in a way that makes him feel comfortable. We wanna keep the lines of communication open, as utterly distasteful as that may be."

"I know, I know. He got exactly what he wanted—struck a chord, got under my skin. I need to take a step back, rely on our experience, and deal with him accordingly. What else?"

"I think we need to be very careful here. I think some of what you said, not all of it, can be communicated. He'll see right through some politically correct, FBI-sanitized message. He loves the game, the mental chess match. While you need to stroke his ego a bit, you also need to ask some probing questions and see what he's stupid enough to cough up. Otherwise, conversation is utterly worthless. Disagree?"

"No, I don't. Keep going."

"Okay," she says. "I'd love to know what his fascination is with movie theaters. Additionally, why the focus on the Northeast, and most importantly, why the gigantic interest in you and your family?"

I nod. "It won't hurt to take a few stabs in the dark. For instance, why don't I tell him that I suspect he lives in Boston or one of its suburbs? If my guess is right, it might unnerve him a bit. And if I'm wrong, so be it. It also won't hurt to lay out our suspicions of his prior abuse and any other profile characteristics that you and O'Shaughnessy feel beneficial. I want him looking over his back. I want him to know he's playing with the best. Know what I mean?"

"Totally. We should call O'Shaughnessy when we land. Let's get back to the profile. Are we missing anything?"

"He's likely educated. My gut tells me he might be a medical professional because of his use of sux, but who knows? He could be a lawyer, a journalist—anything, really."

"I wanna chew on that a bit," D'Antoni says.

CHAPTER 12

He enters JJ Foley's Bar and Grill on Kingston Street in downtown Boston at two fifteen. He's starving and exhausted. He feels comfortable here.

Juggling work and his extracurricular activities is no easy feat. He's been burning the candle at both ends. He's never been busier at work and has fallen behind on his workload.

Focusing on work has become more challenging. He can't get the women out of his mind. Their fear, terror, and helplessness cascade through his thoughts, demanding attention. He snaps out of his trancelike state when he notices the smile on his face in the bar's mirror. *Fuck!*

He's never felt so alive. He can't wait to plan his next move.

The bartender quickly brings him back to reality when she asks him what he wants. "Give me a Sierra Nevada and a shot of Jameson," he answers. "I'll take a cheeseburger, no fries, and a large house salad as well."

"You got it, hun. Where's your sidekick?"

"What—I'm not enough for you?"

She giggles, pours him the drinks, and puts in his lunch order.

He takes a long pull off the Sierra Nevada. *Ah, that's better.* Then he downs the shot in one gulp. The familiar burn brings a smile to his face. Alcohol doesn't affect him the way it does other people. It grounds him and makes him more focused. It pushes the voices and memories to the background. One shot of Jameson helps him, if only temporarily, to ignore the nightmare that was his early life. More importantly, it helps him to focus on his next victim. He finds it ironic that Deke O'Brien allowed alcohol to take over and nearly ruin his life. Deke is a renowned profiler, a great investigator, and a best-selling author. Yet in reality, he's weak. He lacks discipline and willpower. His beautiful wife left him, and he can't see his kids. Frankly, his life's a mess. Now, man, he is going to enjoy making it even worse. What a game this is panning out to be.

Julie delivers his burger and salad. Without asking, she pours him another Jameson. He knows he shouldn't be putting red meat into his body, his castle. Then he shrugs the thought off and digs in, mentally preparing for an additional twenty minutes on the treadmill tomorrow.

He glances in the mirror, and it's as if he has hit the rewind button back to that dark time in his life.

He never knew his father. He'll find him someday, though. No reason not to show him how far he's come. The only role his mother played in his upbringing was in beating the shit out of him or letting one of her countless boyfriends physically or sexually abuse him.

He never got to pay his mother back for all her kindness. Heroin claimed her life three weeks before he entered the home.

She was lucky as far as he was concerned. She would've met a far less pleasant end had she lived. Unfortunately, memory lane will have to be revisited at another time. He has to get back to work. He winks at Julie, plunks a fifty-dollar bill onto the bar, and strolls out to his car.

CHAPTER 13

At the Boston Field Office at 1 Center Plaza, we're ushered into Brian Barnes's office. While D'Antoni and I don't know Brian personally, his reputation as a capable agent precedes him. We waste no time on pleasantries, choosing to discuss progress in the Boston investigation, get Brian up to speed on the other murders, and prepare for our meeting with Slaughter and his partner, which is only an hour away.

Brian asks a lot of questions. He's interested in talking about the killer's texts to me and the body found in Somerville. He's especially interested in the Kips Bay surveillance. He flips back and forth between the Fenway, Boston Common, and Kips Bay photos.

After some time, he stands up and begins to pace, stroking his chin. Then he stops and stares at the ceiling. He opens his mouth to speak but stops himself. Finally, he looks at the two of us.

"Are you certain the killer is telling the truth about not committing the first murder?"

I laugh. "No," I say. "Although I've got to tell you, he was very convincing. Not to mention the body found in Somerville who looks a lot like the perp in the surveillance photos."

"At first glance, it looks like we're dealing with the same guy in all four murders," Brian says. "Shit, look at the surveillance. But look closely at the Fenway photos, and then look at Kips Bay."

We do, and at first, I have no idea what he's getting at. We look up at him, waiting for him to continue.

"In the surveillance from the first Boston murder, he walks with something of a slouch, and there's an air of nervousness about him. Compare that to the footage from the other four murders. The perp in the last four murders is standing straight up, head held high. There's a cockiness coming off him that I don't see in the Fenway footage."

D'Antoni shakes her head. "I may see something too. That said, we can't discount the fact that height, hair, physical build, attire, and, most importantly, MO are identical. And it would certainly make sense that the perp would gain confidence after each crime. Deke?"

"Gimme a sec." I flip through the photos. "I can't believe I didn't pick up on this before the killer reached out to me. Brian, you may be onto something. I don't know what it is, but something feels different. If it were just confidence and cockiness, I would chalk it up to experience."

"Oh shit," Brian says. "They'll be here in less than five. Let's grab coffee first."

+ + + + + + +

The coffee is Starbucks Keurig, and while it's not great, it's leagues above what we get back at Quantico. I'm suddenly exhausted.

"What are Slaughter and his partner like?" D'Antoni asks.

Brian looks up from his cup. "Just be prepared. It's almost comical how different they are."

Minutes later, Slaughter and Bronstein knock on Barnes's office door. Brian's description of the two detectives is spot on. Slaughter is muscular and tall—taller than I am—and dressed to impress. His bald head is so shiny you could check your teeth on it. Bronstein, on the other hand, wears rumpled chinos, a threadbare button-down, and a faded navy blazer that I'm not sure he could fasten over his ample belly. His shoes are black sneakers. Yes, I guess you could say they are polar opposites.

We move to an adjoining conference room where there's more room. Slaughter wastes no time in taking the floor. He starts asking questions rapid fire about the Kips Bay murder and the texts I received from the likely killer. When he finally stops to catch his breath, I clear my throat and address the table.

Slaughter opens his mouth to object with a look of defiance and annoyance on his face. "What makes you so certain this jackoff didn't commit the first Boston murder? I mean shit, just because he killed some anesthesiologist who appears to be of the same height and build? That proves nothing. The surveillance doesn't lie."

I cut him off before he can say anything further. "First of all, we never get a good look at the killer's face. Secondly, DNA proves the same killer is responsible for the Philly, Albany, and New York City murders. We don't have a DNA connection to either of the Boston murders."

Slaughter glares at me.

"I know, I know," I say. "Surveillance footage could support one killer. Again, however—and it's a waste of breath to argue this point—there's no forensic proof linking the first Boston murders with the other four murders. There's a load of video footage and eyewitness testimony supporting the one-killer theory for all four murders. I just ask you to keep an open mind for a couple of minutes and listen to what Brian has to say. Sound fair?"

I speak more firmly than I intend. Grudgingly, Slaughter agrees to listen. Bronstein hasn't opened his mouth once; he simply nods and smiles. I like him.

Brian hands out enlarged surveillance photos from the Fenway, Boston Common, Philly, Albany, and New York City murders and spends the next twenty-five minutes rehashing what we discussed earlier. Slaughter looks bored, skeptical, and borderline unimpressed. For the first time, Bronstein perks up, his attention on the photos.

"Look. We have nearly identical MOs, and look at the pictures," Slaughter says. "It looks like the same guy, right?"

"No, wait a minute," Bronstein says. "I see the same thing Brian does. Granted, he could be holding himself differently on purpose, or maybe the bastard is more confident—proud of himself. But I see it."

"It won't matter for long anyway," I say.

"Come again?" says Slaughter.

"We have a forensic odontologist comparing the bite marks from the Fenway and Kips Bay murders. We'll have our answer soon."

Slaughter is taken aback, his face reddening. "You probably should have led with that, don't you think? No point in sitting here guessing, right?"

"Yeah, you're right. I just felt it was important that we don't go into this with blinders on. We can't afford to make any assumptions."

"Understood." Slaughter nods.

"Anything else you guys can bring us up to speed on?" D'Antoni asks.

Bronstein assumes the floor. "We went back ten years and looked at all unsolved sexual killings in Boston and the surrounding suburbs. As you probably know, we haven't had many sexual homicides with asphyxiation as the MO—not since Albert DeSalvo, the supposed Boston Strangler.

"More than seventy percent of all homicides in Boston occur in Rayburn, Dorchester, or Mattapan. Seventy percent of those killed are black males, who die in drive-bys or gang-related violence. We didn't limit the search to Boston either. We also looked at Rhode Island, Connecticut, New Hampshire, Maine, and Vermont. It all led to a giant dead end, but we left no stone unturned.

"We also checked for homicides in which succinylcholine or another paralytic was involved. We found some of these, but none fit our perp's MO. Another dead end. On the positive side, we were able to retrieve additional surveillance footage of our Fenway perp from two establishments near the Fenway cinema."

Barnes stands up. "Why am I just hearing about this now?"

Slaughter shrugs. "Easy does it, man."

"Just hear me out," Bronstein says. "It'll all make sense in a minute." He pauses and then goes on. "We obtained a very grainy image of our perp walking by Citizen Public House and Oyster Bar at four minutes after midday. It's definitely him, but enhancing the picture was no help. He was walking quickly with his head down, and the image is too grainy and distorted. However, he was also captured entering Basho Japanese Brasserie on Boylston Street at thirteen minutes past twelve. This footage is clear. While he never looks directly at the camera, his height, approximate weight, hair color, and clothing make it easy to identify him. It's definitely him, but it has no more probative value than the theater surveillance."

Bronstein hands out blowups of the photos: images of the perp entering the restaurant, taking a table in the back, and exiting. Amazingly, he never looks directly at the camera. He seems nervous, and he slouches, even when seated; it's obvious he's going out of his way not to be seen. I don't see the same posture, the same confidence, I see in the surveillance photos from the other murders. The perp here is obviously uncomfortable and nervous. In all other ways, however, he appears identical.

Barnes has calmed down at this point, and we spend the next fifteen minutes discussing all aspects of the Fenway photos, including the perp's apparent nervousness. Before we know it, almost two hours have passed since our meeting began, and we decide to take a quick break to check emails and grab coffee.

I follow Slaughter to the break room. He seems like a smart, competent detective, and we need him on board. I find it incredibly beneficial to work closely and equitably with local law enforcement— if they're good. These two definitely are.

"Hey, Slaughter, Brian tells me you guys have made a hell of a name for yourselves here in Beantown."

He takes his time to turn around to face me. "Yeah," he says. "It's not New York, and we certainly don't see the same things you guys see, but we do okay." He gives me a smile.

"I look forward to working with you guys."

"Me too," he says. "I've followed your career for several years. Very impressive. I've also read all your books; I'm a huge Sean Patrick fan,"

I laugh, genuinely flattered. "Thanks. I'm very late on the next installment in the series, and my editor is close to having a coronary.

This case is certainly not helping." I laugh again. "D'Antoni and I haven't had a lot of sleep the last couple of days, as you can imagine. And we're trying to get a profile out today. Listen, again, my partner and I are really looking forward to working with you guys and will keep you in the loop every step of the way."

"I appreciate that. That hasn't always been my experience with the FBI."

We shake hands warmly, and I make my exit to check my email and voice mail.

I search frantically for anything from Catherine. Nothing. I try her cell again, but the call goes directly to voice mail.

"Catherine, please, please let me know how Patrick is doing. I'm dying here. Thanks."

The first email I open is from O'Shaughnessy. He requests a call at eight in the evening to finalize the email response to the perp. Next, I open a text from Griff. He asks me to call him as soon as I can.

He picks up on the first ring. "Hey, pal. How's Beantown treating you? Are you taking D'Antoni to Grille 23 tonight? I fucking love that place."

"It does bring back great memories. Best martini in Boston."

"I'm salivating now," he says. "Listen, we got a potential break. My guys found a Montblanc store in the Copley Mall in Boston that sold three Meisterstück Platinum Line Classique ballpoint pens with the engraving WAS on them about six weeks ago. That's the type we found at Kips Bay. I have two of Barnes's guys over there now, talking to store employees. I'll text you their info."

"I know that store. I've bought pens there. You're the man, Griff. Call me later."

I turn quickly to run down the hall and bump headlong into Barnes. We both laugh.

"You hear about the Montblanc store in the Copley Mall?" I ask. "This could be a huge break."

"We'll hear from my guys in the next hour or so," he says.

"Awesome."

Back in the conference room, Barnes brings everyone up to speed on the Montblanc connection. Even Slaughter's and Bronstein's interests are piqued at this point.

"I guess this means our perp could be from Boston," Bronstein says. "Son of a bitch. Just what we need. The city practically shut down when DeSalvo was running loose. People stopped going out, changed their locks, and stopped answering their doors."

"D'Antoni and I think it's possible, maybe even likely, the killer resides in Boston," I say. "We were just discussing it on the ride in. The first two murders and the killing of the anesthesiologist all occurred here. It makes sense that the perp would start where he's most comfortable and then branch out to deflect attention. That being said, he could also be a professional traveling up and down the East Coast. It's too early to tell. I just hope he was dumb enough to use a credit card at the Montblanc store. At a bare minimum, maybe the store has surveillance that's backed up."

D'Antoni spends about a half hour walking Barnes, Slaughter, and Bronstein through the Kips Bay murder. Barnes has already provided Slaughter and Bronstein with all the FBI's intel on the Philly and Albany murders. We sometimes get a bad name for our cooperation with local law enforcement, but this case is turning out to be the polar opposite. If D'Antoni and I have anything to do with it, this teamwork will continue.

D'Antoni spends a lot of time focusing on the crime scene. Particular attention is paid to the location of the body in the theater, whereabouts the killer must have been seated, and everything else needed to paint an accurate picture of the crime scene and the surrounding area. Bronstein peppers her with questions, comparing and contrasting the Kips Bay scene to that in Boston. It's obvious he's a sound, detail-oriented detective. Slaughter is too; his style is more in-your-face but equally effective.

D'Antoni moves on to the items we recovered at the crime scene. Bronstein is incredulous that the New York City crime-scene techs missed the pen and the note on the first pass through.

"How's that even possible?" he asks.

Who says the New York–Boston rivalry only extends to baseball?

I lay out the condition of the body and all the details we learned from our meeting with the ME. Slaughter lets me finish before asking some questions.

"Where was the injection site?" he asks.

"Right side, upper neck. Same as the others," I say.

"Are you guys considering the potential medical-professional angle?" Slaughter asks. "This guy is obviously well versed in paralytics—everything from appropriate dosing to timing and effect."

"That's a good point," I say. "It's definitely something we have been thinking about. At this point, nothing has been ruled out."

"Good," Slaughter says. "The internet can help anyone with half a brain to become an expert in anything."

"Exactly."

D'Antoni hands out enlargements of the picture sent from the victim's phone. Slaughter can't take his eyes off it and studies it intently for a few minutes.

Barnes's phone rings; he grabs it and exits the room. He returns a couple minutes later with a grim look on his face.

"What's the word, Brian?" D'Antoni asks.

"Store surveillance only goes back four weeks, and it's not backed up or stored. So we have no visual. The store manager actually made the sale, and he remembers the buyer. He described him as tall and well dressed, with wavy dark hair, and wearing sunglasses and a baseball hat. To make matters worse, the individual paid for the pens with cash. However, he did leave a name, a phone number, and physical and email addresses. Nothing pans out, though. Everything's bogus."

"What name did he give?" I ask.

"It's fake," Barnes says.

"Humor me."

"Morris T. Killstein."

I exhale sharply, stand up, and stretch.

"What?" Slaughter asks. "Killstein?"

"Just think about it for a second."

"Holy shit!" exclaims D'Antoni. "Movie Theater Killer."

When we break again, I check for any update on Patrick while gazing out the conference room window. Nothing.

D'Antoni spends the next forty-five minutes discussing our preliminary profile. Bronstein and Slaughter ask questions, adding their two cents along the way. Based on his questions, it's obvious Slaughter doesn't have a lot of faith in the profiling process. He's not alone in his lack of belief.

"So you guys actually think this is going to help us catch our guy?" Slaughter says. "I'm just struggling to see it. It seems so slick and convenient, like you dusted something off from your archives. There are plenty of sickos out there who had completely normal childhoods."

Bronstein tries to persuade him to let the point drop and listen to what D'Antoni has to say, but Slaughter isn't done yet. He goes through the text the killer sent me in agonizing detail. "This is the key," he says, locking eyes with me. "You know this guy. He certainly knows you. How else can you explain his knowledge of your personal life and your family? He knows everything about you. You need to take a step back, clear your mind, and think long and hard about who this sicko is. You're the key. Everything else is secondary."

"Secondary?" D'Antoni asks. "Do you have any idea how important every detail, every tool we have at our disposal, is to a serial investigation?"

Slaughter throws his arms up in mock surrender. "I'm just frustrated. I want to get this guy."

"We all do," D'Antoni says.

"My partner doesn't always play well in the sandbox, especially when the FBI is involved," Bronstein jokes. Everybody, including Slaughter, laughs at this, and it lightens the mood so that the meeting closes without any fireworks. We walk Slaughter and Bronstein to the elevator and promise to provide them with updates.

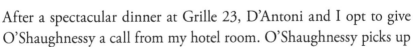

"I can't believe those two are partners," D'Antoni says. "Slaughter looks totally put together, and Bronstein looks like he slept in his fifth-grade Catholic school uniform."

"I told you," Barnes says.

"They're both good cops," I say. "Slaughter's a little territorial, and maybe he's wound a bit tight. The good ones always are, though. I really liked Bronstein."

Barnes and D'Antoni laugh and nod.

It's now a quarter before eight in the evening, and I'm hungry. "Brian, you want to join us for dinner at Grille 23?" I ask.

"Thanks for the offer, Deke, but I haven't seen a lot of the wife and kiddies lately, so let me take a rain check."

"You got it, pal."

He walks us to the elevator. "Any chance I can see the preliminary profile when you finish?"

"You'll be on the initial distribution list."

"Thanks, guys. Enjoy Grille 23. It's my favorite restaurant in the city."

I like this guy.

After a spectacular dinner at Grille 23, D'Antoni and I opt to give O'Shaughnessy a call from my hotel room. O'Shaughnessy picks up on the second ring. Surprisingly, I detect no irritation in his voice.

"How was Grille 23?" he asks. "D'Antoni, you have the beef tenderloin? Damn fine dish."

"I did, sir."

"I spoke to Griff and Barnes and decided you guys needed an hour to catch your breath. Sounds like we're making real progress. Are we assuming this guy is from Boston or one of its suburbs?"

I clear my throat. "It makes sense. It's certainly possible he could just as easily be a regular business traveler. But we're leaning toward a medical professional who would clearly have a home base."

"*Regular* may be a poor choice of word, Deke."

I laugh. "You got that right."

"So where are we on the profile? Are we still planning to circulate something tonight?"

"I'll email a draft before hitting the hay," D'Antoni says.

"Good. Everyone is anxiously waiting. Let's reconvene at eight in the morning." He pauses and then is struck by another thought. "Shit. Hold on a second. Deke, we need to discuss what you're going to say if and when the perp reaches out to you again. You think about it yet?"

"Yeah. D'Antoni and I have spent a considerable amount of time discussing it."

"Let's hear," he says.

I take a moment to collect my thoughts. "The key is to make him comfortable and encourage ongoing dialogue—to probe without being invasive and to suck up just a little without feeding him a pile of FBI-sanitized bullshit. That being said, I want to address bits and pieces of our profile with him and see if I can rile him a bit."

"Anything to add, D'Antoni?"

"No. We're on the same page."

"All right. I really can't think of anything else," O'Shaughnessy says. "Wait. Except that the same goes for you, Louise. This guy may reach out to you as well. Just be prepared." He yawns. "Use my regular call-in number tomorrow morning at eight. I'll make sure Griff and Barnes are available as well. I want to disseminate the profile nationwide by noon. Thanks, guys."

The line goes dead. I stifle a yawn and glance over at D'Antoni. "You want help with the profile? The two of us can bang it out quicker together."

"Get some sleep, twinkle toes," D'Antoni replies. "I've got this. It'll be exactly what we discussed earlier. If I need anything, I'll call."

✦✦✦✦✦✦

When I check my inbox, I see that Catherine has emailed me twice. Patrick is fine, happy and having fun. She says it's impossible to get him to sit still. He's totally back to himself. In fact, he walked right up to the checkout girl in the grocery store of Catherine today and gave her a hug. *Thank God!*

I look through the rest of my emails. There's a terse and, in fact, downright rude note from my editor, Connor Watson. He indicates his firm will consider suing me for return of the advance if a draft is not received within the agreed two-week time frame. *What agreed time frame? Fuck him.* That's exactly what I email him in response. I add that there are plenty of other editors and publishers out there who would love to have me as a client. Then I close—but not before I let him know that my lawyer and I will look closely at the viability of the relationship, keeping all our options open.

This act brings a shit-eating grin to my face. In truth, I love working with Connor. I'd follow him to the ends of the earth. I also love pulling his chain. He's such a nervous Nellie, scared of his own shadow. My message will likely keep him up all night, but he deserves it.

Finding nothing else of note, I flip off the light, hoping sleep comes quickly.

CHAPTER 14

D'Antoni gives the profile write-up one last read-through. It's half past one in the morning, and she has agreed to meet Deke at seven for the world-famous Ritz breakfast buffet. That son of a bitch has to have his breakfast, or his whole day is shot. Louise D'Antoni would rather sleep in.

The profile starts with the obvious—approximate age, race, hair color, height, and build—and then moves on to the less obvious and more significant deductive observations.

The killer comes from a broken home. He wasn't wanted, never mind loved, by his birth parents. He spent considerable time in foster or state-sponsored care. He was subject to abuse, including sexual abuse, as a child and into early adulthood.

He was in trouble from early on, committing everything from theft to the abuse of animals and people. He was known by local law enforcement. He's in the system, though probably only the juvenile system, meaning he's kept his nose clean as an adult as far as law enforcement is concerned.

He's affable, well spoken, and intelligent. He interacts well with others but prefers to be by himself. He's probably highly educated and likely has a good professional job. Given his knowledge and effective use of paralytics, he could be in a medical profession; he might even be a doctor. His job might afford him the ability, or require him, to travel. It's likely he resides on the East Coast, probably in Boston.

She nods out for a second but catches herself before she can fall out of the chair. Nothing else will be accomplished tonight—nothing helpful anyway. She saves the document and then sends an encrypted copy of it, draft-stamped, to Deke, O'Shaughnessy, Griff, and Barnes. She reminds everyone that there's a call at eight to discuss the document.

She's asleep before her head hits the pillow.

CHAPTER 15

The TV coverage of his latest accomplishment is beginning to wane. It's still the lead story, just not 24-7. He needs to change that. He loves being the center of attention, seen and heard by all. His mind drifts, as it often does, to his early formative years.

That fucking cunt Jane Martin floats across his vision. He still has nightmares about being trapped at the bottom of the pool. He can see the surface and all the people horsing around—people smiling, laughing, and having fun. He could swear they're all laughing and pointing at him. Then they start to fade away.

She pushed him in and never looked back. Now he's paralyzed by fear—the fear of not being able to breathe, of being trapped. The fear still cripples him, invading his thoughts daily.

He refuses to this day to go anywhere near a pool. It's not just pools either. The last time he rode an elevator, something he's expected to do almost every day now, he sweated through his shirt.

He almost came undone a few weeks back while working in the basement of an old brownstone in Southie. Every step he took down the stairs into that dank, claustrophobic space sent jolts of panic through his body. Breathing techniques he's perfected and continues to work on daily helped him fight through the fear and panic to do his job that day.

He has that fucking cunt to thank for all of it.

That said, she's also responsible for who he's become—for his sick, twisted fascinations and, most of all, for his fascination with asphyxiation. Watching someone slowly choke to death is the most incredible thing. It's beautiful, captivating, hypnotic, and orgasmic. It's all he lives for. He can no longer climax without it. Shit, he can barely get hard without it. He's forced to re-create it over and over to satiate his desires.

Jane is now a stay-at-home housewife in Weston, Massachusetts, a wealthy suburb of Boston. She married into old money. She's done well for herself. She has two screaming brats, a dog, a huge backyard—the whole fucking American dream. Who better to turn the dream into a nightmare than him?

He owes her.

She has it coming.

He has been saving Jane for a special occasion. A smile creases his face as he revisits his plans. It has been years in the making, but that's what makes it so special. The crescendo of anticipation is like rushing water coursing through his veins.

This will fill the void—until his next big adventure. This will quiet the noise in his head that increases in volume each day.

He feels better now—content.

It's time to sleep and rejuvenate.

CHAPTER 16

The alarm trills at five in the morning. I'm dead tired, but I need to spend some time with the profile. I start the coffee maker, boot up my computer, and dive right in.

D'Antoni did a great job. She hit most, if not all, of the salient points. I will begrudgingly compliment her on a job well done. She is one hell of a profiler—maybe even better than I am. That I won't tell her.

I meet D'Antoni in the dining room at seven. We briefly discuss the profile but spend most of breakfast bullshitting and joking around. It's important to keep things in perspective during an investigation. Working all day every day is ineffective. You need to take a step back to regroup if you want to stay sharp.

We take the eight o'clock call from my hotel room. O'Shaughnessy asks for a quick progress update, and D'Antoni spends ten minutes on that. Then we dive into the profile. Everyone gets a chance to comment. The conversation is productive, and we decide on a few minor changes and additions.

One thing we all agree must be addressed is the sexual sadism component. This is a guy who can't get off sexually unless he's controlling, dominating, and hurting women. He's sexually obsessed in an unhealthy way and views women as objects, not as equals.

This affliction wasn't developed overnight. It was nurtured and learned over many years. In all likelihood, there are women, such as former girlfriends, who remember the perp in an unfavorable way.

The perp lives to fulfill his sadistic desires. Because of this, he sticks out. Try as he might, he can't hide his hypersexuality. It's who he is. It's part of his everyday life. He can no more run from it than he can refuse to breathe.

D'Antoni agrees to make the suggested changes and recirculate the profile to the extended team. We're making progress, and I feel motivated and energized.

Thank God for this job.

I give D'Antoni a half hour to push through the suggested tweaks and get the profile out to the team. We then head over to the Copley Mall to see if there's anything the Montblanc store manager can add to what he already told Brian's people. I tell D'Antoni to pick up whatever she needs clothes-wise at the mall, and I'll handle the store manager interview. She agrees with thanks.

The manager is just opening the store as I approach. I show him my creds and ask him for fifteen minutes of his time.

His physical description is basically a verbatim repeat of what he told Brian's team and confirms what we already know. He does, however, make some useful observations about the perp's manner. He describes the perp as intense, wired even, with an air of cockiness and superiority. It's obvious he didn't like the guy.

"He got right up in my grill," the manager says. "He spoke to me very loud, slow, and deliberate. He treated me like some kind of moron. It really pissed me off, to be honest. He demanded to see more than twenty different pens before settling on the one he eventually chose. He paid for the three pens in cash on the spot and turned around without so much as a 'Thank you for the help' and walked out. He picked the engraved pens up three days later."

"You notice anything different about him when he returned to pick up the pens?" I ask.

"No, nothing. He was dressed almost identically, including the baseball hat and sunglasses."

"Thanks." I hand him one of my cards and ask him to call if he thinks of anything else or ever sees the man again. We shake hands, and I head out in search of D'Antoni.

I dial her cell, and she picks up on the second ring.

"Where you at?" I ask.

"I'm in Neiman Markup—I mean Neiman Marcus. I'm in line to pay. I'll be ready in five."

"Wow, I'm impressed. That was quick. I'll meet you out front."

CHAPTER 17

He's been observing Jane and her family fairly regularly for the past eighteen months. He knows their routines and patterns. He knows when Jane drops the kids off at school, when she goes to the gym, and on which day she picks up her dry cleaning. He knows the days on which the cleaning lady comes and when Jane's friends come over for wine and gossip. He knows the ins and outs of her entire life. Shit, he knows when her next bowel movement will be.

Most importantly, he knows when Jane is all alone in that big house. He's left nothing to chance. His plan is foolproof. He has worked it through from start to finish dozens of times in his mind, and now the day has finally come. The pain of waiting, of anticipating, will finally be eased. That fucking cunt will feel what he felt.

He exits the Mass Turnpike, brimming with excitement. Ten minutes later, he's driving through the quaint village of Weston. *Where the fuck do these people get all this money?* He pulls up in front of the Starbucks and parks. This is a perfect time for a dark roast.

He opens the front door and scans the room. There she is—in the back left corner with a venti skinny latte in her right hand, her eyes glued to today's *Wall Street Journal*. He chuckles to himself. She's a stay-at-home mom. What the fuck does she know about money and investing?

He steps up to the counter, places his order, and waits. Then, coffee in hand, he selects a table a safe distance from Jane. It's possible she might recognize him, although he doubts it. He's several inches taller and at least fifty pounds heavier than he was when she knew him. Countless hours in the gym have given him the V-shaped frame of a professional athlete, a body he's proud of, a body that others envy.

She also knew him by a different name.

She glances up when he pulls out his chair to sit. They lock eyes, and he holds her gaze until she looks away. Did she recognize him? Did he see something in her eyes? No. But she would remember him soon enough.

She's wearing Under Armour workout clothes. She works out at Longfellow Sports Club on weekdays from eight thirty in the morning until about ten. She never misses a day, and her tight body attests to this. She's had work done as well—breast augmentation for sure. He can't wait to put his hands on her body.

He's pulsing with excitement, when he notices her staring at him. He's careful to avoid eye contact. *Shit*. Does she recognize him?

He waits a couple minutes before stealing a look her way. She's packing up, getting ready to leave. Her routine is to head home to shower, sometimes stopping at the Brothers Marketplace to pick up groceries on the way. She's a true creature of habit. It almost takes some of the fun out of what he's planning.

Sure enough, she stops at Brothers. He continues on, without slowing, to her development. The neighborhood consists of about twenty well-built custom homes, each on an acre and a half of land. Of course, Jane's house is one of the nicest.

How fitting.

He's surveilled the house more than fifty times and been inside on five separate occasions. Once, he stole a set of house keys, which he copied before returning the originals. He even knows the alarm code. Like many other stupid homeowners, she has written the code on a piece of paper she keeps in a drawer in the kitchen.

He's even studied her immediate neighbors. He knows with little doubt when they will be home and when they will not.

Now's an ideal time to make his move.

She has a routine she follows upon returning from the gym. Before showering, she strips off her sweaty clothes, sits down on the carpeted floor in the master bedroom, and goes through a series of stretches.

Once, he watched her from her husband's closet. He was mesmerized by her movements and her flexibility. She tucked both legs behind her head, holding the pose without appearing to expend any energy. He almost came just from watching her. Fuck, she turned him on. When she padded off to the bathroom, he picked up her sweaty panties and breathed in her musky aroma. It was all he could do to stop himself from taking her that day.

Twenty minutes later, she pulls into her driveway. One of the garage doors goes up, and she parks. He watches her leave the vehicle with groceries in hand. The garage door slides down.

He reflexively taps the steering wheel and then looks down at his hands and notices they're shaking badly. Actually, his whole body is shaking, as if it is wired to explode. This day has been a long time coming. He's going to take his time and savor every second.

He adjusts his Swarovski binoculars until the staircase from the first to the second floor in Jane's house comes into view. He'll enter from the back after she puts away the groceries and heads upstairs to the master bedroom.

He taps his front shirt pocket, confirming the presence of the sux-filled syringe. *What's taking her so damn long?* Impatience threatens his self-control.

Suddenly, her lithe body comes into view on the stairs. She ascends slowly, absentmindedly staring at her phone. If she only knew what he has in store for her.

He's speaking out loud now to nobody.

"Be there soon, baby. I think I'll just let myself in and join you upstairs. Get limber; you're going to need it."

He spends the next five minutes glancing furtively up and down the street, looking for anomalies or for anyone who might see him. Luckily, he doesn't have to worry about landscapers or lawn-service companies thanks to the late November date. The street is quiet. He gives it one more minute and then gets out of the car and approaches the house.

He walks casually, pretending to partake in an animated conversation on his cell phone. His plan is to go in through the back door, which is out of view of any neighbors' prying eyes. In the backyard, he'll have total privacy.

He sees nothing out of the ordinary in his peripheral vision and makes his way without incident to the back of the house.

He slips the key into the lock and silently enters the house. He stills himself, listening for noise. The faint sounds of a TV reach him from upstairs. Carefully, he slips off his shoes, leaving them by the door. Slowly, he walks to the front of the house. He spends another minute looking up and down the street—looking for anything out of the ordinary. Seeing nothing, he heads to the stairway and makes his way up. He ascends one step at a time, stopping at each step to listen. All he hears is the buzz of the TV—some stupid talk show favored by housewives.

At the top of the landing, he waits, listening intently. The door to the master bedroom is fewer than ten feet away. He crawls to the door, thinking it'll be quieter than walking. He peeks around the doorframe—and there she is, in all her naked glory. Her back is to him; her eyes are glued to the TV.

Should he make his move now? He's completely out of her line of sight, and her neck is exposed.

No, he will stick to the plan and make his move when she gets out of the shower and comes back into the bedroom. He hasn't gotten this far without careful, precise planning, and he isn't going to drop it now.

She stretches for another eight minutes and then jumps up and heads to the shower in the master bathroom. When he hears the shower door open and close, he steps into the bedroom and quickly makes his way to the other side of the room. He positions himself on the left side of the bathroom door, completely out of view. Next, he takes out the syringe and uncaps it.

Let the party begin.

She takes her time, spending nearly twenty minutes in the shower and another ten in front of the vanity before stepping back into the room. He's waiting. He clasps her mouth with his left hand and plunges the syringe into her neck with his right. The move is fluid and silent. She never sees it coming.

The large bath towel she's wrapped around her falls lazily to the ground. She stares at him in dumbfounded, bug-eyed terror. He gently eases her to the floor, affectionately caressing her hair. He whispers in her ear. "Jane, remember the good old days at Rayburn House?"

He asks her if she remembers him.

Tears blot her eyes. She looks as if she might pass out at any minute. That won't do. She has to be awake for this.

He hungrily touches her at will, and he's not gentle about it. It's not romantic or caring in any way. She stares wide-eyed, her heart pounding out of her chest, which only increases his desire. He spends the next fifteen minutes exploring every inch of her beautiful body. Oh, how he wishes he had more time. The things he wants to do.

He looks deep into her eyes. She's still conscious, fully aware, filled with terror.

He wants to mount her, but he's transfixed by her eyes, unable to move.

His hand lazily trails from her head down to her perfect ass, where it lingers. *You could bounce quarters off this rear. What a beautiful physical specimen.* She was all legs and arms back at Rayburn House, but money and free time have transformed her.

He laughs out loud. "You never should've thrown me into that pool, honey. All you had to do was help me get back to the side. I'm just repaying the favor. No hard feelings, right? Ha-ha!"

When it's obvious she's on her last leg, he kisses her on the lips and watches the light fade from her eyes.

She's gone.

CHAPTER 18

We spend the next couple days in Philadelphia and Albany, interviewing witnesses, meeting with local law enforcement and FBI colleagues, meeting with MEs, visiting crime scenes, studying surveillance, and comparing and contrasting these murders with the others. We also try desperately to glean anything new, anything that will get us closer to catching this guy. I'd like to say we're rewarded for our efforts, but I can't. Little progress is made; little new information is learned. It's as if we're stuck in quicksand, sinking fast. It's damn frustrating.

Man, a stiff drink would hit the spot now.

With all leads exhausted, we head back to DC with our tails between our legs. I'm dead tired and mentally shot. I desperately need a night in my own bed and at least seven hours of uninterrupted sleep. D'Antoni feels the same way. We both need to take a step back, recharge, and attack the case with a fresh set of eyes.

Little is said on the flight back to Quantico. The cloud of frustration and helplessness is palpable in the cabin. I stare absentmindedly out the window. Bits and pieces of the last several days flash through my mind like a motion picture in reverse. *What am I missing? There has to be something there. Has to be.*

We land in Quantico and prepare for what's to come, the inevitable O'Shaughnessy debrief. This is not going to be fun. In all honesty, he has every right to be frustrated. We aren't a whole lot closer to identifying and apprehending the perp than we were a few days ago. His A team is coming back empty-handed.

I close my eyes and try a breathing technique that's designed to promote relaxation. Who am I kidding? I've tried the same technique dozens of times to no avail. I'm not wired that way. My mind races perpetually, even in sleep. Booze was the only thing that ever helped to shut the noise off, and that's not an option now.

I snap back to the present when D'Antoni touches my shoulder. "Time to rip the Band-Aid off. Better to do it quickly, right?"

"I guess," I say. "Did you bring the lube?"

"Nope. This will be a lube-free ass fucking."

"My favorite kind."

We enter O'Shaughnessy's office prepared for the worst. His back is to us; his right hand is stroking his chin. He takes almost a full minute before turning around. He's dramatic, if nothing else.

D'Antoni takes the initiative and the floor, but O'Shaughnessy cuts her off abruptly with a wave of the finger. "Me first," he says.

Oh man, this is not going to be good.

"Guess who I just got off the phone with?" He looks like a cat with the proverbial canary dangling from its mouth.

D'Antoni and I exchange glances and shrug. "No idea, boss," I say.

"The forensic odontologist—that's who. We'll have his report soon."

That's all he says. He spends the next thirty seconds leaning back in his chair with his hands behind his head, staring at the ceiling.

The silence is deafening. Finally, D'Antoni clears her throat. "And—"

"We've got ourselves two killers. The bite marks from the first Boston murder don't match New York City. He's positive—zero doubt. We are checking the teeth marks against our Somerville victim as we speak."

"He was telling the truth," I say under my breath.

"So the perp who committed the second Boston murder and the Philly, Albany, and New York City murders is both a serial killer and a copycat," O'Shaughnessy says.

I'm having trouble focusing. I'm too damn tired, and mental overload has set in.

"You guys are useless to me right now," O'Shaughnessy says.

"What's that supposed to mean?" D'Antoni says testily.

"What it means is that you look dead on your feet. You look like someone shot your puppy. Both of you get the fuck out of here right now. Go home, and get some sleep. I need you sharp. I don't need to tell you the pressure I'm under from upstairs. We can game-play tomorrow morning at nine. Now, get outta here."

That's exactly what we do.

CHAPTER 19

I walk through the front door to my townhouse a few minutes after eleven. I pray for uninterrupted, dreamless sleep.

The next thing I know, my cell phone trills. I wipe the sleep out of my eyes, trying to focus on the alarm clock and the time. Eventually, the blurriness clears. It's four thirty in the morning. This can't be good.

"O'Brien," I answer.

I'm greeted by a metallic whirring sound, but just as I'm about to hang up, a voice on the other end of the line addresses me by name. Whoever the caller is, he's employing some kind of voice-altering device to mask his identity. *Well, well. It's about time.*

"Do you know who this is?" His words are garbled. I fumble with the speaker button on my cell phone and grab a pad and pen from the table. I'm wide awake now, with adrenaline coursing through me like electricity.

"Yeah, I know who it is," I reply.

"Good. I hope I didn't wake you. A good investigator never rests. You've been busy, huh? Boston, New York, Philly, and Albany—all in two weeks. Tell me—did you learn anything interesting? Were your travels fruitful? Do you feel closer to apprehending me than you did a few days ago?"

"Not really," I say. "You've done a good job of hiding your face. Your DNA is not on file anywhere, but you know that. It's just a matter of time, though. You'll make a mistake, and I'll be there to correct it."

Loud, distorted chuckling echoes in my ear. "Oh, Deke, I admire your drive and your tenacity. We both know I'm in your head. I'm fucking playing with you. I'm the cat, and you're the mouse. You're the only reason I'm still playing the game, because frankly, I'm bored with it. I have much bigger things planned; I've already done much bigger things. The first murder in Boston presented an opportunity I simply couldn't pass up. Here's a guy who kills a young woman in the middle of the day in a very public place. It took either enormous balls or sheer stupidity. And the way he chose to kill her was so fucking poetic, don't you think? Watching someone's light go out up close and personal is just so amazing. It's mind-blowing. Nothing else compares."

"I know you didn't do the first Boston murder," I say. "What I can't figure out is why you became a copycat. Where's the originality? The creativity? You would think a smart, capable guy like yourself could come up with his own plan and would want to leave his own mark. Do you feel a little bit guilty about taking credit for everything?"

More loud chuckling comes through the phone. "Deke, you do not disappoint. I'm going to have a lot of fun with you. I simply seized an opportunity, a chance to become infamous and to instill public fear. Would you not even give me that? Have you not been watching the TV? The fear is palpable. I'm invincible, and my journey has just begun."

"Yeah, people don't like seeing women preyed on in the dark. Famous? Nah. You'll be nothing more than a blip. You're more pathetic than scary. You can't even write your own script. You plagiarized it. Just a fucking copycat. Where's the originality? Why should you be remembered as anything else?"

More laughter erupts. "Oh, Deke, this is better than I even imagined. Is D'Antoni as good as you are? Who cares, right? She's such a fine piece of ass. You ever tap that, partner? Maybe back when you were drinking? You can tell me. Maybe we'll get to compare notes someday—maybe sooner than you think."

"What happened to you?" I ask. "Did you completely strike out with the ladies? Probably pissed you off, huh? Big, strong guy like you can't even get a date, never mind laid. So you decide to prey on helpless women. That's what you get off on. You're not wired right. You're a freak and need to be put down like a rabid dog."

He laughs again. "How is the little retard doing? You blame yourself for his condition, don't you? You were drunk, weren't you, when he fell? It's your fault he's a little halfwit. He's cute—looks a lot like you—but he's dumber than a post. You can't take care of yourself, never mind him. He should be put out of his misery. I can do that for you if you want."

I need to focus, do my job, and stop letting emotion get in the way. "Why the focus on the Northeast? Is that where you're from? Probably Boston, right?"

"You know that Catherine is dating someone, don't you? It looks like it's getting pretty serious. She and your kids went to his vacation home a couple weeks back. I wonder if they'll call him Dad. It's probably for the best. Don't you think?"

"Oh, lest I forget, you might want to check in on a Jane Birnbaum in Weston, Massachusetts. I knew her as Jane Martin. Man, did she she fill out nicely. Payback's a bitch. Ha ha!

CHAPTER 20

I grab the notepad and head downstairs, where I start the coffee maker and sit down to digest what has just transpired. I could have handled the conversation more professionally. Once again, I have let the creep get to me and this time in a big way. My head is pounding, and my pulse is racing. I want to punch a hole in something. What he said about Patrick was downright cruel—inhumane. I realize now that I would do anything for the chance to choke this freak out.

Five minutes later, with sufficient caffeine coursing through my veins, I call D'Antoni. She picks up on the third ring, sounding groggy and annoyed.

"What do you want at this hour?"

"He called me," I say. "We talked for almost twenty minutes."

"Give me a sec." I hear her moving around, switching on a light. "When?"

"Just now."

"Don't leave anything out. Even the smallest thing could be important."

I recount the conversation. She stops me frequently, asking pointed questions and often making me repeat things. I implore her to be extra vigilant and self-aware going forward, given the killer's unhealthy interest in her.

"He's going to contact you," I tell her. "He told me as much. For all I know, he could be watching you—watching both of us."

"Let him," she says. "I have plenty of things I wanna talk to him about. I'm not scared of this creep, not in the slightest."

"That's fine," I say. "But I've got a really bad feeling about this guy. He's been watching Catherine and the kids. What the fuck am I supposed to do about that? Do I tell Catherine? Will O'Shaughnessy okay a protection detail for a while? Does it even warrant protection? Fuck! Of course it does. It's my fucking family we're talking about!"

"Hey," she says soothingly, "your family is safe. Worst-case scenario, you pony up yourself for some protection. Do whatever you feel you need to so we can focus all our attention on catching this sicko."

"Yeah, you're right. I'd better wake O'Shaughnessy up."

"Patch him in," she says.

I do, and O'Shaughnessy picks up on the fourth ring. I tell him immediately about my conversation with the killer and what he said about Jane Birnbaum and he tells D'Antoni and me to get into the office immediately. Minutes later, I am doing more than a hundred miles an hour on the highway while scenes of my family—playing at the park, walking to school, walking the dog—flash through my mind. Is my family in danger? What have they done to deserve this? Absolutely nothing.

My cell phone is ringing when I reach my desk. The office is deserted at this hour.

It's Barnes, and he wastes no time. "Jane Birnbaum of 1 Riverbed Drive in Weston, Massachusetts, was killed in her house sometime after 1100 hours yesterday. Her naked, lifeless body was discovered by her husband around eight in the evening, when he returned home from work. Neither the nanny nor the kids were able to tell the husband where his wife was when he arrived home. He got worried and began combing the house for her. He finally found her tucked into the back corner of her walk-in closet. She was naked, and officers noted that an object, likely some form of paper, had been shoved into the woman's vagina. They didn't remove the object, per the ME's instructions. An autopsy will be performed first thing this morning. You should get up here as quick as you can."

"I will. What else can you tell me?"

"A puncture mark was also found, on the upper right side of the victim's neck. The MO looks identical."

"Keep going," I say.

"There was no evidence of a break-in. Zero. The husband and nanny were both adamant that Jane was very security-conscious, probably overly so, and the doors were always locked—always, without exception."

"Any of the neighbors see anything?"

"I was just getting to that. A woman staying at a house two doors down on the opposite side of the street said a dark sedan was parked directly across the street from the Birnbaums' house for an extended period of time. She was drinking coffee and reading a newspaper in the front portico of the house when the sedan parked near the Birnbaums' and idled for almost forty-five minutes. At that point, a tall white male dressed in a dark suit came out of the car and approached the Birnbaum house. She could see the man perfectly; he had his phone to his ear and appeared to be engaged in a conversation. Trees then blocked her view of the man, and she never saw him enter the house. She was adamant to point out that she wasn't being nosy. It was a beautiful day, and she was enjoying the scenery.

"She never saw him leave the house either. She went upstairs to shower and get ready for the day, and when she returned downstairs, the car was gone. When pressed by local law enforcement to describe the make and model of the car, she represented it as a nondescript, midsize black sedan, probably American."

"We need to talk to this woman," I say.

"What time can you be here?"

"Let's shoot for eleven o' clock. D'Antoni and I will need a lift from wherever we land, if that's okay."

"Just drop me a text with the time and location, and someone will be there waiting."

"Thanks, Brian. See you soon."

Seated at my desk, I map out a plan for the day, but the conversation with the killer continually echoes in my mind. I'm worried sick for my family's safety. He's obviously been watching Catherine and the kids for some time. I can't do my job effectively if I'm worried about them, so I decide to lob a call to a former colleague, Jim Conolley, who now owns and operates his own security firm. If anyone can keep my family safe, he can.

I call his personal cell, and he picks up immediately. "O'Brien, long time, pal. What's shaking?"

I spend the next ten minutes bringing him up to speed. I painstakingly walk through the killer's physical attributes and promise to send a copy of one of the surveillance photos over. I let him know it's also possible the killer has a proxy doing his dirty work. When I'm finished, breathless, Jim lets out a loud sigh. *Oh no. Maybe he can't help me.*

There's a long, uncomfortable pause before Jim speaks. My heart is pounding in my chest; a sheen of sweat coats my forehead.

"Shit, Deke. This is really a bad time. I have foreign diplomats straight through for the next three weeks. Shit! Oh man. I'll try to bring on some additional help. I'll have someone watching your wife and kids if I have to do it myself, pal."

Relief floods through me, and my heart rate normalizes within seconds. "I don't know how to thank you, Jim."

"You might not thank me when you get the bill," he says.

I laugh. "Listen, Jim, O'Shaughnessy might authorize some protection. But as we both know, it'll be limited. If you can fill in the gaps, I'd really appreciate it."

"Will do. And, Deke, don't worry, pal. We've got your family's back."

I feel as though a heavy weight has been lifted from my chest. I clasp my hands behind my head and lean back in my chair, staring up at the ceiling. When D'Antoni touches my shoulder, I nearly flip over the chair.

"Sorry!" she exclaims, her hands up in the air.

"I hate it when people sneak up on me," I say.

"Brian told me he spoke to you. Looks like we're headed back to Massachusetts. O'Shaughnessy in yet?"

"I don't think so. Let's grab a coffee."

We make small talk in the coffee room for the next ten minutes, neither of us ready to dive back into the investigation just yet. Just as I'm finishing off my coffee, O'Shaughnessy bursts into the room at a jog with his own coffee cup in hand. His forehead glistens with sweat; his eyes are blazing with stress.

"My office in five minutes," he says.

◆◆◆◆◆

We spend the first fifteen minutes discussing the Birnbaum crime scene. O'Shaughnessy paces back and forth with coffee in hand, brown liquid sloshing out at the sides as he gesticulates. "Well, it looks like our serial killer is most likely from the Boston area, even though he wasn't responsible for the first murder. The pen purchase in the Copley Mall, the Boston Common murder, and now this certainly supports that premise. Agreed?"

We nod in unison.

D'Antoni speaks up. "We need to focus on the killer's relationship with Ms. Birnbaum. He told Deke that he knew her as Jane Martin. We need to dig into her life, especially her life before she got married. Maybe she had a relationship with this sicko that ended badly. At the very least, their paths crossed."

"I'll get a team on it pronto," O'Shaughnessy says. "Deke, let's get back to the call. Give it to us from start to finish again."

I do, and I make sure to highlight the danger I see to my family, D'Antoni, and anyone working on the investigation. "This guy either has help or the ability to cover a lot of ground in different states. I truly believe he's a danger to those close to me. He's fixated on hurting me; I don't know why. He's focused on fame and notoriety; I really got under his skin when I called him a copycat and unoriginal."

"I just hope that tactic doesn't come back to bite us in the ass," O'Shaughnessy says.

"It won't," I say, sounding more sure than I am. "I don't know that he would've revealed the Birnbaum murder if I hadn't pushed him. He likes the give-and-take. It's all a big game to him. He's not going to succumb to any mental jockeying. Too damn smart."

I notice I've been talking much more loudly than I intended. I take a deep breath, count to five, and continue. "I think it goes without saying that my family should have around-the-clock protection." I thrust my hand out to silence O'Shaughnessy. "Before you answer, hear me out. I've got a really bad feeling about this guy, boss. He's hell-bent on hurting me and knows where to focus his attention to get the biggest bang for his buck. It's not a question of if he does something but when. You need to fully comprehend what I'm telling you before you give me your answer. I'll not have my family in danger."

O'Shaughnessy leans back in his chair and regards me. I can see the compassion and concern in his eyes. Temporary relief floods my body.

"D'Antoni already requested the same for your family," O'Shaughnessy says. "It's already in the works. I don't know for how long, but I'll do everything I can."

I glance at D'Antoni and wink appreciatively. Then I tell O'Shaughnessy about my arrangement with Jim Conolley. "He'll fill any gaps in coverage. Coordination with his team would be much appreciated. I just need to know that it's covered."

"Rest assured," O'Shaughnessy says.

I sigh and let out a deep breath. Now I can put 100 percent into catching this guy. What a relief.

There's a knock at O'Shaughnessy's door.

"Yeah?" O'Shaughnessy says. The door swings open, and a forensic tech, whom I recognize but whose name I've forgotten, enters the office.

"Tell me," O'Shaughnessy barks.

The tech clears his throat and nervously addresses the three of us. "It's a burner cell. The call originated from Copley Place in Boston. We'll do everything we can to figure out who purchased the phone, but it's a long shot."

"Fine," O'Shaughnessy says dismissively, and the tech is gone.

When the tech shuts the door, I address O'Shaughnessy. "This guy has shown a real unhealthy interest in D'Antoni as well. I would feel a whole lot better if we had someone on her place too."

D'Antoni flushes with anger. "What the fuck, Deke? I can take care of myself, tough guy." She glares at me, daring me to disagree.

I put my hands up in mock surrender.

"We'll revisit that later," O'Shaughnessy says. "Right now, I need you wheels up on the way to Weston. One of Barnes's guys or Barnes himself will be waiting for you at Logan." He stands up. "If you can, meet with the ME in Boston first before going to the crime scene in Weston. Report back the second you've got anything."

"Will do, boss," D'Antoni says, and we're gone.

✦ ✦ ✦ ✦ ✦ ✦

Traveling in the Gulfstream is utter luxury, and we settle in for the trip. D'Antoni obviously isn't ready to let me off the hook for the incident in O'Shaughnessy's office and glares at me. I do my best to pretend to be reading emails, but she does not avert her gaze.

When I can no longer avoid her, I look up with a huge smile on my face. "Sorry, partner. I'm just worried about you. This guy has really gotten under my skin. I'm not thinking straight. I know you, of all people, can take care of yourself."

"You're damn right you're not thinking straight," she says. "Don't pull that shit again."

"Deal."

We both decide to catch a little shut-eye. It's going to be a long day.

CHAPTER 21

Barnes himself is waiting for us at Logan. His company-issued SUV is idling curbside.

"Thanks for grabbing us," D'Antoni says. "What's the game plan, pal?"

"Unless you guys have any objection, I thought we could head to Albany Street to meet with the ME first."

"Perfect," I say. "You speak to Slaughter and Bronstein?"

"Yeah. They're comfortable that we're dealing with two killers and that the Fenway killer is likely our deceased anesthesiologist. Slaughter wants to talk to the two of you as soon as possible."

The trip to the office of the chief medical examiner of Massachusetts on Albany Street takes just ten minutes. Brian informs us that the CME himself is performing the autopsy.

"He started at seven this morning," Brian says. "He should be done now, or very soon. He's expecting us."

Fifteen minutes later, a shortish, pear-shaped man in scrubs enters the waiting room. He appears to be in his early sixties.

"Hey, Brian," the man says. "How's the wife and kids?"

"Good, Charlie. How does Stella like Boston College?"

"Loves it. And the fact that she can hit up Grandma and Grandpa for a home-cooked meal whenever she wants is an added bonus."

"Smart girl," I say, extending my arm. Dr. Charles Moriarity's handshake is dry and firm. There's something comforting about his presence that I can't put my finger on. I have a great respect for those who can dedicate their lives to the role of medical examiner; it would not suit me. The dead torment me enough in my dreams as it is.

We head down the hall to one of many autopsy rooms. I consciously start breathing through my mouth. My heart begins to race as we enter the room. It always does.

A covered body lies on a table in the middle of the room. The doctor lowers the sheet to reveal a beautiful woman in her early thirties. Her eyes stare blankly at the ceiling. Dozens of little red pinpricks dot her eyes. Her face is a mask of terror.

After we've all had time to view the body, the doctor tells us his findings.

"Time of death was between midday and 1400 hours yesterday. The cause of death is not yet known, but there was a needle mark just below her right ear." He pauses. "This woman asphyxiated, as confirmed by the petechiae in her eyes. You can see the needle mark on the upper right side of her neck if you look closely. While sux was not in her blood, high levels of succinylmonocholine and choline acid were. Sux would have paralyzed her quickly. She couldn't even close her eyes during the attack.

"She was sexually assaulted, though unlikely raped. There is no bruising or other trauma present. The assailant left a note inside the woman's vagina. It's addressed to you, Special Agent O'Brien. It's over here on this tray. The ink has run a bit, but it's still legible."

I slap on a pair of latex gloves, handle the wrinkled note with care, and begin reading. I don't look up or address the others for several minutes. Its message is clear. I read it aloud for the benefit of Barnes and D'Antoni:

> Hey, Deke. I've been planning this one for years. This cunt got exactly what she had coming. She almost killed me when I was just a kid. Never even told me she was sorry—totally self-absorbed. She almost ruined my life and never gave it a second thought. She didn't deserve

her opulent lifestyle, her kids, or her perfect husband. This was my most gratifying kill to date. I enjoyed every second of it. Almost came as the light faded from her eyes. So poetic, don't you think? What a great body. Not an ounce of fat on her. Well, let's catch up soon. I need to vacate the premises before the nanny gets here. I left my Montblanc in a special spot for you. Talk to you soon. Give my regards to D'Antoni. Tell her I can't wait to meet her. Your most interesting perp yet, the Movie Theater Killer

The doctor clears his throat. "A pen was recovered from the victim's rectum. It's in a plastic bag on the tray."

No one says a word for a full minute. At last, the doctor clears his throat again and continues. "I don't know how important it'll be to your investigation, but the victim had several healed fractures, and I mean several. All of them were old, likely suffered in adolescence."

The doctor thumbs through some x-rays and stops at one of interest. "This shows a pronounced spiral fracture of the forearm. A simple fracture of the forearm in isolation would not raise concern, but given the number of fractures and the severity of this one in particular, I'm certain"—he glances at each of us individually—"this girl was abused as a child or young adult. Hers wasn't a happy home. No doubt about it."

The doctor answers all of our remaining questions. It's obvious he feels for the victim and cares deeply about his job. Compassion isn't something I'd normally associate with an ME, so it's refreshing. Actually, it's amazing, given all he has probably seen in this life.

We wrap things up and head out to the SUV for the short ride to Weston. The first five minutes of the trip are spent in complete silence. Everybody is mentally digesting what we've just learned.

Barnes is the first to break the silence. "We need to dig into this woman's background, and I mean dig deep. She knew the perp— maybe even had a relationship with him. She was important to him.

Maybe they both came from abusive homes and met in counseling or some kind of group home."

"We have a team on it," D'Antoni says. "You make a great point, Brian. I have no doubt our perp is from a broken home and was abused. It's certainly plausible that the two of them became acquainted because of this. I'll make sure this angle is thoroughly explored."

"This was more than a casual acquaintance," I say. "This could be a telling lead. It's certainly the best to date."

+ + + + + +

Weston is every bit the high-class hamlet of Boston that it's made out to be. Beautiful homes and high-end retail shops are among its amenities. Murder is certainly not commonplace in a town like this—far from it.

Barnes seems to have read my mind. "We haven't had a murder in Weston in eight years, and that one was a domestic that went too far. This is all over the local news. Shit, it's all over the national news at this point."

We turn into the Birnbaums' upscale development. Barnes pulls the SUV to the curb next to the most impressive home in the neighborhood. My best guess is that it's worth between four and five million. It has a sprawling front yard, impeccable landscaping, and a large fenced-in backyard that affords the Birnbaums a ton of privacy.

I am the first to exit the vehicle, and I take my time in looking up and down the street. The houses are fairly spread out, but the SUV is within view of at least three other homes. "Which house was our witness in?" I ask.

"First one down on the right," Barnes replies.

When I look at the house, I first notice the huge picture windows in the front. "Our witness would've had a birds-eye view of a car parked anywhere near here," I say.

"She said as much," Barnes says.

I walk slowly across the street to the Birnbaums' front lawn, peering frequently over my right shoulder. The view is good until almost the center of the front lawn; from that point, it's fully obscured by trees and vegetation. I point this out to Barnes and D'Antoni. They nod, understanding the implications. There's no way the witness could have seen the man enter the house, whether through the front door or another entrance at the back.

The front door is ajar, with yellow crime-scene tape blocking the entrance. A uniformed Massachusetts State policeman is standing guard in the entryway. We flash our credentials, and Barnes makes introductions. The uniform tells us the lead homicide detective, who's also with the Massachusetts State Police, is on the second floor, examining the master bedroom. After signing the log-in book, we thank the young cop for the information, slip on protective booties and latex gloves, step over the crime-scene tape, and make our way inside.

The entrance hallway is breathtaking. The space rises all the way to the second-floor ceiling; a beautiful wraparound staircase provides access to the second floor. I ascend to the fourth step, stop, turn around, and peer through the front picture window. There, clear as day, is our SUV.

I look at Barnes, and he nods. "I parked exactly where the witness indicated the killer's car was," he says. "It's a perfect vantage point. There's an unobstructed view of the staircase. The killer could have surveyed the property for as long as he wanted, only entering when he knew it was safe."

"True," D'Antoni says. "But he still risked being seen by someone in the adjoining homes. My guess is that he staked it out well in advance, observing everything, including the neighbors, to determine when it was safe to make a move."

"This guy leaves nothing to chance," I say. "Absolutely nothing. Why don't we take a look at the first floor before heading up to the master? I'd like to try to figure out where he most likely entered the house."

We pass through the living room and dining room on the way to the kitchen and the back of the house. The layout is open and modern, and the house is tastefully decorated. Abstract art, most of it expensive, adorns the walls. The kitchen is expansive and airy; stainless-steel appliances reflect the sunlight, brightening the room. It opens onto a beautiful platform deck with gorgeous views of an infinity pool, a hot tub, and a spacious, private backyard. I check the sliding glass door. It's locked. I pop the lock, open the door, and head out onto the deck. The deck furniture screams expensiveness. I descend the deck steps and step into the backyard. The grass feels like plush carpet under my feet, and its green hue rivals that of any high-end country club golf course.

I give the backyard a 360-degree inspection. It provides total privacy. It would be possible to sunbathe or swim nude at will without fear of observation. There's no line of sight into the yard from any of the neighboring homes. I approach the fence that separates the front and side yards from the backyard. There's an entrance gate with a simple pop lock. Accessing the backyard from the front wouldn't challenge even a first grader. I turn around and head back to where Barnes and D'Antoni are waiting patiently.

"Here's my best guess," I say. "The perp left his car; walked across the front yard, per the witness; and entered the backyard through that gate." I point over my shoulder. "Once in the backyard, the perp would've been completely out of the sight of any prying neighbors and could've taken his time in breaking into the house— that is, assuming he had to break in at all."

"The sliding glass door showed no signs of being tampered with," Barnes says. "There's also a side entrance, likely to the basement, and I saw nothing indicating a break-in there either. You guys ready to head back in?"

We spend another five minutes on the first floor, walking from room to room, looking for anything of note. Then we ascend to the master bedroom on the second floor. I take my time, stopping frequently, listening for any creaking sounds that might give away an intruder's presence. Each stair is adorned with an oriental runner that does a decent job of muffling any noise, but one would still need to be extra careful to escape detection. Voices can be heard coming from one of the rooms off the top landing, and we follow the noise into the master bedroom. Entering the room, I'm immediately assailed by an acidic odor.

Three individuals are in the room, including two crime-scene techs and a plainclothes detective who is down on one knee, examining something on the rug. He turns at our approach, gives us the once-over, and then stands up and approaches the three of us with his hand extended. He's short and square, almost bulldog-like, but he has a kind face and a nice smile.

"Hey, guys, I'm Homicide Detective Kevin Timmons with the Massachusetts State Police." He's already met Brian, so D'Antoni and I introduce ourselves. The guy's handshake is as hard and firm as a vise, and it takes a couple seconds to get feeling back in my right hand.

"I hear you guys have experience with the perpetrator here," Timmons says. "I just can't believe we have a serial killer running around these parts."

"We think it likely he's local," D'Antoni says. She explains to Timmons our thinking behind this conclusion.

"Hey, Kevin, why don't you run them through what we talked about this morning?" Barnes says.

"Sure thing, Brian. My best guess is that the perp jumped her after she showered. Probably lay in wait for her in the bedroom and surprised her. Her terry-cloth bath towel was found on the floor right in front of the door to the bathroom. It was still slightly damp when I arrived. He then incapacitated her. There was a large urine stain just inside the bedroom that we're pretty certain came from the victim. We'll know for sure today." He points to the spot next to his right leg, which explains the smell I detected. "No weapons were found. CSI found what looked like a piece of paper sticking out of the victim's vagina."

"We saw the body earlier," D'Antoni says. "The ME said the assailant subdued the victim using a powerful paralytic."

"What a sick bastard."

"And getting sicker by the minute," I add. "We're seeing a definite escalation pattern."

I bring Timmons up to speed on our other investigations and my interactions with the killer. I wrap up with what we learned from the ME this morning.

"This guy has a real hard-on for you, huh? What'd you do to piss him off?"

I laugh. "No idea. He likes the control aspect. Wants to show everyone he's smarter than them. But we can let him keep taunting us and showing off as far as I'm concerned. An open line of communication significantly enhances our chances of catching him. He's a narcissistic braggart, and he'll make a mistake eventually."

"Can you walk us through a timeline of what you learned about the deceased's day yesterday?" D'Antoni asks.

"Sure," Timmons says. "This is what we know so far. The deceased got up at six, as she does every weekday, and prepared breakfast for her son and daughter. After getting the kids ready and dropping them off at school, she went to her gym in Needham to work out. This was verified with her personal trainer. She left the gym at approximately ten that morning. A credit card receipt indicates she got gas at a Mobil station directly across the street from the gym. She then proceeded to Starbucks. I talked to the barista who served her. He said she was in like clockwork shortly after ten. She was alone and sat at a table, reading a newspaper, as she often does. Here's where it gets interesting. About ten minutes after she sat down, a tall, well-dressed man in sunglasses and a ball cap entered the store, purchased a coffee, and sat a few tables away from the victim. I asked the barista why he remembered this guy specifically, and what he said grabbed my attention. He said the man stared, gawked almost, at the victim. He said it was borderline uncomfortable. And he left right after the victim left, practically running out the door after her."

"Surveillance cameras?" D'Antoni asks.

"Not working. They haven't been working for weeks."

"What else?" I ask.

"A credit card receipt at six minutes past eleven has her in Brothers Marketplace down the road, buying groceries. This is where the hard-evidence trail ends and conjecture begins. It's assumed the victim went home after grocery shopping. Per the husband, the victim had planned on studying all afternoon for an exam in her nighttime MBA program. She had even lined up the nanny to pick the kids up at school so she could focus on her studies. She went so far as to tell the nanny to keep the kids occupied downstairs and not let them disturb her.

"The nanny arrived home with the kids around a quarter after three in the afternoon. She helped them with their homework, let them watch some TV, and prepared their dinner. She then bathed the kids and got them ready for bed. This was around the time the husband rolled in, approximately seven forty-five. He spent about ten minutes with the kids, asked them where their mother was, and then headed upstairs to change. After throwing on some sweats, he decided to check in on his wife. He spent the next fifteen minutes looking for her with no luck. Just by chance, he saw something out of the corner of his eye when he walked past his wife's walk-in master closet. It was his wife's feet that he saw. She had been stuffed in a corner of the closet and covered with a blanket, but her feet were sticking out."

"The kids never once went looking for their mom?" D'Antoni asks.

"Not according to the nanny," Timmons says.

"Did the nanny hear any noises coming from upstairs?" I ask. "Any cars parked out on the street?"

"No, and I asked," Timmons says with slight annoyance in his tone.

Of course he did. Stupid question.

We spend the next hour looking for anything unusual. We find nothing of note and wrap things up with Timmons around one o'clock. We promise to keep each other informed, and we ask him to catch up with Slaughter and Bronstein, say our goodbyes, and head next door to chat with the witness.

I approach the neighbor's house via the front lawn, trying to approximate her line of sight. As long as her vision is decent, she would've had a good look at the perp until the trees blocked her view. I notice someone sitting in the front portico, watching us as we walk up the driveway. The front door opens before I even have a chance to ring the bell. A tiny, bespectacled elderly women beckons us into the house. Sitting on a rolling cart in the dining room are coffee service for five and what look like homemade chocolate chip cookies. I like this woman immediately.

Coffee in hand and fortified with homemade cookies, we get down to business. She introduces herself as Karen Karso, the mother of the homeowner. She's visiting from Toledo. She informs us that yesterday morning, around eleven o'clock, she was having a cup of coffee and reading the newspaper on the love seat in the front portico. She says a car pulled up across the street from the Birnbaums' home at exactly ten past eleven. She's certain of the time because she looked at her watch. No one exited the car. It just sat there with the engine running.

She noticed a man sitting in the front seat. Her vision is perfect, except for the reading glasses everyone of her age needs. She didn't think anything of it and went back to reading her book. When she glanced up next, something struck her as odd. She's almost certain the man was watching the Birnbaum house with a pair of binoculars. She says her view of the man wasn't perfect because his windows were slightly tinted, but she's pretty sure he was surveilling the house. That was when she took more of an active interest in the car and the man inside it.

She saw a tall, well-dressed white male in a baseball cap and sunglasses leave the vehicle around ten minutes before midday.

He had dark hair to his collar and was talking animatedly on his cell phone as he approached the Birnbaum house. Because of the obstructed view, she never saw whether the man entered the house or not. Shortly thereafter, her interest having waned, she headed upstairs to take a shower and a nap. When she looked out the window later, at around two o'clock in the afternoon, the car was gone, and she thought nothing further of it until the police knocked on her daughter's door last night.

Karen Karso describes the car in some detail. It was a nondescript dark blue sedan with slightly tinted windows. She describes it as being American. Unfortunately, she didn't think to get the license plate number at the time, although she states that it was definitely a Massachusetts plate.

We spend the next few minutes with Karen, trying to nail down as many specific details as possible. For the most part, it's an unsuccessful exercise. As observant as Karen is, nothing she tells us sheds new light on the perp's physical characteristics or anything that brings us closer to catching this creep. I leave the house feeling deflated. The interview started out with such promise, and that homemade chocolate chip cookie took me back to my childhood and the delectable treats my own mother always had waiting when I got home from school.

+ ✦ ✦ ✦ ✦ ✦ +

The drive to Logan takes almost an hour in heavy traffic. We spend the time comparing notes on what we've learned today. Snippets of my conversation with the killer early this morning leak into my mind. Will my family be safe? How do I broach the subject with Catherine? She's going to be pissed and rightfully so. She's got enough on her plate these days without having to worry about some deranged serial killer harming her kids. There's no way to delicately broach the issue. I feel acid churning in my stomach. *Fuck.* I am sick with worry about my family's safety, and I'm not looking forward to the world of hurt Catherine will likely unleash on me.

I snap back to the present as we turn into Logan Airport. The Gulfstream is fueled; the crew are ready for our return trip to DC. D'Antoni and I spend almost the entire flight staring out the windows, both of us consumed by our own thoughts.

D'Antoni finally breaks the silence. "What are you going to tell Catherine?"

It takes me several seconds to answer. "I don't know. I guess the truth. What else can I tell her?" I look expectantly at D'Antoni, hoping for a miraculous solution. None comes.

"You've taken every possible precaution," she says. "Your family is safe. There's nothing else you can do, so stop beating yourself up about it."

"A nice stiff Johnnie Walker Black would make the conversation a whole lot easier," I say under my breath.

"Deke, life isn't easy, but you can't hide from it. You know that better than most."

I smile and shrug. "I know, I know."

CHAPTER 22

He walks into JJ Foley's around four in the afternoon. It's been an action-packed few days. He couldn't sleep a wink last night after all the excitement in Weston. He finally gave up at five this morning and went for a seven-mile run along the Charles River, followed by some strength training at the Harvard sports complex.

He graduated from the prestigious university eight and a half years ago, and that gave him lifetime access to the athletic facilities. Yet to be honest, outside of his time on the baseball team, he didn't really enjoy his time at Harvard. He didn't have a dime to his name back then, and if it hadn't been for the baseball scholarship and generous financial-aid package, Harvard—or any college, for that matter—would've been out of the question.

He thrives in situations in which he's smarter than everyone else. He always has. He enjoys situations he can manipulate to serve his needs. Unfortunately, everyone at Harvard was smart; some were even smarter than he was. It was disconcerting. He felt as though he were always on the back of his heels, always trying to prove himself. He doesn't advertise his educational affiliation with Harvard professionally or personally. Especially since he has taken over the life of someone who graduated from Duke. It wouldn't pay. No one seems able to understand how someone with a Harvard degree can decide to become a city employee. At best, he's wasted a God-given opportunity; at worst, he's a failure.

Julie, his favorite barmaid, is working and delivers a shot of Jameson and a Sierra Nevada. Man, he needs it. He quickly downs the shot and takes a long pull of the Sierra Nevada. Julie refills the shot glass without even looking up. He lets the warmth envelop him. His mind wanders, and he's transported back to an earlier time in his life.

He spent two years after graduation playing AA baseball in the Yankees' farm system. Norwich, Connecticut, was home base. He made the decision to continue playing baseball not so much because he thought he had a bright future in it but because he had nothing better to do and wanted to see the country.

Those were pivotal years in his life. It was his first time leaving the state of Massachusetts. He loved traveling to different cities and towns. It was easy to be anonymous and go unnoticed when you bounced around so much.

On one of those road trips, he first fed his homicidal lust. Well, he had killed and tortured countless animals, but that didn't really count. He needed to pop his human homicidal cherry.

It happened in Zebulon, North Carolina. They were in town for a weekend series with the Carolina Mudcats, the AA affiliate of the Atlanta Braves. The first game was on a warm Friday night in early June. He broke up a 2–2 tie in the top of the eighth with a three-run home run that wound up winning the game. He headed out to a bar with several teammates to celebrate. He wasn't particularly close with any—heck, he didn't even like most of them, but people liked hanging out with him. People, especially women, were drawn to him.

It didn't take long to loosen up. Several rounds of shots made that easy. The bar was packed; the music played loudly. If he was going to make a move, now was the time. He told a teammate he wasn't feeling well and needed to head back to the motel. The guy was too busy ogling a group of girls nearby to even acknowledge him, so he ducked out a side door. He didn't go back to the motel, though. Instead, he headed across the street to the only other happening bar in the town.

A group of attractive girls were dancing in the center of the floor. One particular girl grabbed his attention. She was petite, with straw-blonde hair and ice-blue eyes. When she glanced his way, those eyes seemed to pierce his soul. At that moment, he thought she might actually know what he wanted to do to her. It was unnerving and exhilarating at the same time.

She made the first move, approaching him slowly, languidly. He loved the way she moved. She was damn sexy. He never took his eyes off hers as she got closer. Then he noticed how young she seemed. He doubted she was even of legal drinking age. She wore a pale blue halter top that stopped midstomach, exposing six-pack abs. She obviously worked out. Unfortunately, she had a flashy diamond belly piercing. He didn't understand how people could defile their bodies like that. He hoped she didn't have any tattoos.

She wasted no time. "What's your name, big boy?"

Her voice was a soft southern purr—damn sexy. "I'm the guy who hit the home run to beat your Mudcats. You can call me Slugger."

A wide smile creased her face. "Slugger, huh? That's original. I'm Delilah. Why don't you buy me a beer and a shot, Slugger? I'm real thirsty."

He made his way to the bar and ordered her an ice-cold Sierra Nevada and a shot of Jameson. She checked him out the entire time. This was going to be too easy.

She grabbed the shot and threw it back in one fluid motion. Then she grabbed the beer and took a five-second pull of it. She scrunched up her nose and shook her head. "What the fuck is this? It certainly ain't no Budweiser."

"Thank God for that." He laughed. "No one needs to drink that bear whiz. Let me get us both some more firewater."

Several drinks later, they were both good and drunk. She had both hands around his shoulders, leaning all the way in to whisper in his ear. His left hand cupped her right butt cheek. It was as hard as a rock. So was he.

It was time to make his move. She was primed. She sensed his excitement, grabbed him by the back of the neck, and thrust her tongue down his throat, hungrily kissing him. He reciprocated and slipped his hand inside her halter top. Her nipples were rock hard; her tits were like two perfect grapefruits. He thought he was going to rip a hole in his jeans he was so hard.

He broke the embrace and took a half step back. "I've got a little something that's going to blow your mind." He reached into his pocket and took out two small pills. "This will make you feel like you're on top of the world." He popped one of the pills into his mouth, making sure to quickly hide it under his tongue. He handed her the other one. She hesitated.

"What is it?" she asked.

"It's a pleasure pill," he answered. "It'll help you party all night long."

She shrugged, popped the pill into her mouth without another thought, and washed it down with a swig of beer. He coughed the pill out of his own mouth and into his hand without her noticing. She had just taken a powerful quaalude that, together with the alcohol, should incapacitate her.

He needed to get her out of there before the pill started to work. He kissed her again hard and whispered in her ear, "Let's get out of here."

She smiled with a mischievous look on her face. "What do you have in mind, you naughty boy? We can't go back to my place because my mom's home."

"It's a surprise, gorgeous," he said, and they slipped out a side door without a word. It was prudent not to attract attention. A nondescript motel was located directly across the street from the team's motel, and that was where he took her.

It took the better part of ten minutes to walk to the motel. By the time they walked in, she was visibly wobbly on her legs. *Shit*. He needed to act fast. Not wanting to attract any unwanted attention, he sat her in a chair in the lobby and told her to stay put; he'd be right back. Now came the hard part.

He approached the registration desk with an air of confidence. A kid in his twenties sat behind the desk, reading a newspaper, with a bored look on his face.

He cleared his throat, and the reception boy exhaled as if unduly put out. He took his time in folding up the newspaper before glancing up.

"I need a room for two nights."

"You want a queen-sized bed or two doubles?" the employee asked.

"Queen."

"ID and credit card."

He took a fake Massachusetts license out of his wallet. He'd had it made back in Boston a couple years ago. It was in a fake name. Today, he was glad he had it.

He told the kid he was going to pay cash.

"You need to put up an extra night as security if you pay cash."

"No problem," he answered. One hundred fifty-eight dollars later, with room key in hand, he grabbed his by now very impaired companion and headed for the room.

"What took you so long, Slugger?" Her eyes were at half-mast, and her tongue was thick with intoxication.

He had his hand around her waist, guiding her forward. She leaned heavily into him. It wouldn't do if she passed out now before the fun had even started.

The room smelled of mildew and disinfectant. The comforter looked as if it might be the only one the bed had ever seen. He discarded the disgusting blanket in a heap over in a corner and pulled Delilah in close. He kissed her hard, running his hands all over her tight body. She pulled away for a second and asked him if there was anything to drink—a girl after his own heart. He had his trusty flask in his back pocket; it was an item he rarely went anywhere without. She drank deeply from the flask, burped loudly, and started laughing hysterically. He took a quick slug himself and then got back to the business at hand.

There wasn't anything romantic about what happened next. He didn't take his time to seductively remove her clothes; he just tugged and ripped them from her body. He was crazed with homicidal lust. She was a limp noodle to his over-exuberance. She did manage to squeeze out a "Slow down, Slugger," but that was the last thing he remembers her saying. He didn't take her advice.

Everything that happened from then until he left the motel was a blur. He remembers snippets of what transpired rather than whole scenes. He remembers flipping her over onto her stomach. He wanted her to kneel doggy style, but she was too out of it. He slipped off the bed and retrieved his belt. He snapped it loudly, trying to get Delilah's attention, but she could barely keep her eyes open. A stream of drool trailed from her mouth to the pillow. He leaped up onto the bed and proceeded to slap her hard on both cheeks. She simply whimpered, turned her head to the side, and tried to bury her face in the pillow.

He managed to get the belt under and then around her neck. He pulled as tight as he could. No scream escaped her lips. Instead, she made a sickening gurgling sound that went on for almost a minute until her whole body spasmed and then went slack. A sickening smell wafted up to him. She had emptied her bowels in those last terrifying seconds.

He remembers putting the Do Not Disturb sign on the door on his way out. More than anything, though, he remembers being disappointed by the experience. It had happened too fast. He should've played with her more and savored the experience. Much like a first-time lover, he'd been too charged up and too eager.

He would do it right next time.

Now he loves these walks down memory lane. He takes a long pull of the Sierra Nevada. The bartender has been kind enough to refill his Jameson, and he throws that down in one gulp.

His mind wanders back to the weeks after the first murder. He was a basket case, certain the police would knock on his Norwich apartment door at any moment or show up to the team's training complex. Fear invaded every aspect of his life. He had been cocky and stupid. Dozens of people had seen him talking to and flirting with Delilah in the bar. Then there was the man behind the desk at the motel. He had gotten an up-close look at him. Shit, there was probably surveillance footage of him at the motel.

But the police never came.

Somehow, miraculously, he got away with it, despite how sloppy, careless, and unprepared he had been. He vowed to be much more diligent when he did it again. He knew there would be a next time. He was a killer, with the taste of blood still fresh on his tongue, and he needed to kill as much as he needed to breathe.

CHAPTER 23

The atmosphere in the cabin is tense, bordering on electric. I can't even sit; I opt to pace instead, racking my brain. Maybe Jane Birnbaum's senseless, horrific death would spark our investigative efforts and help us catch this creep.

Jane and the killer had a relationship. What type of relationship is anyone's guess. But that's what investigation is all about: uncovering the unknown.

The feeling I have in my gut right now is the same feeling that gets me out of bed in the morning. I thrive on the tension, the whole cat-and-mouse game. I can't imagine working any other job. No, scratch that. I would be ill-equipped to work any other job. Without the constant internal strain, I would end up at the bottom of a bottle of Johnnie Walker Black.

D'Antoni and I talk at length about Jane Birnbaum. When did she cross paths with the killer? The killer himself indicated it was before she married, when she was Jane Martin.

It appears Jane Martin had a difficult and maybe even horrible upbringing. Is that the connection with our perp? Is that why their paths crossed?

D'Antoni feels strongly that the link between Jane and the perp is their shared experience of abuse. Jane's age matches our estimate of the perp's age, and she likely suffered her abuse in adolescence, as the ME said. What else could it be? They must have met in counseling, in a group home, or on the street.

I feel the same way, but my conviction is not as strong. I decide to share this with D'Antoni.

"I don't know how much I would read into the abuse angle just yet. Having all those injuries from adolescence may simply mean Jane had a terrible childhood—a terrible childhood with one family, her birth family. We'll know soon enough. Clearly, she was in an abusive living situation for an extended period of time. I feel strongly—no, screw that. I'm positive our guy spent time in foster care, a group home for troubled kids, or on the street. I'm positive."

"Care to share the reasoning behind your certainty?" D'Antoni asks. "I think it's a plausible assumption, but a certainty? I'm not there yet."

"I would call it a gut feeling, but it's more than that. This may sound weird, and I may be way off base—"

D'Antoni cuts in. "It wouldn't be the first time."

"Just humor me, okay?"

"Why not?"

"The aura of evil and sickness that I sense in this guy is too pervasive and all-encompassing to have been birthed and nurtured in one household. This guy was abused by more than just his birth family. He had it really, really bad. We're talking an abusive upbringing on steroids. So I'm not saying that these guys didn't meet in counseling, in a group home, or on the street. They very well may have, and if they did, our chances of catching him increase dramatically. This relationship, whatever it was, is our strongest lead to date."

"All of this assumes the killer is telling the truth," D'Antoni says.

"Very good point and one that shouldn't be discounted."

Both of us are sitting back in the leather recliners. I close my eyes, trying to clear my mind, relishing the fact that progress has been made.

"What are you doing for Thanksgiving?" D'Antoni asks. "You doing something with Bridget?"

Our eyes meet, and I take several seconds before answering. "Haven't even thought about it, to be honest. I doubt it, though. No. Definitely no."

"Trouble in paradise?" Her eyebrows are raised.

"What paradise?"

We both laugh, and then I clear my throat audibly. "I'll probably just grab a bite around the corner, watch some football, and decompress."

"You're so full of shit they can already smell you back at Quantico. You're going to work, aren't you? I know you, Deke."

"You going to your sister's?" I ask.

"I'm not going into New York for the day. It makes zero sense. The city will be crazy. I need a minute to decompress as well," D'Antoni says. "Here's what we're going to do. You get up and do your little workout thing, and we'll meet in the office at nine in the morning. We'll work until about half past two or three and then wrap it up. We'll get dinner at Ardour in the St. Regis, which you'll pay for and for which you'll make a reservation today. Deal?"

"Deal."

+ + ◆ ◆ ◆ + +

At seven in the evening, the office is still busy, like a hive of bees foraging a clover field in the middle of July.

D'Antoni and I drop our stuff at our workstations and check email. I have an email from Slaughter asking me to call him immediately. I check my voice mail and texts. I have a voice mail from Slaughter too. I decide to call him later when I have more time. I lob a call to Griff to give him an update. The call goes straight to voice mail. "Hey, pal, Deke here. I apologize for not calling earlier with an update. Things have been crazy. Give me a shout when you can."

I almost jump out of my seat when D'Antoni touches my arm. "Whoa, cowboy, you need to take a chill pill." She laughs. "He's ready for us."

"We have time to grab a quick cup of coffee?"

She's still smiling. "You really think that's a good idea? Aren't you already a bit hyped up?"

I don't even answer.

Coffee in hand, we knock on O'Shaughnessy's door. He brusquely ushers us inside, and we spend the next forty-five minutes giving our progress update. Like D'Antoni and me, he's intrigued by the relationship between our perp and Jane Birnbaum—or, rather, Jane Martin.

He stands up and starts pacing. This is vintage O'Shaughnessy. Sometimes I don't believe he can think while sitting down.

"I want you to coordinate with the entire team and map out our game plan. Feel free to include Griff's and Barnes's teams. We need to learn everything we can about Mrs. Birnbaum in the next twenty-four hours. At the very least, let's get a better understanding of where her path most likely crossed with the perp. I'm very intrigued by the juvenile system, foster care, group home, and street angles. It's gotta be one of those. Got to be."

I jump in. "At the same time, we need to focus on male juveniles from Jane's hometown who meet our timing and profile parameters. This guy shouldn't be hard to find. He should stick out. People will remember this kid even today."

O'Shaughnessy nods readily. "I need updates every few hours. Allyson is coming home from Amherst tomorrow night, and I need to spend Thursday with her and the wife, or I'll never be allowed home again. I need people working this through the holiday. I know this goes without saying; I just don't want you two to be the only ones on the ground Thursday. I mean that. You get whoever you need. I've already made the whole team aware. And get out of here at a decent time to enjoy dinner and relax a bit. It's going to be crazy 24-7 around here until we catch this son of a bitch."

He walks into JJ Foley's about eight in the evening, exhausted and stressed out. He's not felt stress like this since Zebulon, North Carolina. He revealed too much to Deke. What the fuck was he thinking? There was no reason to mention a connection to Jane Martin. He was in complete control up to that point. Why hand a nugget like that to Deke without making him work for it?

There's much work left to do. Has he jeopardized his grand plan? Now the FBI is busy digging into Jane's background, knee deep probably, to see if they can get to him through the proverbial back door. In truth, he's revealed enough to let them get close—maybe real damn close. But he's gone to great lengths to distance himself from that part of his life. He changed his name and now looks nothing like that scared, frail wimp from back then. They have an uphill battle—that's for sure. Still, it was stupid to give the FBI anything.

He knows why he did it: the thrill of the hunt. Without it, life is boring and mundane. His advantage to date is too significant. It's killing his thrill factor. Nothing that is won too easily stimulates him.

Julie, his favorite barmaid, slides a Sierra and a shot of Jameson in front of him.

"You need a menu, sweetie?" she asks.

"Nah. Liquid dinner. Rough day. Thanks, though."

She smiles at him warmly and attends to other customers. He notices she's wearing a pair of Seven jeans that grip her athletic ass like skin on bologna. She's five feet ten, statuesque, and a redheaded beauty. Oh, the things he would love to do to her.

He laughs inwardly, thinking about his infatuation with good-looking redheads. In truth, he lusts after all attractive women. Deke O'Brien has a thing for redheads as well, he thinks. His ex, Catherine, is one damn fine specimen. Bridget is stunning. She's also an overbearing, snobby bitch. It's going to be a lot of fun to introduce himself to both of them.

He glances down and notices that his drinks remain untouched. He laughs out loud. Now, that will not do. With a quick flick of the wrist, the Jameson is gone. Then he turns his attention to the Sierra, which he muscles down in three long gulps. He looks up with a smile returning to his face. Julie is already on the way over, Seven jeans and all, with round number two. *Ain't life grand?*

CHAPTER 24

I let D'Antoni run the team meeting; she's a true leader in every sense. The jury is still out on me. I'm terrific at my job, arguably the best in the FBI, but I'm a bit of a lone wolf. D'Antoni has changed that somewhat, but I still like working with me, myself, and I. It's hard to teach an old dog new tricks, especially a flea- and tick-ridden dog like me.

We have eight other team members, including four special agents, working the case full-time. They're the cream of the crop in the FBI. We've commandeered a large conference room that will serve as ground zero from this point forward.

D'Antoni dives straight into the game plan, assigning responsibilities, setting expectations, and getting the cart rolling in the right direction. She tasks two special agents and two analysts with the job of dissecting Jane Martin's life. Everything from birth to death is relevant as far as the investigation is concerned. Special attention is to be paid to the birth family, the foster family, or state-sponsored care, if applicable, plus time on the street; medical history; criminal history; psychological history, including any related counseling; and anything else deemed important.

The rest of the team is assigned investigative responsibilities for each of the specific crimes, including the latest in Weston. They must coordinate with our local office in each instance and with local law enforcement.

The hope is that the investigation runs like a well-oiled machine. Who am I kidding?

I throw in the towel at a quarter past eleven that night. I'm shot, and there isn't a ton I can add tonight anyway. The dark, starless sky mirrors my mood. The last thing on earth I want to do is exercise, but I need to clear my mind, take a step back, and refocus. My gym is open twenty-four hours—lucky me—so I throw on gym clothes and trudge over a little after midnight.

Later, settling into bed, I set my alarm for half past seven. I need every minute of sleep I can get. But first, I send a text to Catherine, telling her we must talk in the morning at her convenience. I try to convey the importance of the conversation without worrying her. I hope the killer doesn't call and wake me up tonight, and I switch off the light, hoping for dreamless sleep.

CHAPTER 25

He climbs into bed around one in the morning in an alcohol-laced haze. He has overdone it and will pay for it at the gym tomorrow. Man, he loves this feeling, though. It's like floating. Images flit across his mind in no particular order. Alcohol tends to make his dreams far more vivid and realistic. He cherishes these moments. They let him instantly transport himself back in time to any point in his life, good or bad.

He's back at Rayburn House now. It's after the pool incident, and he's changed. Jane is gone—off to college, he heard. How the fuck was that bitch able to go to college? He has never even been out of the state. Worcester is as far as he's ever traveled.

He's much surer of himself now—cocky almost. No one will ever take advantage of him again. No one. He controls his own destiny, and it is his right and duty to do anything he fucking wants.

A family has moved into the duplex next door. They have three kids: two girls and a little boy. They seem happy—too happy. They're outside all the time, playing, laughing, and goofing around. He spends hours at his window, just watching them, seething.

The father surprises the family one Friday night that summer with a beautiful golden retriever puppy. The kids are over-the-top excited. They love that dog. They name him Hooligan. They play with him incessantly.

He sits in his window, glaring at the scene in front of him, becoming angrier by the day. These little morons live a life totally alien to him. It's a world he can't comprehend, and because of that, he hates it, and he hates them.

The father builds a beautiful patio and enclosed area for the puppy in the backyard. This way, the puppy can stay out during the day, and they don't need to worry about incessant bathroom breaks.

He studies the family's habits. He knows when the mother and father are at work and when the kids are at day camp. *Easy breezy.* It is so easy that he has a difficult time enjoying himself.

He sneaks next door midmorning on one July day. He hoists himself up and over the fence in one fluid motion. The puppy goes bananas, wagging its tail and licking him all over. *Stupid animal.* He unwinds the length of twine he hid in his back pocket. He has tested its strength several times. He is pretty sure it will hold.

He picks the puppy up, petting its head affectionately. The animal cranes its head to look at him and try to get in a few more licks. He walks over to the swing set in the center of the yard. He has to stand on his tiptoes to toss the twine up and over the center bar. He makes a knot and tests its strength. It seems fine. He makes a rudimentary noose out of the other end, which falls about three feet below the center bar.

Next, he lazily makes a 360-degree turn, still petting the puppy. He is looking to see if anyone is watching him. He spends several minutes doing this. When the coast seems clear, he slips the noose around Hooligan's neck, tightens it, and lets go.

What happens next is incredible. He is mesmerized, unable to take his eyes off the puppy. It begins to kick frantically, making weak choking and whimpering sounds. Its eyes become twice their normal size. He is so close to the puppy, wanting to look right into its eyes, that when it releases its bladder, the contents hit him right in the face.

Then it is over. It has been an experience he knows he will have to replicate.

He leaves the puppy hanging from the swing set and hurries back to his room. He cleans himself up quickly and then moves a chair in front of the window. He sits there for hours, staring at Hooligan, waiting for the family to return home.

The mother pulls into the driveway with the three kids in tow about half past four that afternoon. Fifteen minutes later, the back door opens, and the three children pile out of the house to play before dinner. What happens next is forever burned into his brain. The wailing, the crying, the screaming—it is magnificent. The young boy is inconsolable, thrashing around on the ground, convulsing with sobs. It is even better than he imagined. He has snuffed out their happiness. He has done that—no one else.

CHAPTER 26

On the ride to work in the morning, I figure it'll be prudent to get the call with Catherine out of the way. I ring her cell. The call goes about as badly as expected—no, worse. She sheds some tears, but mostly, she just screams at me. This is not the first time my family has been affected by one of my cases. She makes sure to remind me.

In the end, I agree—promise, actually—to have security coverage 24-7 for her and the kids. That means coverage when going to and from school, grocery shopping, walking the dog—whatever. That means full-time coverage for all three simultaneously. What else can I do?

I call Jim after getting off the line with Catherine.

"Hey, Jim, glad I got you. Listen. Catherine is totally freaked out by what's going on. She wants, and I promised, 24-7 security for the three of them. They're all in different spots during the day, which I realize will be a pain in the ass. After six thirty, they're all in the same location. Can you coordinate with O'Shaughnessy's detail so any gaps are covered?"

"Already covered, Deke."

"I wired twenty-five thousand dollars to your company account yesterday. Let me know when and if we burn through that. Also, could you have one of your guys introduce himself to Catherine and try to put her at ease?"

"You got it, Deke. No worries, pal."

I hang up just as I pull into my parking spot at Quantico. I'm relieved. Jim is a good friend. Now I can focus on the investigation, and I'm amped to do just that.

I actually feel refreshed when I sit down at my workstation. After grabbing a coffee, I devote a half hour to cleaning out my inbox. I chuckle inwardly upon seeing seven separate messages from Connor, my editor. To say he is groveling is an understatement. By the last message, he's begging me to call him and telling me not to worry about timing—not to worry about anything.

Chuckling, I pick up the phone and dial Connor's cell. Predictably, he picks up on the first ring.

"Deke, my God, man, you had me terrified. Is everything okay? What can I do? Anything. Anything at all. Just name it."

"For starters, Connor, stop giving my ass a tongue bath. It doesn't suit you."

"Well—"

I cut him off. "I only have a minute, Connor, so listen up, and listen good. I'm working around the clock on a new serial case. The book is nowhere near done, nor will it be in the next four to six weeks. If that's a problem and you guys want the advance back, that's fine. You can have it back, but I'll no longer be your client. I hope that's not the case because you're the only one in the business I want to work with. I consider you a friend, but business is business. If you need to check with management or need more time to think about it, that's fine, but I have to get back to work."

"No, no, Deke. You take as much time as you need. Within reason, obviously. I'll not lose you as a client or as a friend."

"Thanks, Connor. Be good."

"You too."

I'm already gone.

No sooner do I hang up than my cell phone begins ringing. I check the number and answer.

"Hey, Griff, what gives?"

"A little of this and a little of that. I have my sister putting pressure on me to go into Darien for Turkey Day. She even got the nephews and nieces involved. I hate traveling on Thanksgiving. It's total amateur hour. I think I'll probably opt to do something local with Colleen so I can get some work done. What about you?"

"Working, but D'Antoni and I'll grab a bite end of the day at the St. Regis. Maybe even catch a little bit of the late game."

"Sounds good. Listen, we obtained additional surveillance footage of our perp outside the Kips Bay theater."

I sit straight up.

"He was caught by a surveillance camera at the TD Bank at 12:47. It's about fifty yards north of the theater, if you remember."

"Yeah, yeah, I remember. Is it a better shot?"

"Better? Yes. But still not terribly helpful. He never faces the camera. He knows it's there. He's smirking in the shot. I shit you not, smirking. I just sent the photo to you and the rest of the team."

"Give me a second to pull it up, Griff." I fumble with the mouse and open the attachment.

I'll be damned. The motherfucker is smirking. The shot does offer a much better view of the side of the perp's face than any of the other surveillance photos. I stare at the photo for the next minute, transfixed.

Griff brings me back to the moment. "What do you think?"

"It's the best picture we have of him. There's something oddly familiar about him. I can't put my finger on it. It'll probably drive me nuts all day." I yawn absentmindedly. "I'll talk to O'Shaughnessy, but if we decide to put a picture of this guy out to the media—and I think we should—this is the one to put out. Maybe scare this guy a bit."

"Agreed," Griff says. "What about timing?"

"Let me talk to O'Shaughnessy, and I'll get back to you. I'll call you later."

Just then, D'Antoni pokes her face over the top of her cube. She's smiling, and I find morning happiness annoying.

151

"What the fuck are you so happy about?"

"I got seven hours of sleep. I'm a new woman, ready to tackle a new day."

I take out my phone and pull up the surveillance picture Griff sent. "Take a look at this. Griff sent it earlier. This is the clearest shot of him yet."

"Yeah, I saw it. There's something familiar about this guy."

"I said the same thing to Griff. I don't know what it is, though. If we decide to circulate any picture of him to the public, this is our best choice. You agree?"

"Yeah. And what can it hurt? It'll bring the crazies out of the woodwork, but what else can we do? If we do it, though, we should ask O'Shaughnessy for a couple more bodies to deal with the tip line."

"Good point."

She changes the subject. "What are Catherine and the kids doing for Thanksgiving?"

"Your guess is as good as mine. Maybe they're spending it with her boyfriend."

"Oh, here we go. Can you please stop letting this idiot get under your skin? Seriously."

"Easy for you to say." I know it's stupid, but you can't change how you feel. My phone rings—a 617 number. *Oh shit!* It's Slaughter. I never got a chance to call him back yesterday.

"I have to take this. Do you want to listen on speaker?"

She shakes her head and acts busy, checking messages.

"Hey, Bill. Sorry I didn't get back to you yesterday. Things got crazy. Did you catch up with Barnes?"

"Don't sweat it, Deke. Yeah, I talked to Brian. Listen, Bronstein and I are working around the clock on this but have very little to show right now. Can you please keep us in the loop?"

I stretch in my seat. "We can debrief every day. Feel free to call anytime, especially if something pops on your end. We'll do the same.

"Our serial perp came right out and admitted that the Fenway murder merely presented an opportunity that was too good to pass up. He was impressed by the anesthesiologist's choice of location, the sux element—everything about the crime. More than anything, though, he saw it as a means to gain national attention, and it is attention he craves as much as the kill itself—attention that we feel will lead to his ultimate downfall."

"You seem pretty sure about this. You got all of that from one conversation?"

"I'm not positive about anything. It's too early. This guy is cocky; he's a braggart. He knows he's not in the system, understands forensics, and has no fear of being caught."

"At a bare minimum, your guy probably lives in Boston or one of its suburbs, right? Please keep Bronstein and me in the loop. We can help. Shit, we want to help."

"Absolutely, Bill. Anything new at your end?"

"Not really. Still pushing hard, closing loose ends."

"D'Antoni and I will keep you informed. I feel strongly that this guy is from Boston. We need your help."

CHAPTER 27

The team is assembled for the 10:00 a.m. debrief. Everyone looks tired, but some more than others. Despite his apparent lack of sleep, one of the agents, Chip Donnelley, catches my eye. He looks as if he's about to burst, practically springing out of his seat. *Someone has found something*, I think. *Good. Very good.*

"Chip, you got something you wanna share with the group?"

"Yeah, Deke. Yeah, I do." He pushes out his chair and stands up.

I figure he's going to use the whiteboard, but he doesn't. Instead, he stands in front of his chair. *Wow, this must be important.*

"I'm going to fill you in on everything we've learned so far."

"That would be nice," D'Antoni says.

Donnelley stutters a couple times before continuing. "Jane Martin grew up in Dorchester, Massachusetts. Dorchester was a rough place back then. Still is. She was born in 1981 to a John and Sandra Martin. Both parents have lengthy arrest records, mostly drug-related, although Dad also spent six years in Massachusetts Correctional Institution Cedar Junction for aggravated assault. Mom picked up a couple solicitation citations while Dad was locked up, and several drug citations. They divorced while he was in jail.

"Jane's home wasn't a happy home. Not even close. Child services were called to the home on five separate occasions between Jane's fifth and tenth birthdays. Jane suffered a lot of broken bones during this period, at least five that we know of so far. She was taken away from the parents for three months in 1988. Unfortunately, she was returned to these animals, and the abuse escalated.

"She was finally taken away for good in 1989. She was placed in foster care and bounced from home to home until 1996. We've not been able to dig up a lot about her life between 1989 and 1992, other than information on the families she lived with. It appears, at least on the surface, to have been a quiet, unremarkable time in her life, but we're reaching out to the foster families as I speak. Later, she came back on the radar in a big way. She was arrested seven times between 1993 and1995. What is not sealed is drug- and alcohol-related. We're attempting to gain access to the rest."

"There's no attempting in this case. She's dead, for God's sake!" D'Antoni barks.

"I know, I know. It just takes time," Donnelley replies, his voice shaky.

"Today," D'Antoni says a little too loudly.

Donnelley nods and continues. "In 1996, Jane was removed from her fifth and final foster home and court-ordered to Rayburn House, a group home for troubled teens in Roxbury, Massachusetts. She lived there until 1999, when she left to attend the University of Rhode Island on a full scholarship."

"Looks like someone turned their life around," D'Antoni says.

Hot damn. Now we're getting somewhere. Rayburn House has to be the connection. It seems too easy, though, and easy rarely works out.

"I spoke with the director of Rayburn House this morning, and he promised a comprehensive list of the juveniles who lived in the house during Jane's time there. He also promised to send along any related case files and disciplinary reports. He wasn't associated with the house during Jane's stay, but two counselors still employed in the home were there during that time." Donnelley looks directly at D'Antoni. "I got you and Deke an in-person interview with these counselors on Friday at ten."

D'Antoni jumps out of her seat, claps her hands, and points at Donnelley. "You're the fucking man. Great work, everyone. This could be huge—and I mean huge."

Now seems as good a time as any to add my two cents. "When this list of Jane's housemates comes in, we need to work it hard. Obviously, special attention must be given to the males, but we need to talk to as many people as possible. Split up the list any way you want, and reach out to these people. Donnelley, you run lead on this. We need to make significant headway today. The trail is red hot right now."

"You got it," Donnelley says.

"Also, if any of them live in Boston, see if they would be willing to meet with Louise and me on Friday. What about the parents?"

"Mother's dead; the father still lives in Dorchester."

"See if he'd be willing to talk to us in person Friday. No, scratch that. Feel him out first to see if you think it would be productive. Who knows what role, if any, he played in Jane's life after prison?"

D'Antoni clears her throat. "Let's find out who the director was during Jane's stay. If the person lives in Boston, see if they can meet with Deke and me on Friday. If not, set up a call with the person today if possible. Also, Boston Police Headquarters is in Roxbury. Find out everything you can about the house. There has got to be someone still working there who was on the job back then. Our guy had run-ins with local law enforcement. No doubt about it."

We spend the next thirty minutes fielding questions from the team and discussing strategy. Everybody is awake now, and the excitement in the room is palpable.

CHAPTER 28

O'Shaughnessy becomes free at one in the afternoon, and D'Antoni and I make a beeline for his office. We spend almost forty-five minutes discussing everything we've learned. He debates the efficacy of sending D'Antoni and me to Boston today, the Wednesday before Thanksgiving, to start the interview process, and in the end, he decides that Friday makes more sense. *Thank God.* I feel like a yo-yo. I want to get as much as possible done today and tomorrow with the team to ensure that Friday will be as productive as it can be.

Next, we move to the surveillance footage Griff sent this morning. O'Shaughnessy has seen it and has already decided to run the footage with the media on Friday. It'll run in Albany, Boston, New York, and Philadelphia.

Before we can ask, O'Shaughnessy tells us he's put together another small team to deal with the tip line. Our team is to keep doing what we're doing. What a relief. Lastly, we talk about protocol over Thanksgiving. O'Shaughnessy asks for updates at ten, two, and five. *Fair enough.*

D'Antoni and I swing by the conference room, grab some lunch, and head back to our workstations. We have a couple hours before our next meeting, and there's plenty to do. I spend the next hour and a half researching the medical effects of sux. It's potent stuff, and it's clear the killer did his homework. How did he access the substance, though? Logic dictates that he has to be in the medical profession, unless there is some sort of black market for paralytics. I make a note to have the team examine this angle. Everything about this guy speaks of careful planning. Finding him isn't going to be easy.

In the ten minutes remaining before the four o'clock meeting, I catch up on emails and texts. *Oh fuck.* There are two of each from Bridget. She wants to know my plans for Thanksgiving. She's free and suggests a few different venues. *Not gonna happen.* Even though I lack both the time and the inclination, I call her cell. She picks up on the first ring. Of course she does. I waste no time in getting to the point.

"Hey there, sexy. Sorry for just getting back to you. I'm working 24-7 on a high-profile case."

"It's always something." She sighs.

"I've been traveling a ton as well. I actually have to work tomorrow and then hop on a plane to Boston. I promise I'll call you when I get back. Promise."

"I was really hoping to have dinner with you tomorrow. We haven't seen each other in ages. Not even a booty call. Doesn't that bother you at all?"

An uncomfortable second or two passes before I realize I'm supposed to respond. "Of course it does. I can't wait to see you. I miss you. Let's plan on getting away for a weekend when this thing wraps. Maybe a weekend in New York if you want."

Another audible sigh travels through the phone line. "I'd like that. But can you at least check in now and then?"

"Scout's honor. Can't wait to see you."

I don't wait for her reply.

CHAPTER 29

The conference room is buzzing with activity. I get a cup of coffee and take a seat. D'Antoni has been waiting for me. I give her a quick smile, and she begins.

"Give us the good news. Donnelley, let's start with you."

"We got the list of juveniles from Rayburn House. There were twenty-one—twelve males and nine females. Three of the males are currently incarcerated and have been for at least the last fourteen months. Two of the others are African American. We'll speak to them, but they're off the suspect list, obviously. Five of the boys still live in Massachusetts—three in Boston proper.

"We have contact details for three of the five Massachusetts residents and contact information for four of the juveniles who live outside Massachusetts. We've reached out to all of them. So far, we've only spoken to a Timothy Veerdon, now aged thirty-one, who lives in Boston's Back Bay. He was in the house for Jane's last six months there. He'll do a call on Friday but can't meet in person because he'll be out of town for the holiday weekend."

"Set it up," D'Antoni says.

"You're set for one o'clock on Friday afternoon. Dial-in information has been sent to the entire team. Barnes suggested you do the call from the Boston office."

"Good," I say. "What else?"

Donnelley clears his throat and continues. "We spoke to the former director of Rayburn House, a Mary Morrison. She now runs another group home in Allston, Massachusetts, less than five minutes from Rayburn. You're meeting her Friday afternoon at two o'clock in the Boston office. We'll find contact information for the rest of the juveniles. Also, we're pulling criminal history and any other background we can find on all of them. Social media will be looked at as well. We'll have more for you at tonight's meeting."

"Good work," D'Antoni says. "Focus on juvenile criminal activity. Our boy's kept his nose clean as an adult, it seems. Look for violence and aggression; in fact, look for cruelty in general, including cruelty to animals. Sexual misconduct would be an obvious indicator."

I ask the team to investigate how sux could be attained outside of a medical setting.

Things are moving fast.

CHAPTER 30

I lean back in a leather chair at the Starbucks less than five minutes from the Quantico campus and give in, letting my mind race and going with it. Almost immediately, I hit on something that makes me pause. *The Montblanc Meisterstück pens.* Is it simply coincidence that the killer chose to buy the same make and model as my own lucky pen, the pen I wrote most of my first book with?

I don't believe in coincidences. I never have.

I search my memory for clues. Ten minutes later, with no progress made, I decide to move on.

That's when it hits me right between the eyes.

I had a book signing at the Boston Copley branch of Barnes and Noble almost seven years ago. A reporter who was in attendance asked me how I had written my first book, whether it was written longhand, written in shorthand, or typed. At the time, I thought it an odd question and decided to answer honestly and in some detail. "I wrote it with my lucky Montblanc pen." I then waved the pen for the crowd to see. Nowadays, I draft on my laptop, but my lucky pen is never far away. I touch my left breast pocket and feel its reassuring outline. I've become almost superstitious about it.

Did this animal attend that book signing? Again, I scan my memory for a mental image of someone in the crowd, but to no avail. Too much time has elapsed. That, and too many brain cells have fallen victim to Johnnie Walker Black and his friends. It's frustrating, and I know it'll haunt me for days to come.

Then I realize the killer didn't necessarily have to be at the signing. Given the reporter's presence, there were probably accounts of the event given in the print and digital media. I make a mental note to verify this back at the office. Still, my brain fights to remember the event, including faces in the crowd and people I talked to.

Next, my mind drifts to the killer's last text. Is he actually stalking Catherine and my kids? Catherine hasn't mentioned a boyfriend. Then again, would she? Probably not. I certainly don't share details of my love life with her. This simple revelation, true or not, feels like a stab in the gut, exactly as the killer has intended. Try as I might to ignore it, the pain nags at me like a pesky mosquito on a warm summer day.

It's time to move on to something more productive. Again, my mind races. Why did the killer divulge a prior relationship with Jane Martin? It doesn't make any sense. What could he possibly gain from it? A dull throbbing in the back of my head pulls me back to the present. I should be getting back to the team. I'm not going to find this guy on my own. I get D'Antoni a venti skim latte with an extra shot, extra hot. It's probably the only productive thing I've accomplished.

Immediately after dropping D'Antoni's coffee off at her desk, I scour the internet for any media accounts of my book signing in Boston more than seven years ago. Sure enough, a *Boston Globe* article pops up, and the Montblanc discussion is referred to. So the killer didn't have to be at the book signing.

Still, I have a sneaking suspicion he was.

CHAPTER 31

Lying on my bed, eyes on the ceiling, I replay the day in my head. This one has been fruitful, with real progress made. I feel as if we're finally moving in the right direction. *Progress rather than perfection, right?* I have to keep telling myself that.

So D'Antoni was right. Jane Martin spent two and a half years in a group home for troubled teens. *Dollars to doughnuts she met our perp there*, I think. Nothing else makes sense.

During Jane's time in the house, twenty-one other juveniles lived in the home too. One of these other kids has to be the perp. Or at the very least, one of these individuals knew the perp. Excitement courses through my veins. This is my favorite part of any investigation: when the puzzle starts to take shape.

I need a reality check. There's a long way to go, and everything could blow up at any point.

I can't stop wondering why this sicko volunteered the information that he knew Jane Martin. Why? It makes no sense. Is he playing us? Trying to lead us down the wrong path? This question and the dizzying array of potential answers and motives spin out of control in my brain. I feel dizzy, intoxicated with information overload. I don't want to get too worked up. This is when a Johnnie Black would come in handy to calm the nerves and help me focus on one thing at a time. As it is, two nonnarcotic sleeping pills will have to do.

I'm about to turn off the lights and surrender to sleep, when the familiar tone of several incoming texts stops me.

Please, God, let this not be the killer.

CHAPTER 32

I don't recognize the sender's number. It has a 212 area code. *Fuck. Here we go.*

> Hey, Deke, enjoy the holiday, pal. Take the day off, and rest up. You're going to need your energy. I promise, Scout's honor, to behave myself. You're probably a bit skeptical, aren't you? Why wouldn't you be? No, I'm perfectly content to slob around all day like every other stupid American, getting fatter by the minute. In truth, I simply have a ton of planning to do. I prefer the doing over the planning, but you can't have one without the other.
>
> The Movie Theater Series needs a grand finale, don't you think? I'm so fucking bored with it already. I'm ready to move on to bigger and better things. I've so much planned. So much left to do. I can't function when I'm bored. You don't want me bored—trust me.
>
> When I'm bored, my mind wanders. I find myself thinking a lot about Catherine, Sean, and the little retard. My offer still stands, pal. I can put the little moron down for you. Probably be a huge weight off your chest. No more worrying about who will take care of him when you guys are gone. Cute little fucker, though. I'll give you that.
>
> I've also done a lot of thinking about Bridget. I know you want out of the relationship. She's pushy and

needy. Let's be honest: she's a bitch. I can help with that too. Actually, I will help you with that. Gladly. I've been dying—no pun intended—to get my hands on her. That red hair and perfect ass. Mmm. Lip-smacking good. It'll give me something else to plan and do. Do you have a protection detail on her as well? Not that it'll matter.

I want you to be front and center for the final act of the Movie Theater Series. It's going to be epic. One for the ages, baby.

December always has a blockbuster or two. Maybe I'll choose a big, well-hyped movie opening. Theaters will be jammed to the rafters during the holidays. So many beautiful women to choose from. No one is safe.

Thousands of happy, festive moviegoers. Lots of holiday cheer. Can you think of a bigger stage? Who better to direct the production than yours truly? The day approaches; the excitement gains momentum. Ha-ha.

Oh shit, I almost forgot. Back to originality and creativity. You should check in on a Joseph Wilson from Worcester, Massachusetts. He was a real mouthful. Has not said much the last five and a half years. Not that he ever had anything good to say anyway. You'll find him hanging around behind the shed.

Gobble-gobble, TMK

My frustration brings me back to reality. This guy thrives on control. He's the master manipulator. I feel like a puppet—his puppet.

This guy knows exactly which buttons to push. I've always been hypersensitive when it comes to Patrick. I want to shield him from all the cruelties the world has to offer, both real and imagined. Somehow, this sicko was able to deduce this. It's eerie and disconcerting. It's as if he can see into my mind.

Anger and frustration gradually give way to focus and resolve. I forward the text to the entire team, including the forensic techs.

I call the office. Special Agent Donnelley answers. He sounds way too bubbly for the time of day. I spend the next five minutes laying it all out for him. We need to learn everything we can about Joseph Wilson, probably deceased, from Worcester, Massachusetts. I mean everything. I ask him to bring Detective Timmons of the Massachusetts State Police into the fold and coordinate the investigation with him.

Next, I text Jim Conolley. I tell him I need security on Bridget as quickly as possible. I ask him to please coordinate with another agency if he doesn't have the manpower. It doesn't matter what it costs at this point. I can't have her on my conscience. I need to focus on catching this animal.

CHAPTER 33

He tossed and turned most of the night. The anticipation and excitement were too much. He couldn't stop thinking about her. She is so beautiful. That red hair and perfect body. Her feisty attitude and bitchiness. What more could he ask for? Plus, this will be a direct assault on Deke too. He will be hurting—actually, a lot more than hurting—someone in Deke's life.

He will need to be extra careful. Deke will probably have security protection on Bridget. He isn't the type to endanger his friends. *Fucking Mr. Goody Two-shoes.* It doesn't really matter; he has prepared for every eventuality and put in the surveillance required. He knows her daily habits and the ins and outs of her daily life.

No amount of security will keep Bridget safe. He is a professional. He is the best.

There's no point in staying put in bed. Sleep is for the weak anyway. He has to be at Logan at five o'clock for his six o'clock flight into Washington Reagan. He might as well look through his bag one last time to make sure he has everything needed. He will keep the sux-filled syringe and the small container of chloroform in his pocket in case his bag is searched. Hopefully he wouldn't be singled out and strip-searched.

Nah, he is just being paranoid.

CHAPTER 34

My alarm goes off at 6:15. I feel refreshed after the best night of sleep I've had in a while. Screw the killer. All I need to do is stay focused and work the case. The killer is playing with me, trying to distract me.

I have a renewed sense of confidence. There's a reason I'm good at what I do. I didn't grow into my role; I was born into it. I truly believe this. God has specific plans for everyone. I was destined to be a profiler, and I'm good at it—really good.

＋＋＋◆＋＋＋

His plane touches down at 7:05. Everything has gone smoothly. On the way into DC, he has to check into his motel. It's a real flophouse, but it has external access out of view of the check-in desk. Also, he has disabled the security cameras in the back, having established where his room was located a couple weeks earlier. He needs to make sure they are still disabled.

Ten minutes after leaving the airport, he arrives at the motel. Before heading into reception, he slips the dark-haired wig on. He had the wig made professionally a couple years ago, and it is nearly impossible to tell the wig from genuine hair. He then puts on a Washington Nationals baseball hat and a pair of large aviator sunglasses—his usual disguise. He shows the clerk at the reception desk a fake ID and pays for two nights' stay.

Before entering his room, he inspects the security cameras he previously disabled. All good—they're still off-line. He enters the room, throws his bag onto the bed, and then heads to the bathroom and splashes cold water on his face.

Before heading back out, he checks his disguise one last time in the mirror. Good to go, he hops in the car for the quick ride into Georgetown. He's not going to Bridget's townhouse. Instead, he intends to surprise her at her gym, the twenty-four-hour Georgetown establishment she frequents every day, even on holidays. It's one of those high-end gyms you can access any hour of the day with your membership card.

On her days off, she usually sleeps in, opting to go to the gym around nine in the morning. He will be there early to surveil the parking lot and the surrounding area for any protection detail. He hopes she doesn't have one. If she does, he will have to take her inside the gym, which will be risky.

It's smooth sailing into Georgetown. Most people have already traveled to wherever they're celebrating the holiday. He pulls into the gym parking lot at about eight forty-five and takes a spot in the rear northwest corner. It's an ideal vantage point, providing a perfect view of the entire parking lot.

He spends the next five minutes scanning for anything out of the ordinary.

She pulls into the parking lot at 8:57. He recognizes the navy-blue 3 Series BMW immediately. No other car follows her in, but that doesn't necessarily mean no one is watching her. He needs to confirm that.

She hops out of the car, grabs a bag from the backseat, walks to the door, and swipes herself into the gym. He gives it a couple minutes and then exits his vehicle to search the area. He has plenty of time. Her typical workout lasts seventy-five minutes.

The only other car in the parking lot is empty—probably just another gym rat. He heads out onto Wisconsin Avenue and spends the next thirty-five minutes walking up and down on both sides of the street in front of the gym, looking for eyes on the ground.

The plan is coming together. He detects no security detail. If there is one, he would've spotted it. It's time to head back to the car.

First, he walks past the gym entrance, looking for any obvious security cameras. He doesn't see any, but that doesn't mean they're not there. He takes up position behind a concrete pylon and waits for Bridget.

He reaches into his pocket and removes the rag and small bottle of chloroform. He's never used chloroform before and hopes it lives up to its reputation. At 10:17, Bridget leaves the gym.

He quickly and thoroughly soaks the rag with chloroform, emerges from behind the pylon, and saunters toward the gym's entrance. He looks like any other gym patron in his workout outfit. He doesn't make eye contact with Bridget, but they almost brush shoulders as they pass.

He pivots around as if on a dime and lunges. He has the rag over her nose and mouth in an instant. She struggles in his arms for several seconds before her body goes limp, and she collapses into his arms.

Without breaking stride, he slips his head under her right arm and gingerly guides her to his rental car. He places her in the front passenger seat, ties up her hands and ankles, places tape across her mouth, and then hops in on the driver's side. While chloroform acts within a few seconds of inhalation, recovery from the effects is similarly quick. Not wanting to take any chances, he immediately retraces his steps back to the motel.

Better safe than sorry.

It takes him less than fifteen minutes to return to the motel. She's come to, but she's still pretty groggy. Wanting to take no chances, he hits her with another dose of the chloroform. He spends a couple minutes scanning the motel parking lot for activity. It's quiet. The motel is practically empty. When he decides it's safe, he unbuckles her, places his right arm under her left shoulder, and guides her toward his room.

They're inside twenty seconds later. He places her gently on the ratty, well-used queen-sized bed.

His heart is beating so fast he feels as if it might explode. He's so hard it hurts. He sets about taking her clothes off and untying her. He removes her shoes and socks and then starts on the sweatpants. When he has them halfway down her legs, her eyes fly open. On her face is the wildest, craziest look he's ever seen. She looks like a crazed animal.

Then she lunges at him with both hands, raking the left side of his face with her nails. He feels as though chunks of his flesh have been torn off, and blood clouds his vision. Boiling rage overtakes him. Blindly, he rains thunderous blows upon her face and body. It's almost a minute until he stops pummeling her. Her face is a battered mess; blood pours from her clearly broken nose. Her right eye is swollen shut, the orbital shattered. She's unconscious, maybe dead.

He hops off the bed, breathing hard. The rage is all-consuming; he doesn't even know what he's doing. Somehow, he manages to get out of his clothes.

Syringe in hand, he gets back up onto the bed to finish what he started.

She's come to—sort of—and a low, barely audible whimper escapes her lips. Her eyes open and close slowly. He plunges the syringe into her neck. The fight is gone in seconds, and the rest of her clothes come off without incident. He's still enraged, and the anger blinds him. White lightning bolts flash before his eyes. Somehow, he manages to regain some degree of composure.

He stares intently into her eyes. His hands caress every inch of her body. He cannot enjoy the moment, however, as his rage is still overwhelming.

When she's finally gone, he's disgusted. This isn't going the way he intended. He had such plans for her; he has fantasized about them for weeks. He feels cheated, robbed of something—something he is entitled to. His anger has gotten the best of him, denying him the ultimate satisfaction he craves.

He rolls off her and onto his back. Still breathing hard, he stares at the ceiling.

There's no way to fix this. What's done is done.

Slowly, he comes back to reality. His breathing evens out, and he begins to think more clearly. It's not all bad. He's still managed to kill someone close to Deke, someone Deke cares for. Even better, he told Deke he was going to do it. He warned him—and Deke couldn't stop him.

He leaps off the bed, dresses quickly, and sits at the desk to write a note to Deke. It takes about five minutes. He then folds the note up and walks back to the bed. He positions the body the way he wants it to be found and then places the note inside her. She's still warm.

Man, has he fucked up. Before leaving, he grabs his new burner phone and snaps several pictures.

He remembers to place the Do Not Disturb sign on the door as he leaves. It's time to get back to Georgetown. He takes a healthy pull of Jameson from the flask in his pocket and then another. It's time to find a restaurant or bar that's open in Georgetown. His body and mind crave booze. It's the only thing that will calm the storm.

Then he will pay Chevy Chase, Maryland, a visit. Things are starting to look up again.

CHAPTER 35

I call Catherine on her cell. She doesn't sound happy to hear from me, so I dispense with the small talk. "What are you guys doing today?"

"I'm not really sure what business it is of yours." An uncomfortable pause follows before she continues. "My mother is coming. Rob and Sue too. Sean has been talking nonstop about Uncle Rob. They're both really excited."

"Oh, that's awesome," I say. "I hope you guys have a great day. Anyone else coming?"

"Nope."

"Did the security detail introduce themselves yet?"

"Yeah, last night. Listen, Deke, I really need to get going. I have a ton of prep to do."

"Understood. Happy Thanksgiving."

The line is already dead.

As usual, I replay the conversation in my mind. Was there anything other than anger or ambivalence in Catherine's voice? Fuck, why did it all have to go so wrong?

This thought process only heightens my loneliness and sadness. The answer is obvious and has been for some time now: she doesn't love me anymore. I need to accept this and find a way, no matter how hard, to move on. I owe her that. I owe myself that.

D'Antoni touches my arm. My eyes open. The pity party is officially over.

CHAPTER 36

After a quick coffee run to Starbucks, we enter the conference room and convene the meeting. I look around the table, making eye contact with each member of the team. Everybody looks exhausted. Nobody can question the FBI's commitment. I feel guilty about having left early last night, but guilty or not, there's no time to waste. We need to keep moving forward.

D'Antoni looks at Donnelley and nods. Once again, he stands up to address the group.

"We made contact with four more of Jane Martin's housemates—three women and one man. The women all live outside Massachusetts, so we set up telephone interviews with them for Friday. Two of the interviews overlap with your meetings in Boston, so we'll handle them and fill you in later in the day."

"Sounds good," D'Antoni says.

"The male, Greg Roker, lives in Natick, which is thirty minutes outside of Boston. He's agreed to be interviewed in the Boston office tomorrow afternoon at four. He indicated that he and Jane were pretty close, so this could be big."

I sit up, my attention caught. "Criminal history?"

"Nothing serious. A couple of juvenile drug citations and nothing else. His file looks a lot like Jane Martin's. He was taken away from his birth family when he was nine. Both parents were locked up for drug trafficking. He was removed from the home three separate times before that because of suspected abuse. He bounced from foster home to foster home until he was fifteen, and that's when he was court-ordered into the house."

"No wonder they were close," D'Antoni says.

"I'd be willing to bet that the majority of these kids have similar stories," I say.

D'Antoni nods in agreement. "That's fair."

"What else?" I ask.

"Greg is a partner in a white-gloved law firm in Boston. He's well known in legal circles. He's also an adjunct law professor at Boston College."

D'Antoni whistles. "Everybody loves a good rags-to-riches story."

The attorney angle has me intrigued. The perp is intelligent and knowledgeable about forensics and detective work. Could this be our guy?

Donnelley clears his throat and continues. "He's married, with two kids."

So much for that. I don't see our guy as being married. "This isn't our guy. Our guy is single and never married. He's a loner, a sadistic narcissist without the capacity to love. But maybe he knows our guy. The fact that he was close with Jane could prove beneficial."

"Anything else jumping off the page?" D'Antoni asks.

Donnelley takes a few seconds before answering. "Maybe. We need a little more time. We should have more later today."

"Fair enough," I say. "Why don't we switch direction? What do we know about Joseph Wilson, the man the killer told me to look into?"

Donnelley thumbs through some notes and then looks up again. "Not a good guy. Spent a significant portion of his adult life behind bars. His last stint was a three-to-five for distribution of child pornography. He's not been seen or heard from in five and a half years. I have a call into his probation officer."

Hmm. The plot thickens. "Joseph Wilson was in our guy's life. Probably when he was a kid or in his early adolescence, given his likely past. Maybe even when he was still living with the birth mother. Do we have a last known?"

"We think so. It looks like he was renting a trailer in Worcester, Massachusetts, right up until he disappeared. I have a call in to the current owner of the trailer."

"He didn't disappear," I say under my breath. "You connect with Timmons?"

"Yes. He's taking a team to the last known tomorrow. He's lined up a cadaver dog."

"Good," I say. I glance over at D'Antoni to see if she has anything to add.

"Why don't we reconvene at two?" she says. "Everybody is to be out of here and on their way home to their families by four. No exceptions. The case will still be here tomorrow."

D'Antoni and I need to give O'Shaughnessy an update. We decide to do that from his office so we can use speakerphone with some privacy. O'Shaughnessy picks up immediately. I can hear the alcohol in his voice. Someone is starting early.

We start with the killer's text. O'Shaughnessy starts right in. "What's not clear to me is what he means by saying he wants you to be 'front and center.' Any ideas, Deke?"

"Maybe he plans to do whatever he's going to do in DC," I say. "He'd definitely get off on doing something right under our noses. That's my best guess. Hey, boss, I hate to ask, but you know I have to. You've got to put someone on Bridget. I've already alerted Jeff, and he's agreed to fill in the gaps. I can't be worrying about her safety."

"Already on it," O'Shaughnessy says. "I've got it lined up 24-7, starting tomorrow, so you can let Jeff know you're all set."

"Thanks, boss. I really appreciate it. I still intend to keep Joe on the job as well—it's family."

CHAPTER 37

Sitting in Starbucks alone, my brain on caffeine overdrive, I make myself comfortable and spend twenty minutes going through my case file. I put the file down, shut my eyes, and let my mind race.

The side profile of the killer flashes before my mind's eye. There's something familiar about him. I've seen this man before. Have I met him at an FBI-sponsored lecture, at a book signing, or while working a case or simply passed him on the street? If I met him on a case, was he a crime-scene investigator or an ME? I reach deep into my memory to try to find something—anything. My mind spins and spins, but try as I might to reach it, the answer is always just out of reach. This half-remembered man will plague my dreams and test my sanity. Of this I'm certain.

The store door opens, and a blast of cold air startles me back to the present. My focus shifts to the killer's last text. What did he mean by saying he wanted me "front and center" for his next sick adventure? I'm already right in the middle of everything. D'Antoni and I, two of the best profilers in the world, are running the case. How much more front and center can one get?

Does he intend to kill someone in my neck of the woods, in the nation's capital? Even assuming that's true, does it give me any real advantage? How many theaters does DC have? Would it be practical to put cops at every location? Is there even enough evidence to support doing so? Probably not. No, definitely not. I don't think a gut feeling is proof of anything, but even so, my gut is rarely wrong.

Next, I focus in on the killer's threats. These can't be ignored. I believe as fact what the killer has told me. He will try to hurt those close to me. It's a matter not of if but of when.

I ponder, not for the first time, the question of whether I am morally or professionally bound to make Bridget aware of the killer's threats. There's no easy answer to that question. In her position, I would want to know, and I felt it important for Catherine to know. But my gut tells me that telling Bridget will accomplish nothing other than terrifying her. I'll check up on her on a regular basis and will keep a protection team on her as long as necessary. What else can I do other than completely terrify her?

CHAPTER 38

He's on his third shot of Jameson before his heart rate returns to normal. He really lost his shit back in that motel room. He had some kind of out-of-body experience, becoming a man possessed. Couldn't have stopped himself even if he wanted to.

The lack of self-control scares him a bit. This is how mistakes are made. It ruined a perfectly thought-out plan, one he had fantasized about for weeks. He doesn't like it when things don't go according to plan.

But what's done is done, and Bridget's death will haunt Deke—and rightfully so. He straight out told Deke he was going to kill Bridget, and Deke did nothing to prevent it. That is going to be a tough pill to swallow—and that is the whole point.

He wants Deke to suffer.

He orders another Sierra Nevada and a last shot of Jameson. He will have to find another establishment to continue his drinking. The bartender is already giving him the hairy eyeball, the fat slob.

His mind drifts back to the day he met Deke for the first time.

Deke was giving an FBI-sponsored lecture on the efficacy of profiling. Personally, he thought it was all a bunch of bullshit, just a bunch of recycled generalities. Any moron could see that. Reading tea leaves would be as useful.

He had done his research on Deke before the lecture. He made sure to read all the media accounts of Deke's success as a profiler of serial killers; he had even read the first book in the Sean Patrick series. He didn't like Deke. He didn't like the FBI in general. They were a bunch of pretentious snobs always sticking their noses where they didn't belong.

He attended the lecture with a single purpose in mind, and he came prepared. He had read several convincing articles that questioned the value of profiling and had memorized the key points made within them. His game plan was to attack the efficacy of Deke's argument. He wanted to be noticed, to stand out, to look smart in front of the other attendees. He was very alert to what people thought of him.

Deke was maybe ten minutes into his presentation, when he unleashed his well-rehearsed counterargument. He interrupted Deke and disrupted his train of thought, taking the chance to dominate the floor for the next five minutes. He might as well have stood up on a soapbox. The room was quiet. He had the floor, and everyone was listening. How could they not be impressed?

Deke gave him all the time he needed, not interrupting once. He thanked him for his input and acknowledged that he had made some salient points. Then he slowly, methodically, and convincingly shot down every single argument he had made. He did it without raising his voice and without referring to him specifically. Deke's rebuttals were so well considered and constructed and so well received by the crowd that he didn't dare respond. He felt humiliated. Some of those in attendance even laughed a little. A bunch of morons were laughing at him. He wanted to crawl underneath his chair and hide.

To cap it all off, Deke gave him the cold shoulder later when he attempted to get his attention during the question-and-answer session. The big-time profiler and murder-mystery writer couldn't be bothered with him.

He left the lecture enraged. He had made a fool of himself. That smug fuck had shown him up in front of everyone. Deke had squashed him like a bug and disrespected him.

His anger over the incident and his corresponding hatred of Deke didn't dissipate over time. Rather, his feelings simmered and grew, threatening to boil over at any moment.

CHAPTER 39

When I swing by D'Antoni's workstation to drop off her coffee, she glances up, and our eyes meet. She doesn't say anything for a few seconds. Then she asks, "Everything good? Anything you wanna talk about?"

I shake my head. "Everything's good. We can catch up over dinner. We shouldn't keep the team waiting."

"Thanks for the coffee, butthead," she says.

The meeting is pretty uneventful; there have been developments since the morning. The team continues to read case files, check social media, pore over criminal histories, and do anything and everything necessary to gain a better understanding of Jane's housemates.

I'm proud of the work that's been done. It's amazing, given the time frame. I'm glad everyone will get home to see his or her family and get some much-needed rest.

"Hey, Donnelley, didn't you say you might be onto something this morning?" D'Antoni asks.

"Uh, yeah. Yeah, I did." He fumbles with some papers in front of him. "I don't know how important this might be."

"Neither do we yet," D'Antoni says.

"Okay. Yeah, um, there was an individual who lived in the house for the last eighteen months of Jane's residence. His name was William Sappey. He's got a thick file full of disciplinary write-ups for fighting, stealing, and alleged sexual misconduct, to name just a few. He almost got kicked out of the house one month into his stay.

He was caught leering at a group of girls from the home while they undressed in the girls' locker room. He cut a hole in an adjoining wall to look through. After promising never to do it again and to repair the wall, he was put on probation but allowed to stay in the house. There's another incident in the file that made the hair on my arms stand straight up, though."

"We can't have that," D'Antoni says. This elicits a few chuckles around the table.

"William was accused of killing a neighbor's dog. Puppy, to be exact. The puppy was hung from the family's swing set. The kids found it when they went out to the backyard to play."

I suddenly sit straight up in my chair. "Holy shit!" I say. "And you thought this might not be important?"

"I know, I know. This guy looks like a real bad apple. It's important to note that it was never proven that he killed the dog. He wasn't disciplined for the incident, and the police cleared him due to a lack of evidence.

"What's interesting is that another boy in the house, Todd Johnson, whom we'll talk to tomorrow, swore that William told him he killed the dog. He said that William planned it out for weeks and that he was—and let me quote—'insanely preoccupied with the family.' Apparently, he would sit in front of the window in his room, watching them, sometimes for hours at a time."

Donnelley continues. "It wasn't all bad for this kid, though. He was a straight-A student and a terrific baseball player. He got a partial scholarship and generous financial-aid package to attend Harvard, where he was a middle-of-the-pack student but excelled on the ball field. He even played two seasons of AA baseball with the Yankees. After his stint in professional baseball, things got very interesting. He disappeared off the face of the earth. I mean gone."

"What does that mean exactly?" I ask.

"There's zero—and I mean zero—activity associated with his Social Security number, credit cards, or anything else. He's just gone."

"No death certificate, I assume?" D'Antoni says.

"Nope."

"So what are we thinking?" I ask. "Did the guy create a new identity? Did he assume someone else's?"

"We're working all the angles," Donnelley says. "As you know, it's nearly impossible to disappear."

"I'm not so sure about that," D'Antoni says. "I like this guy. I like him a whole bunch," she says. "He meets all the profile parameters. He fits it almost too perfectly."

I agree with D'Antoni but keep the thought to myself. I want the team to keep an open mind and leave no stone unturned.

Donnelley then passes around copies of Sappey's 2001 Massachusetts driver's license. I place the photo side by side with the Kips Bay surveillance photo and spend the next several minutes comparing the two. I'm not great with faces; D'Antoni is much better.

I turn to D'Antoni. "Louise? Thoughts?"

"Gimme another minute." She squints, shakes her head, and finally looks up. "I can't tell. Maybe? We need to try to do a facial progression. Donnelley, can you take the lead on that?"

"Absolutely," he answers. "There's one more thing I need to tell you. William's middle name is Andrew—William Andrew Sappey. Those initials match the initials on the pens found at the last two crime scenes."

Holy shit. Apparently, I'm slow on the uptake.

"That's great work," I say to the team, and I mean it. "Let's keep working this the way we've been working it. Everyone is a potential suspect—everyone. Everything to do with Sappey could be completely coincidental."

Even as I say it, I don't believe it. We're onto something—no doubt about it. Hot damn, this job can be exciting.

For whatever reason, my mind flashes back to my summer internship at Ernst and Young, and I shudder. I could've been an accountant. *Yikes.*

We spend the next twenty minutes going through what the team has learned about the people we will be interviewing tomorrow.

Donnelley gives D'Antoni and me a folder each, with all pertinent information on the interviewees. I will review it on the plane ride to Logan.

It's 3:55 in the afternoon—perfect timing. We arrange update calls for the next day and send everyone home to his or her family. D'Antoni has to walk Donnelley to the door to get him to leave. I like Donnelly a lot.

D'Antoni and I head to O'Shaughnessy's office for the four o'clock call. It takes the better part of forty minutes to update him on the new developments. He's a little slower than usual on the uptake, probably due to one too many glasses of cabernet, but who am I to judge?

O'Shaughnessy tells us the plane will be ready to go at eight thirty in the morning and will stay in Boston until we leave. Then he tells us to get out of the office and go home.

He doesn't have to tell us twice.

CHAPTER 40

D'Antoni and I agree to head directly to the St. Regis. I realize then that I'm famished. I forgot to eat lunch.

Dinner is even better than I anticipated. The turkey is moist, and the stuffing is perfectly seasoned. Heck, even the cranberry sauce is delicious, and I've never liked anyone's cranberry sauce other than my own. I eat until I can't eat any more, at which point I suggest we take a break before sampling the wonderful desserts displayed in the center of the room.

"You going to take any time after we close this?" I ask her.

"Haven't even thought about it. I'm hoping to get out west to do some skiing at some point."

"You still have the timeshare at Mount Snow?"

"Nah. I haven't done that in a couple of years. Wasn't worth it. You know what our schedules are like."

"Yeah, I do. You ought to try Banff in the Canadian Rockies. It's the most beautiful spot on earth. And the skiing at Lake Louise and Sunshine Village is terrific. You'd love it."

"Yeah, that's what you said a while back. I'll definitely think about it. I can always go to Aspen with my sister and the kids during the week of Presidents' Day for free. The only downside is that my sister will be there." She laughs.

"I doubt I'll even ski this year," I say. "The last couple of years it's been two or three runs tops, followed by way too much fun in the Cloudspin Lounge. I think I know every bartender employed at

Whiteface over the last five years. Once upon a time, and what now seems like a lifetime ago, I loved skiing. I also loved fishing, hiking, and hunting—anything that had to be done outside, really. I still do. It's simply that drinking became more important than anything else."

"I thought Bridget loved to ski."

"She does, and she can ski as much as she wants as far as I'm concerned. I just won't be joining her."

"Does she know? I mean, does she know how you feel? Where your mind is at?"

"No. Probably suspects. I need to get around to telling her."

"You're such a chicken. The longer you draw it out, the worse it's going to be." Her eyes widen, and a smile brightens her face. "You ready for dessert?"

"Why not?"

A piece of pumpkin and apple pie later, I'm disgusted with myself. I need to get up extra early tomorrow to make the gym and burn off at least some of this massive meal.

Thanksgiving has turned out to be the most enjoyable day I can remember in a long time—and I was sober for it. I can't help feeling a sense of pride about that.

CHAPTER 41

He's feeling no pain. He's lost count of the Jameson shots at this point and decides to stick with Sierra Nevada for the rest of the night. He has to be up early tomorrow morning to check things out in Chevy Chase. He needs to know what he's up against. Preparation is the difference between success and failure, and failure is not an option.

He thinks back to when he decided to cease being William Sappey. In retrospect, it was the best decision of his life bar none. At first, he thought he'd simply change his name, get a new Social Security number, move, and start a new life. It was the simplest answer to his problems.

With forged paperwork, he could make the identity appear legal, and from that point on, he could be that brand-new person for the rest of his life. However, there were risks involved when it came to creating and maintaining a new identity, most notably the chance of withstanding a background check. Background checks would delve back further than the new identity, showing clearly when the identity was created, and that wouldn't be good. Given the career path he was on and determined to maintain, background checks were a certainty, so he was forced to consider other options.

The next option he considered was that of borrowing someone else's identity. In taking advantage of another person in this way, he would benefit from the certainty of a traceable past. Yet this solution also would bring problems. In most such cases, the person whose identity has been thus assumed will eventually become wise to the fraud and quickly take steps to shut down everything the fraudster has worked so hard to create.

So once again, he was at a crossroads. Then a brilliant plan began to form in his mind. He was at a point in his baseball career that meant it was time to shit or get off the pot. He knew he wasn't good enough for the major league. He still couldn't hit the fucking curveball. That wasn't going to change. It was time to make a life change.

✦✦✦✦✦✦

As luck would have it, one of his friends—okay, his only friend—on the team was his age and had similar physical characteristics. He was also the only other player with a four-year degree. He had graduated with honors from Duke, which many liked to call the Harvard of the South. How appropriate. He also had the same first name, which would make things easier.

What really convinced him the plan could work was the fact that this friend had no family—none at all. His mom and dad had died in a car crash when he was sixteen, and both parents had been only children. The grandparents were long since dead. At seventeen, he had been legally emancipated and headed off on a full ride to Duke.

It was almost too good to be true.

The plan came together fairly quickly. His buddy had an apartment in the same complex where he lived. He had an end-of-season party one Friday night in early October. More than one hundred people attended, including some hot groupies and hangers-on—but that night was all about business. His buddy got pretty shitfaced. He couldn't hit the curveball either and had recently made the decision to leave baseball and embark on the next phase of his life. Little did he know he would be moving on both literally and figuratively.

The party thinned out after one in the morning, and he realized he wasn't going to get a better chance to make his move. He had bought some Rohypnol on the internet a few weeks earlier, and the so-called date-rape drug was fast-acting and reliable. Two milligrams would eventually completely incapacitate the taker, especially when combined with alcohol. When his buddy's back was turned, he poured a finely crushed pill into his drink, and then he waited until his friend had finished it and poured a drink for himself before saying his goodbyes. He made sure everybody present noticed him leave.

He would be back soon enough. He'd made a copy of his friend's apartment key three weeks earlier, and he planned to come back after the party wound down, by which time his friend would have passed out. Before leaving the building, he made sure to dismantle the security cameras that would be on his exit route later.

At a quarter before four that morning, he placed a shovel and three bags of lye underneath his buddy's Honda Accord. Then he let himself into the apartment, which was now in darkness. He put the rest of his supplies on the couch and then slowly and carefully made his way through the apartment to make sure his friend was alone.

He was.

Game on.

--- ✦✦✦✦✦ ---

What happened next barely warranted revisiting. His friend was passed out, sprawled sideways on his bed, fully dressed. He went back into the other room and retrieved the rope he had brought with him. He slipped it under and around his friend's neck, straddled his back, and then tightened and pulled with all his might. He held on for two full minutes. His friend never regained consciousness. Shit, he wasn't even sure if he felt any pain. That was all right, though, because now he was closer to putting William Sappey to bed forever.

Disposing of his friend's body was no easy task. He scoured the parking lot in front of the apartment, looking for any signs of activity. He looked up at all the windows that had a view of the lot. Luckily, they were all dark. Everyone seemed to be asleep.

It was now or never.

He hustled back into the apartment, retrieved the keys to his buddy's Accord, hoisted the body up and over his shoulder, and went out of the building. He looked both ways and then walked as fast as he could to the car, popped the trunk, and dropped the body inside. Thank God he lifted weights regularly; his buddy weighed 210 pounds, and it had taken all of his strength to lift him. Lastly, he retrieved the shovel and the bags of lye and tossed them on top of the body before shutting the trunk. *So far so good.*

He was nervous. If anyone had seen him, he'd be cooked. He barely took a breath for the first ten minutes of the trip. The destination was Promised Rock Campground, about twenty minutes outside Norwich. It was a 150-acre park with campsites, public pools, a general store, restrooms, and, most importantly, scenic hiking trails and woods perfect for hiding a body. He had spent the Fourth of July weekend there with teammates, barbecuing and letting off steam. Even then, the second he'd entered the park, he had sensed it was a special place, one he would see again in the future.

He reached the park at five fifteen that morning. It was still dark, and he encountered no other cars. Technically, the campground was locked up and closed for the off-season, but he had picked the lock on the security gate a couple weeks back. He got his car in quickly, shut the gate, and hustled to hide the car next to a trailhead he'd scouted, well away from prying eyes. He had to get the body into the woods quickly. If he was trespassing, others could be too.

He'd spent more than two weeks scouting locations in the park, and after choosing one during that time, he had dug a grave. The hole had taken almost four hours to create. The first two feet had been reasonably easygoing, but the next four had been backbreakingly difficult. He'd been sore for days. The movies made it look so easy. What a load of horseshit. He had spent an additional half hour concealing the hole with tree limbs, branches, leaves, and anything else within reach. He hoped no one happened on the spot. A pink ribbon placed on a tree next to the hole marked the spot for his return.

When he reached the chosen location on the day of the burial, he spent five full minutes scouting the area. Only when he was certain he was alone did he pop the trunk and retrieve the body. The next half hour was forever ingrained in his mind. That was how long it took him to get the body the half mile into the woods to the grave he had prepared. He had to drag the body most of the way due to physical exhaustion. Every muscle in his body ached.

After releasing the body into the hole, he concealed it with branches, sticks, and leaves and returned to the car in an all-out sprint. He made it back in four minutes flat. He opened the trunk, grabbed the three twenty-five-pound bags of lye and the shovel, and slowly made his way back to the grave. He opened the bags one by one and dumped lye directly onto the corpse. The empty bags followed. His research had indicated that lye would aid decomposition, counter smell, and prevent disturbance by animals.

It took him a little more than an hour to fill the hole in with dirt and then another twenty minutes to pack the area down flat. When he was finally happy with the results, he covered the area with the tree limbs, branches, and leaves. Then he stepped back about twenty yards to appraise his work. He wasn't disappointed. It would take a well-trained eye to notice anything amiss.

When he neared the road, he heard a group of hikers excitedly approaching, and his heart nearly leaped out of his chest. He had barely enough time to hide the shovel behind a tree before the group was on him. They paid him no heed and were out of earshot less than a minute later. His hands shook like leaves, but he managed to get the shovel securely into the trunk without any further excitement.

He'd never forget the sense of accomplishment and excitement he felt on that drive back to Norwich. He was on top of the world. He could do no wrong. Everything would be okay.

Later that day, he secured all the necessary documentation from his friend's apartment, including his Social Security card, birth certificate, and bank information. He also made sure to grab his friend's driver's license and credit cards. Then he went back to his own apartment and began his new life.

William Sappey was no more.

CHAPTER 42

Dare I hope for another good night of sleep? It's not even nine thirty in the evening yet, but I want to work out in the morning. I set the alarm for 4:50 a.m. and shut off the lights.

Just as I close my eyes, unease comes over me, causing me to sit up again. I grab my cell and call Bridget. The call goes straight to voice mail. I wish her a happy Thanksgiving and ask her to give me a call in the morning. A sensation of unease gnaws at the back of my mind. I can't get comfortable, tossing and turning; my brain is in overdrive.

When I finally sleep for a few hours, that disturbance is replaced by tranquility. My dreams float back to memories of times past, special times I'll always have in my heart.

I need continually to remind myself that life is still full of wonderful, beautiful, simple things. The job has cut me so deeply and scarred me so thoroughly that I often forget. Keeping my children close to my heart is the best reminder I could have.

I'm up before the alarm—exhausted but up. My efforts in the gym are less than stellar, but at least I break a sweat. I still feel uneasy. I can't put a finger on the cause of the feeling, which only makes it more disconcerting. I need to figure a way to shake it. Today is a big day, one that deserves my A game.

I pull into Quantico at twenty to eight in the morning. Before heading inside, I try Bridget's cell again. The call goes straight to voice mail.

CHAPTER 43

He's up before first light. He tries to shake the Jameson cobwebs off with several glasses of water, steaming-hot coffee, and a huge breakfast, but the food and drink just make him feel worse. There's no time to waste, however; his return flight is at three that afternoon, and there's work to be done.

The drive to Chevy Chase takes slightly more than thirty minutes. He's still a little cloudy from his escapades the night before and decides that a stop at Starbucks is in order. This will give him a chance to go over the plan one last time and ensure he's not missing anything.

He can't explain his unhealthy fascination, his obsession, with Deke and his life. He knows the incident at the FBI conference was no big deal—nothing that warranted another thought, really. He assumes it must be an ego thing, something to do with dealing with the best and beating him at his own game. He's always had this gene, and sometimes it dominates his existence. It's more than that with Deke, though. He doesn't just want to beat him; he wants to crush him and humiliate him.

He also realizes his obsession with Deke could ultimately lead to his downfall. That's why careful planning and flawless execution are imperative. He must keep his eye on the prize. No one's better than him when he puts his heart and soul into something. People will be talking about him for decades to come.

The large dark-roast coffee bolsters his spirits somewhat. Today is a recon mission only. This is his last shot at surveillance, though, and he needs to make it count. Planning and preparation make the difference between success and failure. He doesn't have the luxury of failure as an option.

The familiar rush he always feels before embarking on a mission floods his veins again. All he needs to do is focus and stick to the plan. He drains the last dredges of the bold coffee and heads out to the rental car. Catherine's place is only minutes away. The plan is to drive to her neighborhood, park the car a few blocks away, and then go for a run—or, more accurately, what will look like a run. Only it won't be any ordinary type of run.

When he reaches a location that is sufficiently near Catherine's home but far enough away to avoid attention, he pulls over and parks. He gets out and stretches quickly. This is not going to be a taxing run. It'll be a slow, deliberate information-gathering mission. Five minutes later, Catherine's driveway and house come into view.

Focus.

Seconds later, he spots the surveillance. Anyone would. Only three cars are parked on the street, and just one vehicle is occupied. He gets a good look at the guy in the driver's seat but averts his gaze when the man turns toward him. *Deke is getting ripped off,* he thinks to himself.

He jogs past the driveway and the security gate. A code needs to be entered to access the driveway, but that doesn't matter. His plan has always been to go in through the back. Hopefully there will not be security there.

When he gets to the stop sign, he casually takes a left, taking a quick glance at the car to see if he's drawn any attention. None. So far so good, but the most important part of the exercise is yet to come.

A quick left later, he's almost directly behind the house. *Shit.* There it is: a white panel van, totally out of place. He doesn't see anyone sitting in the front seats, but he knows they're there, and he'll need to deal with them eventually. He pays special attention to ingress and egress points as he runs by the fenced-in backyard. It won't be easy to access the property and house, given the security precautions, but he has a plan and is confident he can execute it. Of course he can; he's the best.

Ten minutes later, he's back in the rental. He has barely broken a sweat.

CHAPTER 44

With just a half hour before I need to get on the plane, I dive into the file the team has put together on today's interviewees.

The first person we're meeting is Terry Goddard, one of the Rayburn House counselors. The file doesn't have much of interest on her. She's forty-seven, is married, has three children, and has been employed by the house for the last eighteen years. She was arrested once, more than fifteen years ago, for marijuana possession. The charges were later dropped. There's really nothing else of interest on her. Hopefully she has a good memory.

The other counselor we'll meet with is Tameka Johnson. She's forty-four and single, with no kids. She's been with Rayburn House for the last nineteen years. She's had a couple minor juvenile arrests, all drug-related, but has been squeaky clean as an adult. Yet two things catch my attention. First, she grew up in foster care and group homes, meaning she might have a particular perspective on life in foster care. Second, she was savagely assaulted four years ago when walking from Rayburn House to the bus stop one night.

Her assailant attacked her from behind, knocking her to the ground. He then tied a rope around her neck and proceeded to drag her down the street for more than two blocks. Eventually, she lost consciousness. Her attacker left her for dead right in the middle of a crosswalk.

She suffered life-threatening injuries. Among these were a broken hyoid bone and lacerations and bruising to the larynx, pharynx, and mandible. Her symptoms included dyspnea, dysphagia, and odynophagia. The injuries were serious enough that surgery was required.

No suspect was identified. Tameka was unable to provide a useful description other than to say the perpetrator was tall and white, because he had been wearing a face mask.

Strangulation. Cutting off one's ability to breathe. Just a coincidence?
I don't believe in coincidence.

———— ✦✦✦✦✦ ————

I'm about to flip to our next interviewee, when D'Antoni touches my shoulder. I practically jump out of my seat. My heart is pounding. D'Antoni is bent over, laughing.

Finally, she regains her composure. "Man, you're so jumpy lately. Everything okay?"

"Yeah. Just engrossed in the file. You read up on Tameka Johnson?"

"I sure did. It's eerie—really eerie. Our boy's been operating a lot longer than we initially believed. I don't buy this as something random."

"No way it's random," I say. "No way."

Flying in the Gulfstream is an enjoyable experience. There is plenty of leg room, so you can spread out. The fridge is always stocked with goodies, including booze, which I have availed myself of many times in the past.

I break the silence.

"I called Bridget last night and this morning, and it went straight to voice mail both times. She always takes my calls. I know it's probably nothing, but it's got me spooked."

"Listen, you need to calm down. You're overthinking things, like you always do. She probably just turned her phone off or forgot to charge it. I'm sure she's fine. Call her again later."

"Yeah. Yeah, you're right."

"I always am, partner."

D'Antoni is a calming influence. I tend to internalize and overthink things, especially when working a case. I think it makes me a better agent, but it's not great for my sanity. The best thing I can do now—the only thing I can do, really—is bear down, focus, and catch this sick fuck. There are no other options.

When we arrive, Barnes is waiting curbside for us, and we spend the ten-minute drive into the city chatting amiably about Thanksgiving. I love this town, and the Southie district and Copley Square bring back fond memories as we drive.

"Did your wife let you ride the couch, watch football, and drink beer?" D'Antoni asks.

"I wish. She's an assistant DA, and she's working a murder trial, so she's as busy as I am. I stayed up until half past three in the morning Thanksgiving Day, prepping, so she could sleep in. What'd you guys do?"

"We worked until about four in the afternoon," D'Antoni says. "Then Dipshit and I grabbed dinner at the St. Regis. I know it's not very holiday-like, but hey, the food was great; there was no cleanup; and I didn't have to talk marriage and having babies with my mom and sister. Best of all, Dipshit picked up the check."

Barnes laughs. "Food always tastes better when you're not paying for it."

"Amen," D'Antoni says.

Barnes has secured a spacious conference room for the interviews. Coffee, juice, and water have been brought in. The first interview starts at ten.

Terry Goddard arrives promptly. She's tall, attractive, and well put together. After formal introductions, D'Antoni and I let Brian run the show. He's a terrific agent, top notch.

Terry doesn't wait for Brian to start. It's obvious she's nervous and stressed out for sure. "What's this all about? Why is the FBI interested in Rayburn House?"

Brian smiles warmly. "There's absolutely nothing to worry about, Ms. Goddard. We just have some questions about a woman who lived in the house about fifteen years ago. What was your position or role in the house back then?"

"I was one of two lead counselors. I believe you're meeting Tameka later. We are both licensed social workers."

"Yes, Tameka has kindly agreed to meet with us later today," Barnes says.

"I assume the woman you're referring to is Jane Martin," she says. "It's horrible what happened to her. Just horrible. We sort of kept in touch—less and less of late. I really liked her. She was one of our true success stories."

Brian nods. "Yes. We'd like to ask you some questions about Jane. Anything you remember, anything at all, could help in the investigation."

Terry looks confused by this statement. She glances anxiously at D'Antoni and me. "You want me to tell you what I remember about her from back then?"

"That'd be great," D'Antoni says. "And anything you know about her life after she left the house might be helpful as well."

"Let's see." Her hand goes to her chin, and she looks down, concentrating. "When Jane came to us, she was damaged goods. She was lost and broken. She was tough, though—real tough. I tried to take her under my wing early on. *Tried* being the operative word. She didn't trust anyone—refused to let anyone into her life. At first, she isolated herself and barely said a word to anyone, including her housemates. I don't know. I guess I saw something in her—saw the pain, the fear. I kept at her, even when she lashed out, said mean things, and tried anything to drive me away. She nearly succeeded. Is it okay if I grab a glass of water?"

"Absolutely," Brian says. "The coffee isn't half bad either."

Water in hand, Terry visibly relaxes as she sits back down. She takes her time before proceeding. "It all happened kind of gradually. I noticed that Jane never went anywhere without her journal. And I mean anywhere. I would see her sitting and writing in it for hours. There was a park a couple blocks from the house. That was her favorite place to write.

"I approached her one day and asked her to make sure she was careful in the park. It was well known as an area where lowlifes gathered. She was a pretty girl. Naturally pretty—no makeup, no fancy wardrobe. At first, she brushed me off and tried to push me away. But I kept at it, and eventually, cracks started to appear in her wall.

"In the beginning, we talked only about her writing. I was just happy to finally break through. She loved writing and, as it turned out, loved talking about her writing. She could talk for hours about it, and I let her. Over time, she let me into her life a little bit at a time. It was a painstakingly slow process but well worth it. We became pretty close—like friends, I guess.

"She had a horrible, horrible childhood. The worst. Her father was a drunk and beat her every chance he got. The mother was more or less a prostitute and a drug addict. She played no role whatsoever in Jane's upbringing. When the state finally wised up and took Jane away for good, things didn't get much better. She was sexually abused by the father of the second foster family she lived with. That abuse lasted for over a year. A good deal of her writing focused on this really dark period in her childhood. It sent her into a tailspin, one she almost didn't come out of. Writing became her escape, her salvation.

"Soon after the sexual abuse began, Jane started getting into trouble. Nothing terribly serious, but she was on the wrong path for several years. The usual stuff—drugs, petty theft, skipping school.

"Ironically, the misbehaving and arrests probably saved her. They got her into Rayburn House. Once she got away from the abuse and the clear lack of love, she thrived. I mean really thrived. She loved being in control of her own life; it was like a light had been switched on. Overnight, she became responsible. She was diligent in her studies, her writing, and her mentoring of other young women in the home.

"We're talking about a complete turnaround here. She became a straight-A student and aced the SATs. Heck, she got a full ride to the University of Rhode Island. She was over-the-moon excited about going to college. I was so proud of her."

"What can you tell me about her friends in the house and, more importantly, anyone she didn't get along with?" Barnes asks.

"Jane was friendly with everyone. That being said, she wasn't especially close with anyone, with the exception of Greg. I can't remember his last name."

"Greg Roker?" D'Antoni says.

"Yeah. That's him," Terry says with surprise in her voice. "He was her best friend. They hung out a ton, studied together, and went to the library together—those kinds of things. It was completely platonic, although Greg always wanted more. Jane was never interested in being more than friends. To be honest, I don't remember her ever having a boyfriend when she lived in the house. I think the abuse made it too tough for her to be in any kind of romantic relationship at that time. Her first boyfriend in college is the man she married."

"How was Greg with this?" D'Antoni asks.

"You know, it never stopped him from trying for more. He was like a puppy around her. All he wanted to do was please her. They were friends right up until the day she left for Rhode Island. I really couldn't tell you whether they remained friendly after that or not."

"What else can you tell us about Greg?" Barnes asks. "Did he have any peculiar habits? Was he violent?"

"No, I don't remember that at all. He was kind of a wimp. He wasn't nearly as well liked in the house as Jane. Jane was smart—super smart, actually—but she never bragged about her academic accomplishments. Greg was very bright as well, and he told everyone who would listen just how smart he was. He even got beat up a couple of times as a result."

"Jane ever have any run-ins with a William Sappey?" D'Antoni says.

Terry blinks rapidly, opens her mouth, closes it, and says nothing for a moment. "Him? I really can't say. Not that I ever saw or heard about. I don't remember Jane ever mentioning his name."

"What can you tell us about him?" I ask my first question of the interview.

"He was disturbed—lost. He got caught peeping through a hole in the wall at a group of girls in the locker room. He was probably doing it for weeks before he got caught. He offered no apologies and showed zero—and I mean zero—remorse but somehow managed to get probation rather than get kicked out. To make matters worse, he bragged about what he saw to other members of the house. Much of what he said was very hurtful. From what I heard, he was graphic, disgusting, and it really messed with a couple of the girls' heads.

"He was an introvert, kept to himself, and didn't seem to have any close friends. Like Jane, he did well in school. Extremely well. Unlike Jane, though, he didn't have to lift a finger to get the grades. He was that bright.

"He got picked on a lot by the other boys when he first moved into the home. He was tiny then, probably a hundred twenty-five pounds soaking wet. About a year later, he shot up like a weed and filled out physically, and the bullying stopped.

"I don't know how to explain it other than to say he gave me the creeps—big-time. I'd come out of the bathroom, and he'd be lounging in the hallway outside the door, apparently with nothing to do. He'd stare at me. It made the hairs on my arms stand up. There was a keyhole in the door, and I suspected he was watching me use the toilet, but I could never catch him in the act.

"In case you can't tell, I didn't like him. I was scared of him. That being said, he was touted as another house success because he got into Harvard. He must have pulled a real snow job on whoever interviewed him, because he was normally very confrontational, in-your-face, and opinionated. No one liked him.

"Several months before he left for school, he was accused of killing the puppy of a family who lived next door. The police were involved and everything. I know he did it. He bragged about it to another boy in the house, whose name I can't recall. He hung the puppy by its neck from the kids' swing set. They were the ones to find the poor dog. There wasn't enough evidence to charge him with a crime, but he did it—of that I have no doubt. Just sick.

"But I never saw him interact with Jane. Heck, he interacted with me more than he did with her. I was a bit heavier back then— well, maybe a lot heavier." She laughs. "I heard him call me lard-ass under his breath on a couple of occasions. So you should probably take everything I've told you with a grain of salt. I didn't like the kid, and to be honest, I don't know anyone who did."

"Anything else stick out about Jane or those she interacted with in the house?" Barnes asks.

"No. Not really. She was well liked. Nothing else of note is coming to mind."

"Well then, we'd like to thank you for coming in," Brian says. He pushes his business card across the table to her. "Please don't hesitate to call me if you think of anything else. This was very helpful."

We all shake hands, and Louise walks her to the elevator. I look at my watch. We're already fifteen minutes late for our second interview.

D'Antoni ushers Tameka Johnson into the room. She's tall— taller than D'Antoni. Her hair is buzz-cut short. She's athletic looking and attractive in a tough kind of way. She oozes self-confidence. I like her immediately.

After introductions, we get right down to business. D'Antoni runs point this time.

"Ms. Johnson, thank you for agreeing to talk to us today."

"Can you tell me what this is all about?" Tameka says. "Why does the FBI want to talk to me? Does it have something to do with Jane Martin's death or the assault on me a few years ago?"

"We're investigating the death of Jane Martin, and we're trying to determine, or rule out, any connection to Rayburn House. We'd also like to ask you about the assault, if that's okay," D'Antoni says.

"Sure. No one seems to give a fuck about it anymore anyway. Excuse my language. I'll be up front with you, though. I don't see how much help I'll be."

"Thank you. And there may very well be no connection to the house. Why don't you tell us what you remember about Jane?"

"Let me think for a minute. It's been a long time."

"Take your time."

"Hmm. I remember she was real quiet. She mostly kept to herself, although she did hang with one of the boys in the house quite a bit. I can't remember his name."

"Greg Roker?" D'Antoni asks.

"Hmm, maybe. He was tall, skinny, and a bit of a blowhard. Everyone in the house liked Jane. She always made time for any of the girls who were struggling. She had a good heart, which always amazed me, given what she'd been through. I liked her, but we were never real close. My focus was always on the lost souls. She was very close with Terry Goddard, whom you just talked to."

"What else can you tell us about Jane?" D'Antoni asks.

"She was, and probably still is, the house's biggest success story. She got a lot of local press back then. There was even a local reporter who followed and reported on her college experience."

"Did she have any run-ins with anyone in the house? Anyone she didn't get along with?"

"No, nothing that comes to mind. Like I said, she pretty much kept to herself."

"Any bad eggs in the house back then?"

Tameka laughs. "We always have a few bad eggs. But yeah, we had a couple of them when Jane was in the house. You know, most of the usual juvenile nonsense—drinking and drugging. There was one really bad apple back then that I remember. His name was William Sappey."

"His name has come up in our investigation," D'Antoni says.

"He was a lost soul—damaged. His childhood was the stuff of nightmares. He's probably locked up somewhere."

"Tell us about him."

"All right, but I've got to tell you, I hate even thinking about him. While I tried to empathize with him—I really did—he gave me the creeps."

"It could be important," D'Antoni says.

"I guess you could say we didn't hit it off right from the start. I caught him peeking in on some of the girls in the locker room while they were changing. He drilled a good-sized hole in a wall that gave him a perfect view of the changing area. He probably used it several times before I caught him.

"I'm not sure he even had a month in the house when the incident occurred. Obviously, I reported it, and he was nearly kicked out. But he argued just well enough to get probation rather than expulsion. He never apologized and never showed any remorse. Shit, he openly bragged about it to the other boys in the house. He went so far as to graphically describe some of the girls' bodies, with special attention given to their private parts.

"I paid special attention to him after that. We mandated that he see a psychologist twice a week and put him in programs designed to help adolescents who'd suffered abuse, whether physical, sexual, emotional, or psychological. Not that it did any good. He was too far gone. I'm talking sick and twisted—not right. He killed a neighbor's dog in his last year. It was a beautiful little golden retriever puppy that the father next door had bought for his kids. The sicko actually hung it by the neck from the children's swing set. Diabolical. Utterly diabolical.

"The police got involved, but there wasn't enough to formally charge him. We all knew he did it, though. He bragged about it to another boy in the house. He went into sickening detail about it. Told the boy he looked into the puppy's eyes as it slowly choked to death. The kid had nightmares for weeks."

"You remember that boy's name?" D'Antoni asks.

"No. It was too long ago. I'll tell you this: William did whatever he wanted. No one could get through to him. He felt no empathy toward other people. I'm talking zero. He thought he was smarter than everyone and that we, especially the counselors and administrators, were beneath him. He was openly hostile toward me. He used to call me his 'favorite bull dyke.' He said this in front of other people. It used to really bother me. I was in the closet back then—felt like I had to be. Who knows? Maybe I gave off a gay vibe, but I don't think so. I think the little pervert was watching me outside the house. I never caught him in the act, but I remember being uneasy on multiple occasions, feeling like I was being watched."

"Did Jane have any run-ins with William?" D'Antoni asks.

"Not that I can remember. They certainly didn't hang out. Wait a second. There was an incident that I heard about. One of the other girls in the house told me that Jane pushed William into a pool on a weekend house outing. That shouldn't have been a big deal, but apparently, William couldn't swim. Jane went back to whatever she was doing and never noticed that William was at the bottom of the pool, struggling. When he was finally dragged out, he was unconscious. I think he spent a day or two in the hospital, recovering."

This revelation has my interest piqued. "They have any problems after the incident?"

"Not that I saw or heard about. I know that several girls in the house wished he'd been left at the bottom of that pool, and they were vocal about it."

"Let's change gears for a little while," D'Antoni says. "What are you comfortable sharing with us about your assault four and a half years ago? I apologize up front for asking you to revisit that horrific time. Please know that I wouldn't do so if it wasn't potentially important."

"I don't have a problem talking about it anymore. I did at first. Shit, I had a problem with everything right after it happened. I was terrified—truly terrified. I didn't feel safe unless I was locked up in my bedroom. It wasn't just me it affected either. It damn near tore me and my partner apart. It took a lot of very expensive therapy to save the relationship."

"Were you having problems with anyone in the time leading up to the incident?"

"No, and trust me, I've been through this a million times in my mind. The only weird thing going on was that I was getting lots of hang-ups for two months before the incident. That, or I would pick up, and there would be nothing but heavy breathing on the other end of the line. I was just about to file a complaint with the police, when the calls suddenly stopped."

"Tell us about the incident itself," D'Antoni says with warmth in her tone.

"Okay. Let's see. I was walking to the bus stop after work. It was a little after six and pitch black. I felt him more than I saw him. He came out of nowhere. Best guess is that he was hiding in wait at the playground down the street and made his move when I walked by. He was on me so fast that I barely caught a glimpse of him. Not that it would've mattered. He was wearing a ski mask. He shoved me to the ground hard—knocked the wind out of me. I never even saw the rope until it was wrapped around my neck.

"The next thing I knew, I was being dragged. The rope was so tight. The pain was excruciating, and I couldn't breathe. He had to stop briefly to cross the street, and I was able to catch my breath for a couple seconds before he started in again. The next thing I knew, I woke up in the hospital, in a lot of pain. I think he left me for dead."

"Did he say anything to you?" D'Antoni asks.

She thinks about that for a couple seconds. "Yeah. He did. He said, 'You're going to die, you black lesbian cunt.'"

"Sounds like a nice guy," Barnes says.

Tameka laughs nervously. "Yeah, a real winner. I heard what he said over and over in my head for years."

"Anything familiar about the voice?" D'Antoni asks.

"You know, I've asked myself that same question thousands of times. I've replayed it so often I've lost count. There was something vaguely familiar about his voice, but the harder I tried to place it, the more confused I got. Finally, I stopped trying. It was driving me insane—literally."

"Thank you for sharing that with us. I can't fathom how difficult it is to revisit it. You're a brave woman."

"I don't know about that," Tameka says.

"Well, I do," D'Antoni says. "One last question, and we'll get out of your hair. Is there any possibility your attacker was William Sappey?"

Tameka looks as if she has just been sucker punched in the stomach. She stands up, wobbling a bit, and slowly makes her way over to the water carafe. A couple shaky gulps later, she appears ready to answer.

"I don't know. What would make you think that?"

"We don't think anything. We're simply covering all the bases. Mr. Sappey is someone we'd love to talk to."

"I can't help you with that. I haven't even thought about him in a long time. Unfortunately, now I probably will."

"Ms. Johnson, the last thing we intended was to alarm you. Please don't read too much into the question," I say.

"That's easy for you to say. I, uh, I'm sorry for being bitchy. It's just tough reliving it, you know?"

"You have nothing to apologize for," D'Antoni says. She then pushes her business card across the table. "I wrote my cell phone on that. You can call me day or night if you think of anything else or if you just need to talk. Thank you again for coming in today."

We all shake hands, and D'Antoni walks Tameka to the elevator.

When D'Antoni gets back to the conference room, I suggest ordering in sushi for lunch and making a quick Starbucks run. Barnes runs out to give his assistant the lunch order, and the three of us hightail it to Starbucks. We have twenty minutes before the conference call with Timothy Veerdon, another boy who lived in the house during Jane's time there. We all have a lot to digest.

I need time alone to think.

CHAPTER 45

The call with Timothy Veerdon is quick and doesn't reveal much. He says he barely knew Jane; he only talked to her a handful of times before she left the house for college. He doesn't even recall whom she was friendly with. He says he was too busy getting stoned back then to focus on much else.

When he's asked about William Sappey, his response is a bit more interesting. He recalls that he was warned early on to stay clear of William, and that was exactly what he did. He also remembers the dog-killing incident and says Sappey openly bragged about it. He claims Sappey once recounted the incident in such gruesome detail that another younger housemate threw up on the spot.

We have an hour and a half before the meeting with Mary Morrison, former head of Rayburn House. I suggest the three of us give O'Shaughnessy a call. We spend the next twenty minutes updating him on everything we've learned. He's intrigued by William Sappey.

I try to make it clear that it would be irresponsible to shift all of the focus onto Sappey at this point. There's still a ton of legwork to be done. O'Shaughnessy doesn't want to hear any of it. He's already put together a team that is working around the clock to discover what has happened to Sappey. Nobody can just disappear.

O'Shaughnessy shifts the focus of our conversation. "Deke, did Bridget go out of town for the holiday?"

"Why do you ask, boss?"

"Our security detail has not seen her yet today, and her car isn't in its spot."

"As far as I know, she was staying local. At least that's what she told me. Boss, I haven't been able to reach her on her cell phone. I've left two messages, and she hasn't responded. I've got a bad feeling about this. Tell the security detail to try her office and her gym. Tell them to call her mother. Shit, I don't know. Canvass the whole neighborhood!"

"Relax, Deke. We've got it under control. I'll give you a call later when I know something."

"Please do."

"D'Antoni, can you get this guy to relax? Take him to Abe and Louie's for a big cowboy steak tonight. I want you guys staying put in Boston for now. Call you later."

D'Antoni starts to speak, but the line is already dead. She turns to me. "Maybe just once he could tell us before we go somewhere that it might be for more than a day."

"Don't sweat it," I say. "I'll take you shopping at the Copley Mall. I love that place."

✦ ✦ ✦ ✦ ✦ ✦

Mary Morrison is ten minutes late. She comes busting into the conference room with a full head of steam. It has been a rough day, clearly.

It takes her several seconds to catch her breath. "I'm so sorry for being late. We had an incident at the house. A couple of my boys got into it with a couple of neighborhood kids. One of my kids got beat up real bad. Broken nose and possible concussion."

I decide to run point on this one. "Please don't worry about it. Hopefully the boy will be okay. They usually bounce back pretty quick at that age. Thank you for taking the time to come in and talk to us."

"Sure. I'm guessing this has something to do with Jane Martin?"

"We're investigating her death."

"You see a connection with Rayburn House? That was a long time ago."

"We're just being thorough."

"Okay. What do you wanna know?"

"First, can you confirm your role at the house during Jane's stay? Then tell us what you can about her."

"I was the director, the lead administrator at Rayburn House. I didn't interact with Jane on a day-to-day basis like the counselors did, but I got to know her pretty well. She came to us in pretty rough shape. There was a lot of abuse in her past—physical, sexual, emotional. Life had dumped a big pile of crap on her.

"Early on, she was completely closed off, unapproachable. Terry finally got through to her. They became very close—almost friends, I guess you could say. I had to remind Terry on a couple of occasions to keep their relationship professional, and she did. Without her diligence, I'm not sure if we would've gotten through to Jane. Frankly, I doubt it.

"Jane soon became a mentor to the younger girls in the house. They all looked up to her. She was perfect for the role because she'd lived on the dark side; she understood pain, abuse, and a lack of love. In many respects, Jane functioned as a quasi-counselor in the last year of her stay. The transformation was incredible to see.

"She was an extremely bright and dedicated student. She put in the time. When other girls in the house were punch drunk with thoughts of boys, Jane was studying in the library. She knew her only shot at going to college was a scholarship. She wound up getting scholarship offers all over the country but opted to stay in New England. I found that strange at the time. I thought she would wanna get as far away as possible. I was certain she was going to UC Berkeley. But she opted for URI and even visited the house a few times while in school."

"Was she especially close with anyone in the house?"

"Hmm. She was nice to all the girls, but she marched to her own drummer. She hung out with and studied with a boy in the house on a pretty frequent basis. His name escapes me now."

"Greg Roker?"

"Uh, yeah, that's him."

"His name came up earlier," D'Antoni says.

"Okay. He definitely appeared to be Jane's best friend in the house. He definitely wanted more than friendship, but Jane was happy with the relationship as it was."

"Did that piss Greg off?" I ask.

"If it did, he did a good job of hiding his feelings. I think he was petrified he would lose her as a friend if he pushed too hard."

"So you don't see Greg as a guy who could've held a grudge all these years."

"No, I don't. He was scared of his own shadow."

"Was there anyone in the house Jane didn't get along with?"

Mary takes several seconds to think about that. "Not that I can remember. Like I said, everybody liked her."

"Okay. Let's change gears for a second. What can you tell us about William Sappey?"

At this, the color drains from Mary's face. She looks nauseated, as if she's about to vomit. What the fuck did this guy do to her?

"Can I get you a glass of water, Mary?" D'Antoni asks.

"Yes. Please. That would be great."

I decide that a quick break is what Mary needs, and I go use the lavatory. When I return, it looks as if some of the color has returned to her face, so I decide to dive right in. "So where were we? Oh yeah, William Sappey."

Mary swallows hard and takes a few seconds before answering. "He was unequivocally the most scarred, narcissistic person I've ever met. Bar none. Pure evil from my point of view."

"Can you provide some specifics?"

"I could spend the rest of the afternoon providing specifics, but I'll focus on some of his more memorable transgressions. He was in trouble, or causing trouble, from day one. A month into his stay, Tameka, one of the counselors in the house, caught him peeping at a group of girls while they changed in the girls' locker room. He cut a hole in a wall with this switchblade he went everywhere with. God only knows how long it took him. And I'm sure the day he was caught wasn't the only time he did it. Listen, I know young boys sometimes do things like this. That's why I opted to give him another chance. That mistake is on me.

"He actually bragged about what he'd done and seen to the other boys in the house. He did it in an incredibly malicious way, and everything he said got back to the girls. Girls at that age—well, I guess at any age—are very sensitive about their bodies. I had to talk several girls off the ledge after that incident. I knew then that my decision to give him a second chance was a mistake, but I still didn't know how big a mistake."

Wow, this kid really was a monumental prick. I don't interrupt Mary.

"I wish I could say things got better." She sighs. "But they didn't. He didn't do anything terrible for more than a year after that. He was small when he first moved in, and some of the older boys bullied him. To be honest, it really wasn't even bullying. William just got into it with everyone and everything. He was an instigator. Everyone was fair game.

"The odd thing was that this cancerous presence was also extremely bright. I'm talking straight-A student without lifting a finger. Number one in his class. He knew he was smarter than everyone else. He felt like he could get away with anything simply by being the smartest guy in the room.

"His behavior really started going downhill over time. He was constantly getting into fights. He stole things from other kids in the house. Two girls accused him of inappropriate touching. One of the girls claimed he shoved his hand inside her shorts at a weekend barbecue. Unfortunately, there were no witnesses, and William denied it. I told Tameka and Terry to keep a close eye on him, but it didn't do any good.

"A sweet young family moved into a duplex right next door to the house. A couple of months later, the father surprised his three little kids with a golden retriever puppy. The kids were outside playing with the dog all the time. They let many of my kids go over to pet the dog and play with it as well. This was a beautiful, happy family.

"William waited until they were all out of the house one day, and then he hopped their fence and snuck into the outside area where the dog was kept during the day. He proceeded to hang the dog by the neck from the kids' swing set.

"The cops were all over Rayburn House an hour later. The house was well known to the police and the neighbors. No one liked living next to a home full of juvenile delinquents. The funny thing is, the family right next door couldn't have been more supportive and accommodating.

"I knew William did it. I saw him on two separate occasions, sitting in his bedroom window, watching the kids play with the dog. It was like watching a wolf gazing at a sheep. He caught me looking at him, and I swear he looked me right in the eye and smiled. It sent chills down my spine.

"The police couldn't prove anything. There was no evidence linking him to the crime, and they gave up on it fairly quickly. Too quickly, in my view. But William went ahead and shot his mouth off to anyone who would listen. He described the killing in graphic, horrific detail. Word got back to me, and I figured now was my chance to kick him out of the house—something I should've done long before.

"I had Tameka summon William to my office. I was giddy with delight at the prospect of kicking this kid out on his ass. Literally giddy. I felt a little guilty for feeling that way, but the guilt didn't last long.

"As the house's lead administrator, I had no choice but to kick him out. When William came into my office, he had a huge smile on his face. I was totally taken aback. I had no idea what he was up to. I shrugged off my unease and laid right into him. I told him that I knew he killed the neighbors' dog and that we had witnesses who would corroborate this to the police. I told him he had until the end of the day to pack his things and be on his way.

"The smile never left his face. He actually started laughing. I was really confused and pissed. I asked him what he thought was so funny. I'll never forget what transpired after that."

Mary stands up a little shakily and walks over to the water carafe. She drinks an entire glass in two gulps and then pours more. She turns back to us with a look of genuine concern on her face. "Okay. Here's where I need some assurances from you guys. I'm going to tell you something I've not shared with anyone, not even my current husband. I need you to promise to be discreet with the information I'm about to volunteer."

I glance at Barnes and D'Antoni in turn. Things have taken an interesting direction.

"Mary, it's tough to promise not to reveal something that we don't know. We didn't ask for your help to put you in a bad spot. You have to trust me on that. Please. You have been a tremendous source of information so far. Please don't shut us out of something that might be important," I say.

She looks as if she's about to be sick. Her top lip starts trembling. *Oh shit.*

D'Antoni stands up, approaches Mary, and puts her hand on her shoulder. "Mary, you have nothing to be worried about. You just have to trust us. We'll be as discreet as we can be." D'Antoni pulls a chair over and sits next to Mary, which seems to calm her down a bit.

"All right. Just give me a second. This isn't easy."

"Take your time," I say.

Mary lets out an exasperated sigh. "So like I was saying, I told him I was going to the police with evidence of his confession, and I told him he was kicked out of the house, and he started laughing. Not the reaction I'd hoped for. Then he started shaking his head and saying no. Basically, he said that I wouldn't be going to the police and that he'd stay in the house as long as he wanted. I was flabbergasted, totally caught off guard. And I was getting madder by the second. That was when my whole world came crashing down.

"He started tearing open an envelope he'd brought into my office. Then he slid something across my desk. It was a picture of me undressed, fully naked, lying on my bed, legs spread wide. My eyes were closed like I was asleep. I was so horrified I couldn't speak. The next picture he pushed my way was of the two of us naked in my bed. He had his right hand on my left breast, and my left hand was on his crotch. My face was turned into the pillow. The third and final picture he shared with me was one of me naked with my head buried in his lap. He had an ear-to-ear grin on his face in the picture."

Mary abruptly stands up and begins pacing around the conference room. She takes almost a full minute before continuing. "Needless to say, I was stunned beyond words. I was also shaking with rage. If I'd had a weapon at that point, I have zero doubt I would've used it. I never invited that boy into my house, never mind engaging in any inappropriate conduct with him.

"I couldn't figure out how he had manipulated the pictures. It made no sense. Then it dawned on me like a sledgehammer blow to the head. About three months before, something weird had happened to me. I got home late one Friday night and immediately poured myself a glass of pinot grigio and drew a hot bath. I had an open bottle in the refrigerator. I drank the first glass fairly quickly and poured myself another to enjoy in the tub. That's the last thing I remember of that night.

"The next thing I knew, the sun was pouring in through the blinds, and I was in my bed, naked. I don't make a habit of sleeping naked. My head was pounding, and I was terribly nauseous. I lay in bed the entire day, desperately trying to recall what had happened. Try as I might, I couldn't remember a thing. Eventually, I just chalked it up to a bad reaction to the wine, even though that made no sense. To be honest, not knowing seemed better than the alternative.

"Now everything became clear. That sick, demented pervert broke into my house, drugged me, and then sexually assaulted me. I went berserk. I went at him with everything I had, punching, scratching, and kicking. It was like I was possessed.

"He laughed the entire time. When sheer exhaustion meant I could no longer lift my arms to strike him, things quickly took a turn for the worse. He grabbed me by the throat with one arm and lifted me up in the air. He was incredibly strong. Then he pinned me up against the wall by the neck. I couldn't breathe. I was sure he was going to kill me.

"Just as I started to black out, he loosened his grip. Then he calmly told me that I wouldn't be going to the police, nor would he be getting kicked out of the house. He said he'd made multiple copies of the pictures and put together packages to be mailed to the *Globe*, the *Herald*, and the *New York Times* detailing how I'd taken advantage of him, of how I had raped him, as he wasn't of age to consent. He said that as the head administrator in a state-run home for troubled teens, I'd be vilified, publicly humiliated, and jailed. Then he open-mouth kissed me and whispered in my ear that I was the best he'd ever had.

"He didn't say another word. He just gathered up the pictures and left. I collapsed into my chair and cried for hours. This diabolical fuck had pulled it off. If I went to the police, it was every bit as likely that I'd be arrested as him. So I decided to do nothing.

"I'm not proud of the way I handled the situation. I would probably—no, definitely—do it differently today. It damn near killed me. I started drinking heavily and abusing Xanax. I was a mess for about a year. But I was young and loved my job. I was also far too interested in what people thought of me. I figured that even if I ultimately prevailed, my image would be sullied enough that I would never be allowed to work with kids again.

"I never said a word to anyone. Instead, I swallowed my dignity, my pride, and my sense of right and wrong and looked for a new job. I was offered the Allston position about two months later and accepted on the spot. I didn't even give Rayburn House two weeks' notice. I just packed up and left. I simply couldn't face the prospect of seeing the animal that may have raped me for one more day.

"I never saw or heard from William again. To be perfectly honest, I rarely think of him at all anymore."

D'Antoni stands up and puts her arm around Mary's shoulders. "What do you say we take a five-minute break and then wrap things up?"

Mary just nods, her face expressionless.

Barnes is about to speak, but I put my index finger to my lips. I want to make sure Mary is out of earshot before anything is said. Barnes understands and pauses for several seconds before continuing.

"This has got to be our guy, right?"

I shake my head. "I don't know. We don't even know if this guy is alive."

"We need to figure that out immediately," Barnes says. "This guy was evil personified. He fits the profile like a glove. Sometimes we just have to accept the obvious."

I stare directly at Barnes but say nothing. I don't accept anything until I'm completely certain. That said, on some level, I know this is our guy. Deep in my soul, I know, but my investigative stubbornness requires more proof.

D'Antoni and Mary return to the conference room. I let Mary get settled in before wrapping things up.

I smile warmly at her. "I wanna thank you for being so candid with us. I won't pretend to even understand how difficult that time must have been for you. Nor do I judge you in any way, shape, or form. To be honest, I think it took enormous courage to continue working in your field, given everything that happened. Unfortunately, in my job, I see evil on a fairly regular basis. You shouldn't have to see it."

A small smile comes to Mary's face, but it quickly disappears. "I just hope William had nothing to do with Jane's death."

"There's absolutely no evidence suggesting that he did," I say. "We're just covering all our bases."

She doesn't look convinced, but I move on. "Please know that you have nothing to worry about. We didn't ask you to come in today in order to put you in a bad spot. Not at all. The information you provided may prove helpful, and we'd all like to thank you for that."

I stand, and everyone else follows suit. D'Antoni then walks Mary out.

◆ ◆ ◆ ◆ ◆ ◆

We're running twenty minutes late for the Greg Roker interview. When she returns to the room, I tell D'Antoni to start the interview without me. She doesn't ask any questions, and I leave for privacy. I shakily dial Bridget's cell phone. The call goes to voice mail, and I leave a message: "Bridget, it's Deke. Please gimme a call as soon as possible. Thanks."

I then call O'Shaughnessy. He puts me on hold for a couple minutes. I'm ready to jump out of my skin by the time he comes back on the line.

"Did they find her?" I ask.

"No, Deke, not yet. We found her car parked outside her gym. There's security footage of her entering and leaving the gym on Thanksgiving Day. Unfortunately, there are no security cameras in the parking lot, so we're scrambling at this point."

"Motherfucker," I say. "I fucking told you. I told you this guy wasn't screwing around with me. This is the bureau's fault. Completely. We should've protected her immediately. Son of a bitch."

"Deke—"

"Shut up. You'd better get protection on D'Antoni, and don't say a word to her. And you'd better have the best of the best on my family. Do I make myself clear?"

"Deke—"

I've already hung up.

I feel myself struggle to breathe. I loosen my tie and hit the stairs at a run. I need to get outside.

Once out of doors, I hungrily gulp mouthfuls of fresh air. My head is spinning. I think I'm going to be sick. I grab a utility pole with both hands, close my eyes, and wait. The nausea finally passes. I look around me. There's a liquor store only a few blocks away. I could be there in less than five minutes. Before I even realize it, my feet are moving in that direction. It takes all of my strength to stop, turn around, and head toward Starbucks instead.

I grab a large Pike Place and a single shot of espresso and take a seat in the back, facing the door. I take out my phone and dial Jim's cell. He picks up on the first ring.

"Deke, what's up, bud?"

"Jim, I've got a major problem here. Bridget's missing. She hasn't been seen since yesterday. She went to the gym yesterday, and there's surveillance of her entering and leaving, but her car is still parked in the gym's parking lot, and there's no sign of her."

"Security cameras in the parking lot?"

"No."

"Son of a bitch."

"Yup. Listen, I'd feel a whole lot better if I had your team on Catherine and the kids 24-7, even when the bureau's team is on them. Can you swing it?"

"Consider it done. Hey, try to relax, pal. Maybe she just had car trouble, or there's some other reasonable explanation."

"Thanks, Jim. Please keep my family safe. I'll let you know the second I hear anything about Bridget."

"They'll be safe."

I'm already gone.

CHAPTER 46

His favorite barmaid, Julie, places an ice-cold Sierra Nevada and a shot of Jameson in front of him.

She looks at him with concern. "What happened to your face, baby?"

"Oh, this? I'm cat-sitting for my neighbor, and let's just say me and the cat don't see eye to eye." He laughs.

She laughs too. "Make sure you put some antibacterial on it. You don't want it getting infected."

"I will. Thanks."

Shit, he thinks to himself. *It didn't look that bad this morning.* He'll need to take another look at it. The bitch really caught him off guard.

Man, is he going to ruin Deke's night. He needs to send the pictures before the body is found. He wishes he could be there when he opens them. Deke will feel responsible and blame himself. He should blame himself. He warned him. He came right out and said he was going to harm Bridget. Obviously, the egomaniac didn't take him seriously. A lot of good his profiling skills have done him so far.

Julie has replacements in front of him seconds later. *Ain't life grand?* He craves the high that booze gives him. It calms his brain and helps him focus. He needs to focus. He has work to do.

He savors the second shot. The familiar smoky burn sends pleasure pulsing through his body.

It's time to focus. He's been uneasy all day. He can't stop thinking about Mary Morrison. If the FBI sniff out Jane Martin's connection to Rayburn House—and they will—could she be a problem for him? He decides not. William Sappey no longer exists. How can she possibly hurt him? Still, he can't get her out of his mind. It would be silly—idiotic, really—to think the FBI won't find her and question her. He can fix that easily. But he'll need to act fast.

He knows where she works and where she lives. He will probably rest easier if he pays her a little visit and eradicates any potential risk.

It's time for another round.

CHAPTER 47

I get back to the office just as the Greg Roker interview is wrapping up. I don't even bother introducing myself. I wait for him to leave before catching up with D'Antoni and Barnes.

"You guys learn anything?"

"That guy is a clown," D'Antoni says. "Egomaniac. He spun a tale of Jane Martin being in love with him. When I told him that's not what everyone else in the house thought, he got really defensive. He offered nothing helpful. He didn't know anyone in the house who had a problem with Jane. And he knew next to nothing about William Sappey. Said the guy freaked him out, so he stayed clear. All he wanted to do was talk about himself, so I cut it short."

"So you guys are certain he had nothing to do with Jane?" I say.

"Yeah, absolutely zero," Barnes says.

"What were you up to?" D'Antoni asks.

"I called O'Shaughnessy. Bridget's missing." I spend a couple minutes bringing them up to speed on what I know. "I know something terrible happened to her," I say.

"No, you don't, Deke."

"Yes, I do, and you do too. We'll know soon enough."

"Didn't we have protection on her?" Barnes asks.

I stand up and rub my face, ready to lose it. "It didn't start until this morning. That's on me. So fucking stupid. You know, this sicko went out of his way to promise me he wouldn't do anything

225

on Thanksgiving Day. I actually believed him. Believed a sick, narcissistic serial killer. Who's the moron in this situation?"

"Hey, enough!" D'Antoni says. "We need to stay optimistic. In the meantime, did you tell O'Shaughnessy to put a net around Catherine and the kids?"

"Not yet. I talked to Jim, and he agreed to put a team on them all day every day, even when our team is working."

"Good. He's the best. What do you wanna do?"

"Head back to DC as soon as we can. Maybe you two can give O'Shaughnessy an update on what we learned today. I can't speak to him right now. And please make it clear we're heading back to DC. I don't care if we have to rent a car. I'll call Donnelley and find out what's going on back in the war room."

"You got it."

I leave D'Antoni and Barnes to their call and go in search of a vacant workstation. I find one immediately. It looks as if a bunch of the Boston field agents have availed themselves of the holiday weekend. I quickly draft a text to Jim, letting him know Catherine will have a full house this weekend. Then I ring Donnelley's cell.

He picks up on the first ring. "Hey, Deke, did you get my text?"

"No. We've been a little busy here. What's up?"

"They found a body. It was buried behind the shed. Too early to tell if it's the Joseph Wilson our perp referenced. The coroner indicated there was evidence of blunt force trauma. All the deceased's front teeth were gone, presumably knocked out."

"I assume you're coordinating with Timmons?"

"Yes. He'd like you to give him a call later."

"Okay. Are you guys getting anywhere with William Sappey?"

"We have him for eighteen months after he graduated. Then the trail goes cold."

"We gotta find him. There's a chance he's our guy—a decent chance. We'll explain when we get back. What else?"

"We located a few more people from Rayburn House, and we're lining up calls."

226

"Good. Let's plan on an all-hands-on-deck meeting tomorrow morning at ten. Find out everything you can about this guy in those eighteen months before he disappeared. See you soon."

I try Bridget's cell phone again. The call goes straight to voice mail.

CHAPTER 48

Barnes volunteers to drive us to Logan. He tells us that he can handle any live interviews tomorrow and that we can dial in.

I turn to D'Antoni. "What did O'Shaughnessy have to say?"

"He tried to convince me we should stay in Boston. He gave up without much of a fight, but I got the distinct impression he's not looking forward to seeing you. He seems very stressed out."

"He should be. We should've had protection on Bridget a while ago. It's my fault. I should've insisted."

Barnes jumps in. "Deke, it's no one's fault but the perp's. What I can't figure out is why he has such a hard-on for you. Does he look familiar to you at all in the New York City surveillance?"

"Familiar, yeah, maybe a little. But I just can't place him. It's driving me fucking nuts."

"He looks sort of familiar to me too," D'Antoni says. "I swear I've seen his face recently."

"It'll come to you when you least expect it, when you're focused on something else," Barnes says.

"I hope so," I respond. "There's no time to waste. My biggest fear is that this guy simply disappears, like William Sappey did."

The plane ride home is quiet, so I close my eyes and simply let my mind go. *Where have I seen this guy before?*

Suddenly, as if on cue, an image of a large room with hundreds of seated people flashes through my mind. I'm at the lectern, speaking. *Where am I? What am I speaking about?* But then it's gone. *Damn it!*

CHAPTER 49

I walk into O'Shaughnessy's office at a quarter before seven in the evening. When he glances up, I know immediately that Bridget hasn't been found. He looks worried—scared almost. Good. He should be. I fill him in quickly on my new working arrangement with Jim. He assures me that the agency's team is top notch and that no one will get anywhere near my family.

I look O'Shaughnessy in the eyes without blinking until he finally looks away. "Boss, there can be no more mistakes going forward. We should've had protection on Bridget earlier. You know it; I know it. I accept full responsibility. It's on me. What I'll not accept is anything happening to my family. I'm going to introduce myself to the team tonight. Please let them know I'll be out there a little after eight."

O'Shaughnessy starts to say something, but I'm already out the door.

I head down to the team room about ten past seven. My plan is to stay for about a half hour and then head out to Chevy Chase to meet the two security teams protecting my family. I'm sick to my stomach about Bridget, but I need to push the feeling to the back of my mind. I just feel so damn guilty.

D'Antoni is already seated in the conference room when I enter. I grab a cup of coffee and take a seat.

"We were just getting started," D'Antoni says. "Donnelley, let's start from the beginning again."

"Sure. No problem," Donnelley says. "We've placed a lot of focus on the eighteen-month period after William Sappey left Harvard and before he disappeared. During that period, he played baseball in the Yankees' organization, for their AA affiliate in Norwich, Connecticut."

"Good. That could provide a wealth of information," D'Antoni says. "We should be talking to his teammates, his coaches, and anyone associated with the organization. Someone must know what he did after baseball."

"Agreed, and we're already pressing that front," Donnelley says. "We should be able to get a team picture for the 2002 Norwich Navigators. We're reaching out to the Yankee organization as we speak. We're pulling information on everyone associated with the team and should know a lot more tomorrow.

"We interviewed three women by telephone today, all of whom lived in Rayburn House at the same time Jane did. All three reside outside of Massachusetts now. They had nothing but positive things to say about Jane, but none were particularly close with her. None of them could identify anyone in the house Jane was having problems with.

"When asked about William Sappey, all three gave nearly identical answers: 'He was creepy.' However, none of them knew much about Sappey. They said he was a loner, and they all recounted the incident with the puppy.

"One of the girls, a Beth Moore, said she was in the locker room when Sappey was caught peeping through the hole he made in the locker room wall. She said at the time, it didn't really bother her. She said Sappey was cute, and she was proud of her body.

"Her feelings about Sappey took a one-hundred-eighty-degree turn about three months later. She said he approached her and struck up a conversation at a house barbecue. She said everything was fine at first, but the conversation quickly started to make her feel uncomfortable, especially when Sappey started making disparaging comments about her body.

"He said she had 'nice, perky tits.' That she was fine with. The conversation went downhill from there, though. Sappey said she had way too much 'baby fat' on her. He said she had 'cottage cheese' thighs and described her pubic area as a 'hornets' nest of nastiness.' He told her the house had a Weedwacker in the backyard shed, and he volunteered to help her trim her pubic area with it.

"Needless to say, Janice was pretty upset, hurt by Sappey's comments. What made it—and these are her exact words—'super creepy' was that he had a huge grin on his face the entire time he talked to her. She said she never said a word to him again after that and stayed clear."

I stand up and clear my throat. "Let's work this Yankee angle hard. I wanna know everything about William Sappey leading up to his disappearance. Even though we don't know with certainty he's our perp, he's clearly a person of interest. As you all have probably heard, it's possible—probable—that this maniac has struck again, this time right in our own backyard. The potential victim is a close friend of mine. Time is of the essence, people. This guy is escalating, and more people will die if we don't get him off the street. Keep working it the way you've been working it, and we'll catch him. I have a commitment in Chevy Chase, but I'll see you all tomorrow. Thanks."

D'Antoni follows me out of the conference room. "Are you gonna check up on Catherine and the kids?"

"I just wanna talk to both sets of security."

"I wanna come. Would that be all right?"

I think about that for several seconds. "Yeah, sure. I'd like that."

I'm glad D'Antoni has offered to join me. To be honest, I'm feeling vulnerable, and that's a feeling I detest. I hate feeling weak; it seems to affirm everything the killer has said about me.

What I really want is a bottle of Johnnie Black, a glass, a couple ice cubes, and enough time to totally numb myself, to just disappear and forget about everything that's happened.

D'Antoni interrupts my self-pity. "Why don't you drive? I'll leave my car here, and you can drive me in tomorrow morning."

"Sounds good."

＋＋＋＋＋＋＋

I spend the entire drive to Chevy Chase sharing my burdens and fears with D'Antoni. She knows this is what I need. It's why she volunteered to come. She's a terrific listener; she doesn't judge, and her insights are usually spot on, even when I don't want to admit it. I tell her how guilty I feel about Bridget. I should've gotten Bridget protection at the same time as my family, not days later.

D'Antoni speaks up for the first time. "Deke, we don't even know that anything has happened to Bridget, and if something did, it's completely on the killer, not you. You can't put a bubble around everyone. The world we live in is a dangerous place. We just need to keep putting one foot in front of the other to try to make it a little safer."

I decide to park a couple blocks away from Catherine's house. It still feels weird not calling it *our* house. It probably always will. I figure a surreptitious approach will give us a better opportunity to observe the strengths and weaknesses of the protection teams. D'Antoni agrees.

When we finally get to Catherine's street, I recognize the bureau-issued car immediately. *Why the fuck couldn't they use something less obvious than an unmarked blue Crown Victoria?* It's law enforcement's signature car nationwide.

D'Antoni and I walk up on the car from behind, and the driver's-side window lowers before I can even knock.

"Deke, that you?"

I recognize the voice immediately. It's Greg Segal, a longtime top-notch agency man. Overwhelming relief floods through me when I realize in whose hands O'Shaughnessy has placed my family.

I shake Segal's hand enthusiastically. "O'Shaughnessy give you the 411 I was stopping by?"

"Yeah, but Tommy Selfridge spotted you about five hundred yards back. He's in that set of trees over there, along the fence line."

"Whoa. We got Tommy on this too?"

"Yup. And Nick Devito is set up inside the fence perimeter."

"Nicky is here too?"

"You bet, pal. We aren't going to let anything bad happen to your family, Deke."

I choke up a bit and have to look away for a second. "Thank you, Greg. I owe you huge, pal."

"You owe me nothing. I stopped in and caught up with Catherine yesterday. I just can't get over how much Patrick looks like you. And to think that I was positive she was having an affair with the FedEx guy!"

I laugh and feel good for the first time all day.

"And Sean is a trip. She kept asking to see my gun. When I told her I was a friend of yours, her eyes lit up. She said, 'My daddy catches bad men.' She is very proud of you."

"Greg, I can't tell you how relieved I am that you're on this."

"I volunteered."

"Thank you. I mean that."

"Make sure you wave to Tommy when you head around the corner. Jim's got three guys on the other side."

I clap Greg on the shoulder and thank him again.

"Get this motherfucker," he says. "Just get him."

We slip around the corner and see if we can sneak up on Jim's team. I haven't taken five steps before a man materializes from behind a tree next to the backyard fence. He approaches us casually.

"Checking up on us, Dekey boy?"

"Just making sure you're not napping, Jim. I know how you retirees get."

He laughs, and the three of us catch up for a couple minutes.

"Deke, every ingress and egress to the house is covered. You have two highly capable teams. Don't worry about your family. We've got this. Do what you do, and catch this sick fuck."

I clap Jim on the shoulder and smile. "I will, pal. Count on it."

＋＋＋◆＋＋＋

D'Antoni and I are in the car, heading to Georgetown, a few minutes later. I feel much better than I did a half hour previously. Both O'Shaughnessy and Jim have come up big for my family. Then I feel guilty for feeling this way. Bridget is missing, probably worse.

I drop D'Antoni off in front of her apartment with a promise to pick her up at eight the next morning. I wait for her to let herself in the front door before pulling away from the curb. I spot the FBI-issued car with little difficulty. *Good man, O'Shaughnessy.*

After parking in the driveway, I take my time walking up the steps to my front door. I glance up and down the street, looking for anything unusual, anything out of place. I know it's a waste of time—this guy is too good—but I do it anyway.

＋＋＋◆＋＋＋

It's after midnight by the time I get back from the gym. I make a quick bite to eat and head upstairs. Hearing the faint ping of an incoming text, I glance down at my watch. It's 11:10, not really late. I settle into the king-sized bed with my phone and computer within reach. I want to close my eyes and shut down, completely turn off the brain. I laugh inwardly at the idiocy of the thought. I have zero control over my brain. I decide to go through my unread texts before diving into email. I have a ton of them, but the latest text grabs my attention. It's from a 617 area code, a number I don't recognize. My heart starts pounding; my hands shake. I jump out of bed and pace around the room for a couple minutes. I don't want to open the text.

I try to convince myself I can somehow change the course of history simply by not opening the text.

Eventually, I throw in the towel. The desire to know is too strong. I open the text, preparing for the worst.

It's worse than I could have imagined.

The text is short and straight to the point. There are three attachments.

> For your viewing pleasure. Hey, pal. Hope you had a great Turkey Day. I sure did. I hope you didn't buy into my big promise. You can't be that stupid. Maybe you did. Hmm. You put security on Catherine and the kids but left poor Bridget all alone to fend for herself. That's cold, bro. You could have simply broken up with her rather than getting me to do your dirty work. Too late now. You owe me one. I'll be calling shortly. Enjoy the pics. MTK

With trembling fingers, I open the first attachment. It takes a few seconds to load, but when it does, the room starts to sway. It's a close-up of Bridget's face, although she's almost unrecognizable. Her face is covered in blood. Both eyes are swollen shut. Her nose is practically sideways, horribly broken. I feel dizzy and nauseated. I barely make it to the bathroom before emptying my stomach.

I take my time in splashing water into my mouth and onto my face before returning to the bedroom and the horrible photo. I'm taken aback by the violence and the rage. This is something new, clear evidence of escalation. For a brief second, I entertain the thought that Bridget could still be alive. Maybe he just beat her unconscious.

Yeah.

The second picture is not quite as horrific because the focus is on Bridget's naked body rather than on her battered face. It's just as disturbing, though. The body is posed provocatively. Her legs are spread. The perversity sickens me. Anger floods through me like a rain-swollen river. My head feels as if it might explode.

I sit down on the bed before opening the third attachment. It's more innocuous and less offensive than the other two. The body is visible on the bed, but the focus is on the room itself. It looks to be just a plain hotel room. Is he trying to give me a clue to the location of Bridget's body?

My phone vibrates in my hand. The call is from a 617 area code—the same number as the text. *Here we go.* I struggle to compose myself.

"Yeah?"

Nothing but distortion comes through for the first few seconds. He's obviously using a voice-altering device again. Then there's clarity. "Hey, Dekey, my boy. Did you have a nice Turkey Day? I made my own fun. Turkey and slobbing around in front of the TV is not my thing. I'm a man of action and adventure. You are too when you're not drinking. Are you drinking again, Deke? You can tell me the truth. I know you wanna. You want it so bad it causes you physical and emotional pain. A couple of pulls from the Jameson bottle, and your problems will fade away. I'm having a Jameson straight up right now. I know you drank your fair share of Jameson back in the day before you became famous and felt the need to upgrade to Johnnie Black. You can't upgrade from Jameson, you dummy. It's the best.

"Cat got your tongue or something? Don't you have a bunch of scripted questions to ask me? Let me guess. Did O'Shaughnessy tell you not to piss me off too much and to engage me and keep me interested in talking to you? He's a bureaucratic moron. You know it; I know it. Taking orders from someone who can't hold a candle to you intellectually has got to kill you. I don't know how you work for him. D'Antoni, on the other hand—now, that I understand. Smart, sexy, tough. Mmm. Can't wait to try that one out myself. Tell her it'll be soon."

"You ought to stick to the scared and weak," I say. "More your speed, wouldn't you say? You would embarrass yourself with D'Antoni. She's way out of your league there, Double-A. She's playing in the majors, and you couldn't even get out of the minors. A copycat and a failure, huh? No wonder you prey on the scared and weak."

Loud, distorted laughter comes through the phone. "I love sports analogies. If you were just a little tougher mentally, drank a little less, and had a better second serve, you could've made the ATP tour. Your brain got in the way the same as it does now. You'd better hope Catherine is strong and tough. I'm going to get her, Deke. That's a promise."

Shit. Have I gone too far?

Now I laugh. "Keep telling yourself that. Stick to what you do best: preying on the weak and scared. That's all you cowards can do. You'll never be famous. No one will even remember you when you're gone. I won't give you another thought."

More distorted laughter erupts. "Oh, you'll remember me, Dekey boy. You'll remember me. Every time you think of Bridget, I'll be there. When you dream of your little retard, I'll be there. I promised you I was going to put him down, and I will. I'll put your whole family down before I put you out of your misery. You'll beg me to kill you when everything is said and done.

"Bridget was a feisty little bitch. I can see why you liked her. I wanted to take her for a test-drive before finishing her, but I got too excited. It happens. I still had loads of fun, though. Hey, you should be thanking me. No need to sweat breaking up with her anymore. You're welcome, pal."

"I saw you at an FBI-sponsored event," I say. "You interrupted me. I'm less than a step behind you, jackass. I'm breathing down your back. I know who you are. I know. Enjoy your last minutes of freedom."

"Do you feel guilty about Bridget? What—she didn't warrant protection? You protected your family but not your girlfriend. That's cold, bro. The way I see it, you killed her. I came right out and told you I was going to kill her, and you did nothing. How do you live with that? Maybe we're a lot more alike than you care to admit.

"Hey, I would love to keep gabbing with you, but I have so much left to do. Do you think the retard will cry when I choke the life out of him? Will he even know what's going on? I sure fucking hope so. I'll let him know how ashamed you are of him, how stupid he is, and, most importantly, that you don't love him.

"Before I forget, your girlfriend is resting at the Capitol Acres Inn. It's less than three miles from Reagan. She's in room thirty-seven. I left a note inside of her for you. I even left a little clue because I feel bad for you. I need the game to stay interesting. It's starting to bore me. See you soon, buddy."

As he hangs up, I jump to my feet and quickly dress. Then I call D'Antoni.

"D'Antoni, he called. He killed Bridget. He sent pictures to prove it. She's at a motel near the airport, the Capitol Acres Inn Motel. I can grab you on the way."

"See you in a few," she says.

✦ ✦ ✦ ✦ ✦ ✦ ✦

I'm in front of D'Antoni's apartment five minutes later, and she's already waiting. She opens the car door and leans in without sitting down. "You okay? Want me to drive?"

"I'm fine. I need you to call O'Shaughnessy. Fill him in on what's going on," I say as D'Antoni gets in, buckles up, and shuts the door. "GPS will get us to the motel. It's near Reagan."

She calls O'Shaughnessy from her cell phone. She's on with him until we pull into the motel. It's fairly nondescript as motels go, and I wonder why he chose it—probably the proximity to the airport.

"O'Shaughnessy wants you to give him a call later," D'Antoni says. "He wants you to forward the text to the team and to the forensic techs. He'll take care of the locals, who will likely be here any second."

"Man, I hope someone is at reception," I say.

A young woman—in her early twenties is my guess—sits at the reception desk. She has Bose headphones on and doesn't acknowledge our approach. I place my FBI ID within her field of vision, and she takes her sweet time before looking up. The young woman rudely snaps her gum a couple times before addressing us.

"Can I help you?"

"Yes. We need a key to room thirty-seven. We're investigating a crime. Local police will be here any minute. We need to get into the room right now."

"I can't just give keys out and let anyone who asks into rooms."

"Unless you wanna be arrested for obstruction, I strongly suggest you get off your ass and give me the fucking key right now."

She almost falls out of the chair, but to her credit, she hands over the key without another sound.

"Do you feel better after scaring the shit out of that poor girl?" D'Antoni says. Her grin lets me know she's just trying to calm me in preparation for what's to come.

The first thing I notice is that room thirty-seven can be accessed from the outside. The killer could have parked his car right in front of the door. I'm sure this was planned. When I get to the door, I stop and take in a couple gulps of air.

"You okay?" D'Antoni asks.

"Yeah. I will be eventually."

The door has an old manual key lock. I push the door open and flip on the light. The smell of death, though faint, assails my nostrils immediately. It's a smell I'm all too familiar with. She lies, posed, in the center of the still-made bed. I choke back bile, not allowing myself to be sick again. She was such a beautiful woman. She's almost unrecognizable now. Her face is a mask of blood, broken bones, and bruises.

She didn't deserve this. No one does.

Her eyes are swollen shut, but the pain and horror are evident on her face. She suffered terribly—of that I'm certain. I only hope and pray she lost consciousness before any of the worst indignities.

I notice a piece of paper sticking out of her. I know the note is meant for me, but I won't handle it until the ME has examined the body. Another wave of nausea hits me hard, and I walk away from the bed to collect myself.

"I wish we could cover her," I say weakly.

"Me too," D'Antoni says, her hand on my shoulder. "But she doesn't mind now; she's in a better place, pal."

"I know, I know."

That's all I can say as the lump in my throat grows. I unconsciously wipe at my face, and my hand comes away wet. I have to pull it together. I owe her at least that much.

"We haven't seen this level of rage before," D'Antoni says. "Was it simple escalation? A direct message to you? A reaction to her fighting back?"

"All of the above," I choke out. I walk around the room, collecting myself, while D'Antoni continues to examine the body. Nothing grabs my attention.

Two uniformed DC cops walk through the door. D'Antoni and I flash our creds, and she spends the next several minutes explaining why we're there. They get to work securing the scene while D'Antoni and I continue to process it. It doesn't seem the killer left anything behind. The only obvious things in the room besides Bridget's body are her clothes, which lie in a heap near the bed. The killer's signature pen is nowhere to be found.

Within minutes, the room is crawling with local police. Local homicide detectives introduce themselves, and we spend the next five minutes quickly bringing them up to speed. The assistant ME shows up twenty minutes later, and I tell her about the note. I make plans to visit the morgue at ten in the morning. The scene is chaotic, and D'Antoni and I make our exits. She suggests an all-night diner in Georgetown, and I'm too numb to argue.

There are a couple drunk college students feeding their munchies, but the diner is otherwise quiet. D'Antoni and I take a table in the back, and the tired-looking waitress delivers menus and coffee. She's been working in the diner for as long as I can remember, and she knows both of us by name.

I'm not hungry and doubt I can keep anything down, but I order eggs and toast to be polite.

"I need you to walk me through your conversation with this guy. You up for it?"

"Yeah. You should probably give O'Shaughnessy a quick call first. Let him know I'll call him first thing in the morning. I'm too shot now."

D'Antoni spends the next five minutes getting O'Shaughnessy up to speed. He's not happy with my decision to defer talking to him until the morning. *Fuck him.* It's the bureau's fault Bridget is dead. In reality, I'm to blame, but I need O'Shaughnessy to sweat and keep my family safe.

The food arrives, and D'Antoni digs in. I nibble at a piece of toast, hoping to get something in my now-empty stomach to combat the nausea.

When D'Antoni comes up for air, I talk her through the call. I have difficulty recalling anything other than the morbid threats against my family.

"The most telling takeaway was the killer's frame of mind. He's becoming unhinged, escalating rapidly. He's consumed with the endgame, which includes killing you, my entire family, and, ultimately, me. He's intoxicated by the thought of instilling fear. It gets him off—to see the life fade from their eyes is his orgasm. He wants to be inside my head at all times, and you know what? He's winning on that count.

"What I need you to understand and appreciate is that he came right out and said he was gonna kill you. Said there was nothing I could do to prevent it. He told me he was gonna kill my entire family. He actually asked if I thought Patrick would understand what was going on while he strangled him."

I notice the waitress looking at me. I've been talking much more loudly than I intended to. I suck in a couple deep breaths before continuing in more subdued tones.

"He said that after he accomplishes those two things, killing you and my family, I'll beg him to take my life, and he'll be only too happy to oblige. You know what's crazy, D'Antoni? He's right. I wouldn't wanna live if those things happened. Not at all. Sometimes I feel like he can read my mind, my deepest secrets. It's incredibly unnerving, and it's starting to drive me crazy. I'm sure that's what he wants."

"That's what all these sick, twisted, narcissistic idiots want," D'Antoni says. "You know that, Deke. You're too good and too strong to let that happen. He can't get to you, can't get inside your mind, unless you let him. Once that happens, he's won."

"I'm gonna kill the motherfucker with my bare hands," I say. "That's a promise. He'll never see a jail cell. It's all a game to him, and the only way to win is to kill. That bastard is done hurting people close to me. Done."

I take a few deep breaths. "I know I've seen this guy before. I haven't said anything yet because I haven't put all the pieces together. My best guess is that he attended an FBI-sponsored lecture I presented at."

"Seriously?"

"I keep getting flashes but nothing definite. The harder I try, the less clear it becomes."

"Don't force it. Let it happen."

"Yeah, I know. Easier said than done, though. Time is not on our side. This psycho is out of control, and this thing is gonna play out quickly."

"What did he say about Bridget?"

"Exactly what I anticipated. He blamed me for her death. Told me how selfish I was to put protection on my family but not her. Said I used him to accomplish my dirty work. The scary thing is that he might be right. How else do you explain my decisions? It's driving me nuts. He's obviously been scouting out my family. He knows all about the protective detail. Probably knows exactly what vehicles they're using. I'm sure he knows my family's schedule and when they're most vulnerable. I need to put this guy down now. I won't rest until he's six feet under."

D'Antoni replies in adamant tones with a determined expression on her face. "First and foremost, you had zero—fucking zero—to do with Bridget's death. Stop letting this moron screw with you. Don't give him the satisfaction. Channel the anger; focus it into catching him. Let's get this son of a bitch off the street."

"Listen, I appreciate it, but you're not going to convince me I shouldn't have had protection on Bridget earlier. That one is on me however you slice it. So I'm going to catch this bastard in the next few days or die trying. Bank on it."

"That's what I wanna hear. What do you wanna do tomorrow?"

"Maybe we should push back the team meeting and go directly to the ME's office in the morning. It probably doesn't make sense to go all the way out to Quantico and come back for ten. You agree?"

"Yeah. Why don't you grab me at nine thirty? I'll catch up with Donnelley and the team at eight. Maybe something popped."

"Good. I'll call O'Shaughnessy at eight. Get that out of the way. I don't know why I'm so pissed at him. Mostly, I'm just angry and sad. And I need him to guarantee my family's safety. You know the first thing I thought when I saw Bridget's body?"

"What?"

"It was *Thank God it's not Catherine, Patrick, or Sean.* How bad is that? Bridget did nothing to deserve this. Simply knowing me got her killed."

"So you say, but what I find interesting is that his simply knowing you is what's going to get this guy caught."

"Let's hope so. Now I wanna get back to you for a minute. I need you to listen carefully. Please. This is serious. The guy threatened you again. He was much more direct about it this time. He also threatened my family and me."

"He doesn't scare me."

"Yeah, well, he should. He scares the shit out of me. Terrifies me. He's good at what he does—too good. That's why if either of us notices protection covering our asses, we should consider it a blessing."

"O'Shaughnessy already has people on both of us."

"You knew?"

"I figured it out when you dropped me off last night. You can spot the guys from a mile away. I called O'Shaughnessy on it this morning, and he admitted to having teams on both of us."

"Good for him," I say.

"It's nice not to have to continually be looking over our shoulder. He realizes how serious this is."

"Yeah. I just wish that realization had struck a week ago."

I signal to the waitress for the bill. She brings it right over, and I plunk down cash, including a generous tip.

"You should try to get a bit of sleep," I say. "We're in for some long days ahead."

"Yeah. You too. Let's go."

+ + + ◆ + + +

I'm back in my king-sized bed fifteen minutes later. It's a quarter after three in the morning. I send a text to O'Shaughnessy, letting him know I'll call him at eight. Miraculously, I fall asleep quickly.

I dream of conferences I've spoken at and speeches I've given. I flip through the faces in attendance like pages in a book. *Where are you, you son of a bitch?*

The alarm trills at 6:15. I leap out of bed with a smile on my face.

CHAPTER 50

I know where I saw this guy. I know for certain.

I write a note to Donnelley and other members of the team. I tell them our guy attended a lecture I gave in the summer of 2008 or 2009 on criminal profiling. Maybe he's law enforcement. We need to find a registration list or sign-in sheet—whatever—detailing who was in attendance. It was an FBI-sponsored event, so there has to be a list somewhere. I'm dying to call D'Antoni, but if she's smart, she's still sleeping. She needs all the sleep she can get.

I'm practically skipping as I make my way to the gym. It's packed, but I manage to grab the last available treadmill. Five miles go by in the blink of an eye. I search my memory for specifics about this guy, anything that might be helpful.

Then I hit the jackpot. I remember the exact event. It was in Boston in the summer of 2010. I can't remember the month, but that should be easy enough to determine. He interrupted me early in the discussion. He was a pompous know-it-all who came armed with a ton of naysayer rhetoric. I got the feeling he was trying to impress someone, maybe his supervisor. The guy was dressed in plain clothes but definitely gave off a law enforcement vibe.

He spent more than five minutes on his soapbox, minimizing the benefits of profiling to law enforcement. He was a big advocate of what he called "old-style detective work." He quoted liberally from published works espousing the same viewpoint. In the end, the interruption turned out to be a blessing in disguise. I was knee deep in research at the time for an FBI-sponsored paper on the benefits of profiling, a paper in which I traced the evolution and pointed to several incontrovertible successes, including some of my own. At the Boston presentation, I had a roomful of law enforcement bigwigs to try those arguments on and win over to the right side of the argument.

This guy, therefore, picked the wrong person to screw with— big-time. I gave him all the time he needed to get his point across. I thanked him for sharing his own and many other educated law enforcement experts' views on profiling. I complimented him on his knowledge of the subject. Then I systematically dismantled each and every point he'd made. I did it professionally and courteously but made sure to allude to my personal experience and success in the area. In the end, my opponent was left without any viable counterargument. He looked visibly shaken, embarrassed. Thinking back on it, I realize that embarrassing him was part of my intention.

I took the contest a step further, however. I ignored his repeated attempts to reengage me at the question-and-answer session after the lecture—a petty act, to be sure, but one I took pleasure in at the time. Have I shown my own inflated ego to the wrong person?

CHAPTER 51

I call D'Antoni, and she's as pumped as I am when I tell her what I remember.

"So you really think this guy is law enforcement?" she asks.

"Yes. Most in attendance were."

"Makes sense. You think he was Boston-based? Maybe still is?"

"Definite possibility."

"I'll get the team cranking on this. Between the local, state, and federal databases, maybe we find this guy."

"Sounds good. I don't think he's a fed. I knew all the Massachusetts guys back then."

"All right. This is great news, Deke. See you at nine thirty, partner."

Next, I call O'Shaughnessy. I've made him sweat long enough. He answers on the first ring.

"Deke, how are you doing?"

"I've been better. Listen, he promised me he was gonna kill Bridget, and he did. He beat her so badly she was almost unrecognizable. That's on me. He's promised to kill my entire family. He's also promised to kill D'Antoni. He'll do exactly that if we don't stop him. Don't doubt that for a second. Make sure my family and D'Antoni are safe. I don't care if you have to put an army on them. Just do it."

"Everyone is safe, Deke. He's not getting to anyone."

"I'm gonna hold you to that," I say. "I would get them hidden, but I feel they're safer under our direct care."

"They are. Listen, D'Antoni took me through the call last night, but I'd like to hear your side of things."

"All right." I pause to prepare myself to relive the harrowing conversation. "He was obviously tailing Bridget. He knew there was no security on her. He told me he saw the security on Catherine, so he's obviously invested some time in watching her. I don't need to tell you that freaks me out. He probably knows their vehicles, their schedules, and everything he needs to strike quickly. You need to let our team know this. I plan on spending time out there as well."

"Deke, you have enough on your plate."

"I'm not asking your permission, boss."

O'Shaughnessy sighs and mumbles something incoherent. "All right, all right. What else?"

I spend the remainder of the conversation bringing him up to speed on my recent revelation. He's blown away.

"I'm not positive it's the same guy, but I wouldn't bet against it."

"Holy shit!"

"Yeah. Holy shit. Unfortunately, knowing that I met him doesn't do us any good in and of itself. We still need to identify him."

CHAPTER 52

After showering, I throw on some jeans. I might as well be comfortable. This could be a long couple days, and it's the weekend. Next, I don a button-down, a navy Hickey Freeman blazer, and a pair of well-worn, comfortable Cole Haan loafers.

D'Antoni is waiting when I pull up out front. She's wearing jeans too. Great minds think alike.

We make the drive over to E Street in under five minutes. I find an illegal parking spot right out front and make sure the official FBI decal is visible to thwart any overzealous parking officers.

I've been inside the DC medical examiner's office dozens of times, but it never seems to get any easier. I swear a dark cloud hangs over the building at all times. We make our way toward the chief's office.

I glance at D'Antoni. "I would think the chief would handle this one himself?"

"Probably," she says.

We arrive at the chief's office moments later. His door is closed, and no one sits at his assistant's desk. I knock softly, but there's no answer. We elect to take a seat in the waiting area. It's five past ten, so hopefully we won't have to wait long.

These places creep me out. I turn to D'Antoni, anxious for distraction.

"Yesterday was tough, man. Worst day by far since leaving rehab. I craved a drink more than ever. I was shocked by how overpowering the urge was. I felt helpless, really, like I just wanted to disappear. I convinced myself it'd be all right. If it weren't for this sicko and the dangers he poses to the people I care about, I would've had a drink. I know it. I think I may actually start going to AA meetings. I thought I could do it on my own. I certainly have the motivation, but I don't know, Louise. Yesterday really scared me."

"Deke, you're gonna have tough times—close calls or whatever. Yesterday was a horrible day. It was the trigger of all triggers. You know what you need to do. Anytime you get cravings, try to think about Patrick and Sean. They need their daddy. You know that; I know that. If you decide to go to meetings and you want company occasionally, I can join you."

"Thanks, partner. I'm not going to do that to you. If I need to go, I will."

At that moment, Chief Medical Examiner Thomas Gehraty walks into the waiting area looking haggard. "Deke, Louise, how are you guys?"

We shake hands. Tom is a decent enough man, even though his excellent political connections have helped him to land the job and ensure his job security. As a consequence, he doesn't bend over backward for anyone, including law enforcement. I just hope he's finished Bridget's autopsy.

"Tom, how are the grandkids?" I ask. "Is Katy walking yet?"

"They're both doing great. Katy has been walking since she was ten months. Gives her mom a real workout every day!"

"That's awesome. Sean started walking at ten months as well. It changes everything. You need to grow eyes on the back of your head."

We laugh, and then Tom clears his throat, and the mood alters. "I just finished up," he says. "Give me a minute to check messages, and then I'll take you in to see her."

"Take your time," D'Antoni says.

Bridget is laid out on a table in the center of the room. Tom wastes no time. "Deke, I heard this was a close friend of yours. I'm sorry for your loss."

"Thanks, Tom. She didn't deserve this."

"No one does. She didn't go easily—that much I can tell you. We recovered a decent amount of skin from underneath her fingernails. She scratched this guy good. She also had a number of nonfatal facial injuries, including a serious nasal fracture, a broken orbit, a broken zygomatic bone, and a number of pretty serious blunt force contusions. The blunt force trauma was delivered by the assailant's fists, as I'm sure you expected. We took blood samples from her face to see if any of it was her attacker's.

"I know it goes without saying, but this was a vicious, savage beating, and I hope she lost consciousness quickly. She died from asphyxiation. I found a single puncture wound on the right side of her neck. She was injected with something. Blood work is pending. I'm sure you suspect succinylcholine. Also, she has ligature marks on her wrists and ankles."

"Yeah, that seems to be his trademark," I say. "Was she sexually assaulted, Doc?"

"There's no evidence of rape. However, a note was left inside the victim's vaginal vault—probably postmortem, but we have no way to be certain. It's in a Ziploc bag on the tray next to the sink. The note was addressed to you, Deke."

I'm relieved to turn away from Bridget's battered body; I don't want to remember her like this, but I know the image will forever haunt me.

I slide the paper out of the Ziploc into my latex-gloved hands. I take a deep breath before starting to read.

Hey, Dekey boy,

You can thank me later. No uncomfortable breakup necessary. Personally, I would've kept a piece of ass like that on the side for a while longer. What a body. No body fat whatsoever. Small tits, but I'm not a breast man. And I love the tiny little patch of fire-engine-red pubic hair. Fire in the hole, baby.

You would've been proud of her. She went down fighting. Scrappy little bitch. I bet she was awesome in bed. I should've taken her for a test-drive, but all in all, things worked out. Then again, why test-drive a Mercedes when you can test-drive a Rolls-Royce? Tell D'Antoni I'm coming.

If I were you, I would try to get on Catherine's good side as soon as possible. I want you to be able to say goodbye to the little retard and to Sean. I'm not a monster. Anyway, looks like we're headed to the fifth-set tiebreaker, and I'm still fresh and loose. Good luck to you, pal. Do you know who I am yet? If you were as good as me, you would. Johnnie Black forever, baby. MTK

I feel a bit light-headed and dizzy. More than anything, though, I'm pissed. No one threatens the people I love. No one.

I slip my cell phone out and snap several pictures of the note. Everybody needs to see this to get a true picture of this sick monster.

I make my way back to Tom and D'Antoni. "He's quite the linguist," I say.

"I'd like to read it too." D'Antoni frowns.

"I took several photos of it."

I hand D'Antoni my phone. She pulls one of the pictures up and takes her time in reading the note. She shows no outward emotion whatsoever. *Man, she's tough.*

"Tom, anything else we need to know about?" D'Antoni asks.

"No. I'll email you the lab results."

"Hope your weekend isn't wrecked. Have fun with the grandkids. That age is so much fun," I say.

We say our goodbyes, and D'Antoni and I begin the trek out to Quantico. It's a beautiful, vibrant area when the leaves are on the trees. Now, however, it simply serves as a stark reminder of the precarious situation we're in.

"I have to give Catherine a try," I say. "I don't wanna. I think I'd rather choke on a dog turd. But I have to."

"Go ahead, pal," she says.

"This is going to suck," I say out loud as I dial her number. Catherine answers, and we exchange small talk for the first minute or so.

It's time to rip the Band-Aid off.

"Catherine, it'd be better if you guys stay around the house this weekend. I know the kids have activities, but I need you to stay put."

"Yeah? Why is that?"

"I've received credible threats against you and the boys. This man killed a close friend of mine yesterday. He warned me he was going to kill her, and he still pulled it off. The guy is unhinged, and he knows I'm closing in on him. If he's going to make a move, it'll be soon."

Her response is a mixture of anger and horror, and I have no choice but to listen. "What have you gotten us into, for God's sake? How could you do this to Patrick and Sean? If you love them at all, you'll protect them. You protect them, Deke."

"You guys are safe. I have the best of the best watching you guys. I'll be joining them tonight and until we catch him."

She gives a sarcastic laugh. "Is that supposed to allay all my fears? That the great Deke O'Brien is watching over us? He's probably drinking, but fear not, as he's all-powerful. Keep your kids safe."

Click.

"Well, that went better than expected," I say shakily.

D'Antoni puts a comforting hand on my shoulder. "Deke, she's just scared. You can't fault her for that. She doesn't do this for a living. She doesn't deserve this. Not at all."

"What did the team have to say this morning?" I ask.

"They're making tremendous progress. They have a list of the names of everyone associated with Sappey's baseball team—players, trainers, coaches, medical staff. They also have a team photo, and they already have someone working on an age progression of Sappey. They have even talked to a couple of Sappey's teammates."

"Dynamite," I say.

"Hey, I forgot to tell you. I talked with Barnes, Maeve, and Griff this morning. Everyone has been updated."

"Awesome. I was going to do that later today."

———— ✦✦✦✦✦✦ ————

The conference room is bustling with energy and excitement. Every member of the team seems engrossed in his or her work. Although the team must have been working flat out, I don't see a bunch of overtired, under-appreciated people; I see people dedicated to their jobs—jobs that often take them away from their families and put them in harm's way.

D'Antoni and I take seats on opposite sides of the table. She clears her throat to get everyone's attention and wastes no time.

"Donnelley, you wanna run lead?"

"Sure. Let me start by passing out a blown-up picture of the 2002 Norwich Yankees. This is by far the best picture we have of William Sappey. I'm also going to send around a computer-generated age-progression photo of Sappey as he might look today. I'll give everyone a couple minutes to review the photos."

I look at the photos intently. As Donnelley resumes his update, I leave my chair and then the room and dash to my workstation; I need my file with the New York surveillance photos of our killer.

I sit down and compare the pictures Donnelley handed out with the New York surveillance photos. I spend nearly twenty minutes comparing the two. Finally, my vision blurred, I head back into the conference room.

Everyone looks up when I walk in. D'Antoni has a smile on her face. "Well?" she says.

"Well, I'm not one hundred percent sure, but I think Sappey is our guy."

"You didn't need to leave the meeting to figure that out. We all figured it out."

I smile. "I've always been a little slow on the uptake."

"We know," D'Antoni says. "You're going to wanna buckle your seat belt for what we've got next."

Donnelley resumes. He points out Sappey's teammates by name. The last name he mentions causes my heart to skip a beat: William Slaughter.

I look quickly to D'Antoni, but she's enjoying herself too much to give anything away. I look back to Donnelley, my eyes pleading for an answer.

"Yup," D'Antoni says. "Our asshole detective from Boston was a teammate of William Sappey. What are the chances, right?"

"Which one of these guys is Slaughter?" I wave the team photo at Donnelley frantically.

"The guy to the left of Sappey."

I spend the next several minutes studying the team photo. Slaughter and Sappey are both tall, at least six feet two; both are muscular and have full heads of wavy dark hair. They could be brothers. In this picture, Slaughter looks different somehow from the man I met in Boston. Maybe everyone looks different when bald. This is weird. What are the chances that Slaughter and our perp played semipro ball together?

"Are we sure it's our Bill Slaughter?" I ask.

"Positive," D'Antoni says.

"I'll be damned. I wouldn't have made the connection simply by looking at the team picture."

"Me neither," D'Antoni says.

Then Donnelley jumps in. "We've spoken to two of Sappey's teammates so far. Both of them said he wasn't an overly friendly guy and mentioned that the only person he ever really hung out with was Slaughter."

"Are you shitting me?" I say.

"Nope," D'Antoni says, the smile back on her face.

"I owe Bill a call anyway to update him," I say. "Let's hope Billy takes our call. He's got some explaining to do."

D'Antoni rummages through her purse and retrieves a card with Slaughter's information. We elect to put the call on speaker for the entire team's benefit.

Dispatch puts us through to his direct dial, but he doesn't pick up.

D'Antoni then tries his cell, which goes directly to voice mail. She leaves a message: "Bill, it's Louise D'Antoni with the FBI. Hope you're well. A lot has happened since we last spoke. Can you give me or Deke a call at your earliest convenience? We have some questions we need to ask you about one of your former teammates, William Sappey, from the good old days. He's a person of interest—one we need to find."

CHAPTER 53

D'Antoni's cell phone rings, and a quick look at the caller ID reveals the caller to be Slaughter. "Let's find an empty office and take it on speaker," she says.

Moments later, we have found an office and are taking the call. "Bill, I have you on speaker with Deke. Thanks for getting back to us so quickly. Things have gotten really crazy on this case."

"No problem, Louise. Barnes has been nice enough to keep us lowly city cops in the loop."

She laughs. "We asked him to keep you up to date every step of the way."

Slaughter laughs as well. "Well, we sure do appreciate it. Now, which one of my Norwich teammates were you asking about?"

"William Sappey," D'Antoni says. "A couple of your teammates said you guys were pretty tight."

"Really?" Slaughter chuckles softly. "Not that I remember. He was a loner. Mean son of a bitch. He lived in my apartment complex, so I used to hitch a ride with him now and then, but he mostly kept to himself. He freaked me out a bit, to tell you the truth."

"How do you mean?" I say.

"He was always staring at people, especially women. He wouldn't talk to them, just stare. And he had a hair-trigger temper. Got into it with a couple of my teammates. Good-looking guy, but I never saw him have any luck with the ladies. Couldn't get lucky in a

Mexican whorehouse with a fist full of fifties. He was just too weird and creepy."

"Hmm," I say. "That certainly fits our profile."

"Barnes has shared the profile with me," Slaughter says. "It seems a bit general. Almost any educated man between twenty-five and thirty-five who had it rough as a kid would fit it."

D'Antoni and I look at each other, confused.

"So you think he might be your serial killer?" Slaughter asks.

"I know he is," I reply.

Slaughter absorbs that statement for several seconds before responding. "Well, he was a bit of a dick, but a serial killer? I don't know. We never kept in touch when I moved on to the real world. Never even thought about him again, to be honest, so I don't think I can be a lot of help."

"What you have already said has been helpful," D'Antoni tells him. "If nothing else, you've corroborated what we already knew."

"Always glad to help my law enforcement brethren, even if they're FBI," Slaughter says with a laugh. "Please keep Bronstein and me in the loop. We will help you in any way we can."

"Thanks, Bill."

Click.

"I still don't like that guy," D'Antoni says.

"I get it," I say. "He's just ambitious—wants his input to be heard. In fact, I see a little bit of myself at his age in him. He loves the job but wants to do everything on his own. If he wants to grow as a cop and advance, he'll have to change. Easier said than done, though. There's something that's been nagging me about him and Sappey."

"Other than the fact that they look alike?" D'Antoni says.

"I don't know what it is. My gut says it's something obvious, and it'll come to me with time, but who knows? It's probably nothing."

"It's rarely nothing with you," D'Antoni says with a wink.

CHAPTER 54

He paces around outside the precinct. *Fuck, fuck, fuck!* Things are moving too fast. Deke and D'Antoni are even better than he expected. He'll need to act quickly because his identity could be discovered soon.

He heads back into the precinct; he needs to come up with a credible excuse to get out of there. His shit-bag partner will likely give him a hard time. He heads into the men's bathroom and looks at himself in the mirror. Fear and stress are written all over his face. He must pull it together. Failure is not an option. He splashes water onto his face, hoping it looks like perspiration. He's never called in sick in his life, but today he's going to use the sick card.

His partner couldn't care less. He lays it on thick, saying it must be the stomach flu that's going around. He's careful not to exaggerate the act, and he's pretty sure the fat little prick buys it. His partner promises to let the boss know, and he's out the door seconds later.

He wants to head to JJ Foley's for a few drinks so he can calm down and come up with a plan, but it's too risky. It's a cop bar, and his partner eats there at least once a week. Instead, he decides to head to one of his favorite bars, the Red Hat, a century-old icon over in Beacon Hill.

He doesn't recognize the bartender. She's young—mid twenties at most. She wears a tight V-neck T-shirt that barely contains her surgically enhanced breasts. There's only one other patron in the bar, and having served the other customer, she sidles over to him seconds later. *Damn, she's sexy.* Then she ruins everything by opening her mouth.

"What can I get ya, mister?" she says, her hillbilly redneck accent destroying the illusion completely.

"I'll take a Sierra Nevada in a cold mug and a shot of Jameson." *No one can screw that up,* he thinks to himself. She does, though—too much head on the beer. The key to pouring into an ice-cold mug is patience. Disgusted, he grabs the shot of Jameson, downs it in one gulp, and pushes the glass back to her.

"Another, mister?"

He looks her in the eye. The look clearly speaks louder than words, because she quickly takes the glass, refills it, and leaves him in peace. Again, he grabs it and throws it back in one deft motion. Then he bangs the glass down a little too hard and takes pleasure in seeing the redneck flinch. Man, he loves screwing with people. He drains his partially filled mug of beer in one sip.

He finally starts to calm down. His blood was practically boiling when he walked in; now it is time to sort things out. In his gut, he already knows what he's going to do, but he feels obliged to go through the motions.

Deke and D'Antoni have moved faster than he anticipated, and he has nothing but his own ego to blame for that. He never should've revealed his prior connection to Jane Martin. His lust for always upping the stakes got the best of him. *So stupid.*

There's probably no point in worrying about Mary Morrison. For Deke to be locked on William Sappey already, the FBI has already talked with her. That sucks. He has been looking forward to catching up with that bitch. If he finds a way to pull through this, he'll pay her a visit eventually. He sees no reason at this point not to mail the packages he has made up for the major local and national newspapers; they contain the lewd photos of Mrs. Morrison. She can say goodbye to that cushy job in Allston and life as she knows it. He chuckles to himself. *Ain't life grand?*

He orders two more drinks, resisting the urge to pour the beer himself. He tries to convince himself that even though the FBI is onto William Sappey, it's possible they'll never make the connection to him. He thinks about it, drinks the shot of Jameson, and thinks about it some more. *Nah, they'll make the connection.* He's on borrowed time. He needs to act now. The endgame hasn't changed.

He takes out his cell phone and opens the Delta app. He buys a ticket on the shuttle into Reagan that night at six. He uses a credit card in his own name to book the ticket. He thinks briefly of using one of his aliases, but what's the point, really? They will make the connection soon enough anyway, and he has to identify himself as a Boston city policeman in order to check a bag with a firearm.

He quickly drains the beer, leaves a fifty-dollar bill on the bar, and heads out the door. Now he's a man with a plan.

CHAPTER 55

The conference room is still buzzing on our return. Little has happened since we left, so I head back to my workstation to make some calls and think. My first call is to Joe. "Hey, Joe. How are things?"

"Decent. What's up, pal?"

"This sicko has directly threatened the lives of Catherine and my kids again. He's definitely going to make a move, and it'll be soon. No question about it."

"We're ready for him, Deke."

"I know, Joe. I know. If it's all the same to you, I may spend some time on the property during the next couple of nights. Can you tell your team that an extra good guy might be running around tonight?"

"You got it, brother."

"Thanks, Joe. Talk soon."

I decide to see if O'Shaughnessy is available. I knock on his door and poke my head in. D'Antoni is in with him.

"You want me to come back?" I say.

"No," O'Shaughnessy says. "Come in. Louise was just catching me up."

"Can you please let Catherine's security detail know that I'll be nosing around the property the next couple of nights and that they are not to shoot me?"

"Shit, Deke. That's not a good idea. You're just going to get in the way."

I look O'Shaughnessy in the eyes. He shakes his head, picks up the phone, and does as I asked.

"Thank you," I say.

He simply shakes his head again. "So Sappey is definitely our guy? You feel confident about that, Deke?"

"It's him. He's not William Sappey anymore, but that won't matter. We'll get him."

"I just wish we had some inkling of what happened to him. No one can just disappear."

"I don't know about that," D'Antoni says. "With planning and money, you can do just about anything."

"How are we going to catch him then?" O'Shaughnessy asks.

"He will come to us—and soon," I say.

CHAPTER 56

He gets back to his apartment and immediately gets to work. Financially, he can afford to disappear for a long time. He's had five big financial coups in his time as a cop. It's amazing what criminals will pay—or sacrifice—for their freedom or their lives. Most of it is hidden in untraceable overseas accounts, but he has $45,000 in a shoebox in the closet. He'll definitely need some walking-around money.

He takes the three big boxes he's already packed out to the unmarked car. Then he heads around the corner to the UPS store. He uses one of his two aliases to send the boxes to the little town on the Venezuelan coast where he owns a small shack right on the water. He'll be calling that shack home for the foreseeable future.

He knows he could leave right now. He could simply disappear; he's that well prepared. The FBI would have little chance of catching him. But no, there's work to be done before he can disappear—important work.

He could care less whether the FBI figures out who he is. He's ready for new and more challenging adventures. Life would be drab if you couldn't reinvent yourself every couple years.

Next, he packs a bag with about five days' worth of clean clothes and several other essentials he will need on the road, including, of course, several hundred-milligram doses of sux. He takes his sidearm out of his shoulder rig and secures it in its hard, rectangular travel container. He locks the container and puts it in his travel bag. Being a law enforcement officer definitely has its perks.

Then he secures a dozen empty magazines inside his pistol case and places that in the bag as well. Finally, he places three unopened boxes of nine-millimeter ammunition in the bag.

He opens the liquor cabinet, selects three unopened bottles of Jameson, and places two of them in the travel bag. The third bottle he pours into three flasks, two of which he stows in the backpack he will carry onto the plane. The third one he puts in the right breast pocket of his blazer. He then pours three fingers from an open bottle into a tumbler and sits in a chair from which he can look out on the public park below. He takes a healthy pull from the glass, closes his eyes, and goes through the plan from start to finish again.

CHAPTER 57

Donnelley has news when we get back to the conference room. D'Antoni and I both pour ourselves coffee and take a seat.

The ME's report on the body from Worcester has just come back. The deceased has been positively identified as one Joseph Wilson. Blunt force trauma removed Mr. Wilson's missing teeth, and apparently, even the few that were left were splintered. The cause of death is listed as possible strangulation, evidenced by a pronounced fracture of the hyoid bone. However, too much time has elapsed to indicate a definitive cause of death.

Donnelley speaks. "We've spoken to Sappey's baseball coach in Norwich. He didn't have anything good to say about him. According to the coach, he was a loner with a giant ego who thought his Harvard degree made him better than everyone else. He said the only player he hung out with was our very own Bill Slaughter. He said that Sappey would've made the big leagues if he could've hit the curveball."

This makes me smile.

"Anything else?" D'Antoni asks.

"Yeah, we talked to a Mary Cross of Knoxville, Tennessee. She was in the house at the same time as Sappey. She says she still has nightmares about him to this day."

"Why is that?" D'Antoni asks.

"She claims Sappey sexually assaulted her in her last year in the house. Lay in wait in her room while she was at soccer practice. She says he choked her with a belt while assaulting her. She blacked out a couple of times. When he was finished, he told her he would do the same to her as he'd done to the neighbors' puppy if she said anything. She's now a youth counselor in a group home."

+ + + ◆ + + +

He's in full disguise when he boards the plane. Checking his bag was a pain in the ass, but he needs access to a firearm. He's excited and takes a seat toward the back of the plane, minimizing the risk that someone will sit next to him.

It's time to solidify his plans for tonight. He needs to create a distraction that will keep Deke and D'Antoni preoccupied tomorrow while he gets to work putting the finishing touches on his master plan. He takes the flask out of his breast pocket and takes a three-second gulp from it.

Perfect. Now he can concentrate.

CHAPTER 58

I spend the next two hours racking my brain for anything useful, but I have nothing to show for it except frustration. I decide to head home. Maybe the change of venue will spark something.

The drive into Georgetown takes less than forty minutes. The streets are eerily quiet. Traffic will pick up tomorrow with the end of the holiday weekend. I promise to check in with D'Antoni later that night and head to my place. Today I pick up the surveillance immediately. The dark, unmarked Crown Vic sedan is two houses down on the left. I'm glad to have the extra set of eyes watching out for me.

I'm too wired to simply sit around my townhouse, so I put on some workout clothes and head to the gym. Maybe a good sweat will jar something loose.

Five miles later, I'm no closer than when I started. Why can't it ever just be easy? Time is not on my side. Rather than trying to force it, I decide to head home, grab a quick bite, shower, and then head out to Catherine's.

+ + + ◆ + + +

I get to Catherine's shortly after nine. After checking in with both security teams, I take up position in the pool house. It's a decent vantage point because it has viewing access to both the front and back yards. The place creeps me out a bit with all the lights out. It has more than its fair share of cobwebs at this time of the year, and the evening is cold. Luckily, I have opted to wear my black Bogner ski jacket over a blazer. I settle in a recliner in front of a window that gives me a perfect, unobstructed view of the backyard.

Boredom sets in quickly. I've always hated surveillance; it does not suit my hyperactive nature. I try to get more comfortable and settle in for what should be a long night. I have made the rookie error of not bringing coffee. What was I thinking?

I'm not sure when I doze off, but thank God I do. What I've been searching for comes to me as I sleep. Its impact hits me like a locomotive, and my eyes fly open. I leap out of the chair and frantically search for my phone with shaking hands.

Holy shit, holy shit, holy shit!

D'Antoni picks up on the first ring. "What's up, dipshit?"

I have trouble getting the words out, but finally, I pull it together. "I figured it out! I fucking figured it out!"

"What? What?"

"Slaughter is Sappey. Bill Slaughter is William Sappey, the baseball player. I'm positive. I have no idea what happened to the William Slaughter in the team photo. Just look at the picture. There's no doubt in my mind. I can't believe it took me this long to figure it out. I knew the picture of William Sappey looked like our perp. I also felt like I had seen him before, though. I never made the connection to Slaughter because of his bald head. But look at the picture. Granted, the two of them look a lot alike—eerily so. Focus on the smile. There's no doubt. I should've realized earlier. Son of a bitch."

"Holy shit. Holy shit!" D'Antoni exclaims. "I don't believe this!"

"I'll call Donnelley," I say. "You call O'Shaughnessy. We need to track Slaughter's every move. He knows we're closing in, and he'll be desperate."

"Okay, call me back."

I call Donnelley and lay out our game play. We need to monitor Slaughter's every movement. He knows we're close—maybe not how close, but he knows he's on borrowed time. If he's going to make a move, it'll be soon.

Donnelley agrees to check air-travel logs out of Boston into DC and return flights for the periods immediately before and after Bridget's death. He'll also check with car-rental agencies. We need to know in real time if he's on the move. Of course, he could be driving his own car, but we can track him via E-ZPass if he's using it. I tell Donnelley to update me immediately if anything pops.

Next, I call Barnes. It's late, but he picks up on the first ring. I apologize for the hour but get right down to business. Barnes is blown away.

He pauses for several seconds before saying anything. "Wow. He's a colossal asshole, but I never would've guessed this in a million years. You're sure?"

"No doubt."

"Really. I don't see it. I don't have the pictures with me, but to be honest, I'm at a complete loss. It never even entered my mind."

"Listen, I didn't make the connection either. His bald head throws you off immediately, and he's also put on some muscle since then."

"I'll put a couple of my guys on him immediately."

"Perfect. At this point, we need eyes on him at all times. He knows that we were onto William Sappey. He's got to know it's just a matter of time until we make the connection to him."

CHAPTER 59

He's in his silver Nissan Altima rental, heading out to Tysons Corner. It's a little less than thirty minutes from the airport. He's booked a room at the Ritz Carlton, which adjoins the Tysons Corner Galleria, one of the most upscale malls in North America. He books the room in the name of James Reardon, which is one of his aliases—one that will cease to exist tomorrow. He needs to keep Teddy Winks clean because his overseas accounts are in that name.

He's stayed at this Ritz before, when he was surveilling Deke, Bridget, Catherine, and D'Antoni. It's luxurious, and he might as well close this chapter in style. He has the car valeted on arrival. The concierge recognizes him and greets him warmly. He's in his room on the club floor just a few minutes later.

He makes a quick inventory of his bag. He loads one of the empty magazines and puts it into his city-issued nine-millimeter, which he lays on the nightstand next to the shoulder rig. Then he takes a bottle of his salvation out of the bag and pours himself a few fingers. He's too hopped up. He needs to calm down and focus so he can truly appreciate the moment.

He doesn't really hate Deke personally. He feels jealousy, sure, but hatred presupposes caring, which he doesn't feel. To borrow from addiction parlance, he is addicted to more. It doesn't matter whether it is exercise, drink, work, or killing—more is better. It's what his body craves—demands. Ultimately, he is powerless to deny it. It's better to embrace it.

His addiction to Deke is also out of his control. He wants to work with and beat the best. He needs to, really. He craves fame, even if it takes the form of infamy, and what better way to achieve it than by beating the best in his own backyard?

He's a control freak. He loves getting inside others' heads and taking over their lives. He's deep inside Deke's head now. He loves the cat-and-mouse game. The intention has always been to play with Deke until it ceases to be interesting. That always happens. It's happening now.

He savors the last sip of the smoky amber liquid. He's much calmer now, almost serene. He dials the number he knows by heart. She answers immediately.

"Hey, sweetheart," she says. "I've missed you. You want some company tonight?"

"Always, Jen. Why don't you meet me for a cocktail at the Palm around ten?"

"See you there, gorgeous," she says.

He quickly pulls off his clothes and turns on the shower. He looks in the mirror, appraising himself. Damn, he's a nearly perfect physical specimen. The testosterone and human growth hormone treatments have helped for sure, but mostly, it's just hard work. Maybe genetics plays a role too, but his mom was a waif, thin and short. He's never met his asshole of a father.

He luxuriates in the hot, steamy shower. Tonight will at least provide entertainment, a delicious distraction.

He met Jen for the first time almost two years ago in the Palm Bar, where she was trolling for a well-heeled senator or lobbyist looking for a good time. Instead, she landed him. She is five feet eleven, blonde, and gorgeous. She is also $3,500 a night but worth every cent. Her skills beneath the sheets are unmatched. Most importantly, however, she lets him entertain his fantasies to his heart's delight. *What a woman.*

It's a shame she has to die tonight, but it's for a good cause.

CHAPTER 60

My cell rings, and I practically fall out of the chair. I'm wound way too tightly. It's D'Antoni.

"What's up, partner?" I say.

"O'Shaughnessy is on this like stink on shit. He's authorizing four separate two-man surveillance teams on Slaughter. He acknowledges we don't have enough to arrest him yet but that we need eyes on him 24-7. He wants you to call him."

"Okay. Anything else? Does he think we should head to Boston if they locate him?"

"Not yet. He wants to meet tomorrow at eight."

Relief floods through me. I can't leave DC and my family right now. He'll be here soon enough—of that I'm certain.

"Are you still out at Catherine's?"

"Yes. I'm going to head home shortly. See you bright and early."

"Hold on a second."

"What?"

"Be careful."

"Always. You too, partner."

My mind drifts to Slaughter. The thought helps take my mind off how cold and quiet it is in the pool house. What made this malignant piece of garbage what he is today? Could upbringing, potential brain abnormalities, and life experience create someone this evil? Several highly regarded medical studies support that malignancy is either present at birth or formulated through abuse, neglect, and a lack of love and nurtured and fed throughout life. There's little doubt Slaughter's childhood was horrible, but that's not what made the monster in front of us today. The evil monster might have always existed; his childhood and lifetime experiences simply allowed the monster out of its cage.

CHAPTER 61

Freshly showered, he decides to throw on jeans, a starched white button-down, and a blazer. A guy with his physique and looks has to dress well. When he finishes primping in the mirror, he grabs his cell phone and makes a call. The gentleman on the other end picks up the call but says nothing.

"Hey, it's Teddy. Is the AR15 ready to go?"

"Da."

"Night-vision scope and noise suppressor assembled? And it's been sighted in?"

"Da."

"I'll be by about nine to pick it up."

He takes his blazer off for a second so he can put the shoulder rig on. He's famished and hopes there's a seat at the bar so he can order a nice steak and a glass of wine immediately.

He calls downstairs to the concierge and orders a bottle of Joseph Phelps 2013 cabernet to be delivered to the room. He lets the concierge know he'll be next door at the Palm, having dinner, but requests that the bottle be opened to give it ample time to breathe. Then he heads out.

He gets the last seat at the bar. It's hopping with well-heeled politicos, lobbyists, and the occasional high-priced call girl, as usual. He loves the atmosphere. The smell of power permeates the air. He starts to order a Jameson neat but quickly changes his mind; tonight is a special occasion. "Give me a Johnnie Black, two ice cubes." He smiles to himself. That's just how Deke likes it. *Perfect.*

His twenty-ounce ribeye and large tomato-and-onion salad arrive. The tomato-and-onion salad is to die for. It's probably not the best choice in some ways, given his impending entertainment, but he doesn't care. His great is going to be the least of her worries. He laughs out loud.

Jen arrives about a half hour later. As usual, she's stunning. Her silver sequined cocktail dress fits her body like a glove. She looks so elegant that he forgets for a second who—and what—she is.

She leans into him and kisses his cheek. She smells of jasmine and mountain air. Oh man, he's missed her. He orders her an extra-dry Ketel One martini with olives and a side of ice. Even her choice of drink is sexy.

"Oh, that hits the spot," Jen says. "Frankie really knows how to pour a martini."

"You hungry?" he asks.

"Just thirsty, baby," she replies.

Good answer. "I have a nice cabernet breathing back at the hotel."

"Perfect."

+ + + ✦ ✦ + + +

They're back in the hotel a half hour later. They get in the elevator at the ground floor. He hopes it doesn't stop at floor two, which is where reception and the restaurant and lounge are located. Keeping a low profile is key. He keeps his head down, not wanting to be seen by the camera. He pulls his ball cap lower.

The elevator goes right to the seventh floor. He hustles Jen to his room, careful to keep his gaze down as they pass the surveillance camera. He knows that extra precautions are meaningless at this point, but it's better to be safe than sorry. He might still have some time, and it would be best not to waste it.

He fixes Jen a glass of wine and a small plate of berries and whipped cream. He loves watching her eat and drink.

He excuses himself to use the bathroom, where he takes the syringe and vial of sux from his shaving kit. He loads the syringe with exactly one hundred milligrams and places it in the pocket of the robe he'll be changing into. He'll then hide it in the bed. He takes a large swig from the flask. Now's the time to focus but not at the expense of enjoyment.

He takes off his clothes, which he folds neatly in a pile, and then he puts on the luxurious, heavy terry cloth robe the Ritz is famous for. *Damn, that feels good.*

He rejoins Jen in the bedroom. She has a speck of whipped cream on her upper lip, so he kisses it off. She smiles. "I wanna get comfortable too. I'll just be a minute, darling."

"Take your time, gorgeous. The night is young."

She comes back into the room wearing nothing but an understated pearl necklace and a beautiful diamond tennis bracelet, both of which he purchased for her on a prior visit.

He appreciates the dichotomy of the situation. She presents as an elegant, sophisticated, gorgeous woman, but in reality, she's a whore—a high-priced whore but a whore all the same.

She picks up her wine glass and settles next to him on the bed. Her aroma is intoxicating. She leans in for a kiss, which he hungrily accepts.

The desire to elicit terror and pain courses through his body. He whispers in her ear. "You okay if I record this, like last time, for future viewing enjoyment? I'll make it well worth your while financially."

"Of course, baby. I trust you. Are you going to wear the face mask like you did last time?"

"Nah. I wanna star in my own movie. Damn, you're so hot."

He jumps off the bed and walks over to the desk to retrieve his phone. He positions it perfectly on his overnight bag, facing the bed, and then hits the video record button. Then, after taking up his wine glass, he walks back over to the bed and lets his robe fall to the ground.

He turns full-frontal toward the camera and winks. Then he mouths silently but clearly, "Deke, I'm gonna do this to Catherine."

He turns his attention back to his current companion. He kneels on the bed, and she sidles over and then expertly and gently takes him into her mouth.

Nothing she does arouses him. The sex act—any sex act—is meaningless now. Inflicting horror and panic is the only thing that excites him. He reaches behind him, grabs the syringe under the duvet, and quickly injects her.

A tiny cry escapes her lips.

He looks over to the camera, placing his left hand on Jen's head. He mouths, "D'Antoni, I'm pretending this is you."

When the drug takes effect, he straddles her, looking deep into her eyes. The wide smile does nothing to hide his excitement. At that moment, he realizes just how addicted he has become. Sex itself means nothing to him. He has a beautiful woman who is willing to do anything he wants, and he couldn't have cared less. Arousal and sexual release are no longer possible unless he's hurting someone—badly.

Her desperation and her certainty she will die exhilarate him. He continues to stare into her eyes until the light fades away. When it's over, he turns around and takes a bow for the camera.

He figures an encore-worthy performance deserves one.

CHAPTER 62

I wake with a start. *Shit.* I must have dozed again. I'm clearly not suited for surveillance. Apparently, I did more than doze. It's 5:15 in the morning. I fumble for my phone to check my email and texts. Donnelley sent me a text at 2:47. I quickly open it: "There is no record of Slaughter flying from Logan into Reagan and no record of any rental cars in his name, but we'll be showing his photo to all the rental agencies. I'm heading into the office now."

I quickly dial Donnelley's cell. "Have you notified the rest of the team about Slaughter?"

"Of course," Donnelley says. "I talked to O'Shaughnessy live five minutes ago. D'Antoni too."

"Good. Let's bird-dog the rental-car angle. See you in the office."

It's definitely time to check in with the security teams and then head home for a shower and change of clothes, but I opt to check in with Segal first. He looks dog-tired; his eyes are a puffy mess. He's instantly invigorated when I tell him about Slaughter.

"Bring it on, baby," Segal says.

"You have night optics?" I ask.

"Yes. And I have an extra set if you need them."

"Perfect," I say. "I'll see you later." I clap Greg on the back and make my way over to Jim's team. They are ready and waiting to help however they can.

I call D'Antoni once I'm on the freeway.

"Hey, where are you?" she says.

"Just leaving Catherine's."

"You get any sleep?"

"Believe it or not, yes. So what do you think? Does Slaughter know we're onto him?"

"Maybe. Probably. Thank God we're not in Boston."

"Have you talked to O'Shaughnessy?" I ask.

"Yes, a few minutes ago. He's heading into the office shortly. What about you?"

"I'm heading home for a shower and a change of clothes. I'll pop into the office for a bit to catch up with O'Shaughnessy and the team, but I intend to spend some more time at Catherine's later."

"Good. I figured as much. See you in the office, partner."

CHAPTER 63

He sleeps until seven thirty. He's relaxed, calm, and satiated after last night's activities. Now it's time to break a little sweat and get the blood pumping.

He gets down on the floor and proceeds to do ten sets of a hundred push-ups. The first five sets go smoothly. The next five ignite the fire in his arm and chest muscles.

He loves this pain.

He goes to the minibar, grabs two bottles of ice-cold Evian water, and drains one of the bottles in a single sip. He's parched from the Jameson and wine of last night. He takes his human growth hormone, testosterone supplement, and creatine and washes them all down with the second bottle of water. Then he heads back into the bedroom to do sit-ups and squat thrusts—ten sets of a hundred each.

He removes three airplane bottles of Ketel One and a small bottle of grapefruit juice from the minibar. Then he rinses off his wine glass from the previous night and heads down to the ice machine. Upon his return to the room, he pours the drink slowly, savoring the process. He opens up the blinds to let in some sun, switches on the TV, and scrolls through the channels to NBC. He then flips through each of the major networks, looking for anything related to the Movie Theater Killer, as the press is now calling him. He knew the catchy moniker would be leaked to the press by someone. It was just too deliciously salacious to keep bottled up.

Today has been a long time coming. Countless hours of planning and preparation have gone into this. He needs to execute the plan flawlessly if he is to have any hope of success. Deke has made his job much more difficult, but that means success will be that much sweeter. Oh, he cannot wait. He's ready to move on to the next phase of his life now. Boredom has always been his worst enemy. That's when his mind overwhelms him.

He needs to pick up the long gun from his contact around the corner. Then he'll head to Chevy Chase, where he'll hang out for the day, grab some lunch, and get situated in the woods across the street from the rear of Catherine's house.

It is important that he get settled in the woods by midafternoon. He will need plenty of time to scout the exact location of every single member of the security team at the back of the house, because that is where he intends to breach. He'll deal with security at the front of the property on a need-to basis only. The noise suppressor will minimize sound as he approaches.

Adrenaline courses through his veins. This is what he lives for. It has become crucial to him; it is now what he needs to do merely to survive. He takes a small, clean glass out from the bathroom and pours a couple fingers of Jameson. He is going to have to be careful with the drinking. Even though alcohol doesn't affect him as it does other people and even though his body needs and craves it to calm his mind and simply to function, even he has a saturation point at which it no longer helps. He's been drinking more over the last few weeks—too much, actually—and he needs to watch it.

After showering and dressing from head to toe in black, he heads into the Galleria in search of some more essentials. A short time later, he exits with various complements to his ensemble: a black baseball cap, black bandana, and black eye shade he will use to further obscure his face. Now he's ready.

He quickly packs up when he gets back to the room. He loads the night-vision goggles, bottled water, a bulletproof vest, rope, a flask, syringes, and several loaded magazines into his knapsack. He secures the shoulder rig and razor-sharp eight-inch hunting knife and places his bags in front of the door.

Finally, he goes into the closet to retrieve the body. Rigor has set in, and the corpse is now cold to the touch. Getting her out is awkward, and he's not gentle about it. *She won't mind*, he thinks to himself, and laughs.

It takes a couple minutes to get her onto the bed and underneath the covers. This way, if a cleaning lady ignores the Do Not Disturb sign, she'll simply assume she's walked in on a sleeping guest.

He leaves the hotel with a wide smile and an extra spring in his step.

CHAPTER 64

Supercharged on fear and adrenaline, I enter the office. I call Griff and Barnes; both will be at the Quantico campus by early afternoon. Mobilization is well underway. *Good.* This should free me up to focus on my family's safety.

I grab D'Antoni's coffee and head down to the conference room, which is bustling with activity. It's standing room only. Even O'Shaughnessy has graced us with his presence. The room gradually quiets after my entrance. I hand D'Antoni's coffee to her, and O'Shaughnessy takes center stage.

He gets straight to business. "We have visual confirmation that Slaughter boarded the 1800-hour Delta shuttle flight out of Boston to Reagan last night. Barnes's team has reviewed the video security tapes, and he definitely got on the plane, obviously wearing a wig. Our team has confirmed that he got off that plane at Reagan. We're talking to employees and reviewing security tapes at the car-rental agencies to see if he rented a car. If he did, we can use LoJack to monitor his movements."

I interrupt. "He may have rented a car as a diversionary tactic. Certainly, we'll need to monitor LoJack, but it won't guarantee the perp's location. We're dealing with a seasoned, highly intelligent law enforcement officer. He's well aware of the danger that LoJack poses."

"Very good point," D'Antoni says. "Let's move on to the next item in the order of business. We're going to station additional agents at the residences of those people our perpetrator has threatened, to include at least one agent inside every residence. Agents are already on the scene at each location."

"Tell whoever got my place that I'm sorry the fridge is so empty," I quip. "Also, we need to make it clear to each team that Slaughter has scouted every location already and probably knows exactly where the surveillance has been positioned."

"We may also ask local law enforcement to provide security at all DC-area movie theaters," D'Antoni says.

"I should hear back from the police commissioner shortly on this, but it's a prudent idea," O'Shaughnessy says.

"Slaughter's picture, with and without hair, has been disseminated to local law enforcement and airport security," D'Antoni says. "Hopefully this makes it tougher for him to run."

"He's not running anywhere. He'll die playing his sick, twisted game before he runs. The endgame is all he cares about now," I say. "Let's keep doing what we're doing and monitor developments in real time. He'll make a move today. It would be his ultimate fuck-you to the bureau to take action successfully even though we know he's going to. We're not gonna let that happen. Also, my time is best served at my family's place. We have things under control here. I'm worth a lot more on the ground than I am here, stressing out."

"Does it matter what I think?" O'Shaughnessy asks.

"Not really" is my brutally honest reply.

"We have your house locked up like a drum," O'Shaughnessy says, but I'm not convinced.

"It doesn't matter. He's that good. If he wants to get in, he'll find a way."

"And I guess you're saying that you're better than the agents I've already deployed?"

I look O'Shaughnessy directly in the eyes and wait an uncomfortable few seconds before responding. "I'm not saying that. I'm saying that I know this guy better than anyone else. I need to be on the ground. I intend to be."

O'Shaughnessy opens his mouth, closes it, and opens it again. He glances at D'Antoni. "What do you think?"

"He should be on the ground. I intend to join him."

"You do, huh? Fine. Make sure you get fully outfitted before leaving. Vest, night-vision optics, long guns, radio capability, and whatever else you think is necessary. I want you checking in every hour."

"You got it, boss. And thank you."

Within seconds, I've left the room.

CHAPTER 65

He drives around, looking for a suitable spot in which to pull over. The AR15 transaction went off without a hitch. The guy squeezed him for an extra $1,500, but it was well worth it. His new scope has night optics, and the gun has been expertly sighted in.

It's almost time to party.

He spots a large shopping plaza and decides to pull in there. He must get to work on disabling the LoJack device. Instead of removing the device or covering it in a lead or brass mesh, he installs and implements a GPS tracking jammer that will override any incoming signals and prevent anyone from reaching the device. The jammer will also cancel any outgoing signals and, via software, send a false location to the GPS satellites. That false location will be this, the main shopping center in Tysons Corner.

Sometimes it pays to have techie friends.

Installation takes about forty minutes. Now he can drive to Chevy Chase without fear of being tracked. He reaches into his right breast pocket, takes out the flask, opens up the top, and inhales the savory aroma. Then he takes a three-second gulp. *Oh, that burn is heavenly.* He picks up the sign he has had made up and places it in the parking space.

Man, he loves it when a plan comes together.

CHAPTER 66

D'Antoni pokes her head up over her cube. "I'm leaving with you. No point in sticking around here twiddling my thumbs. You okay with that?"

"Of course. We're gonna set up at Catherine's place?"

"I'm with you, partner."

"Good. Let's get out of here and grab some Starbucks and sandwiches. Before we head out, though, let's stop down at tactical. There are a couple of MP5s with our names on them."

Having met with both teams, D'Antoni and I make the trip to Catherine's and settle into the pool house. Everyone is on high alert, amped on a mix of caffeine and a healthy dose of fear. We're all made aware of both communication channels to ensure coordination. My earpiece irritates me, but it's a necessary evil if I am to stay in touch.

D'Antoni excuses herself and goes into the bathroom to change. I take off my jacket and put my tactical vest on. I check my ankle holster to ensure my .38-caliber is secure. I set my binoculars and infrared optics on a coffee table near the window. The MP5 leans against the wall next to the window. I'll be perched in front of the window for the next several hours.

D'Antoni comes out of the bathroom, dressed head to toe in black. *Damn, she might just be the sexiest tactical operative on Earth.* She sets up much the same as I have, on the opposite side of the room.

"Damn, it's cold in here," she says.

"I know. We never winterized it. I'm surprised she hasn't turned the water off yet."

I get up and pour each of us a large cup of coffee, and then we settle back in.

My phone rings. It's Donnelley. "What's up?" I ask briskly.

"He rented a car from Avis, and we've tracked that car to Tysons Corner," Donnelley says. "We're converging on the exact location now."

"Good. Keep me on speed dial. I doubt you're going to find him there."

CHAPTER 67

He's chosen a remote dirt road that runs parallel to Rock City Park, a forever-wild national park that was created by Congress in 1890, preceded only by Yellowstone and Sequoia. It's a huge tract of land, more than twice the size of Central Park, and has hundreds of hiking and biking trails. Given its close proximity to DC, it gets a lot of foot traffic, but there's still plenty of dense, inhospitable forest that's rarely visited. Most importantly, the park runs to the rear of Catherine's property, where he intends to breach.

He's spent countless hours exploring the park. He's identified a virtually fail-safe way to navigate through it to a wooded spot with excellent views of Catherine's backyard. It's approximately 150 yards from Catherine's property line. There, he sets up a tree stand, which will provide an excellent vantage point.

Preparation is everything.

He spends nearly fifteen minutes surveilling the area in which he intends to leave the car and enter the park. The car is almost invisible, within the tree line. When he's sure the coast is clear, he jumps out of the vehicle, grabs his gear, and heads into the woods at a trot. It takes forty backbreaking, grueling minutes to bushwhack to his hidden spot.

The forest has changed a great deal since he was here last. The beautiful fall foliage has been replaced by stark gray openness. He needs to be careful. The cover the leaves once offered is gone. The heavily leaf-blanketed forest floor will mask his approach, and the more quickly he gets to his secluded location the better.

He's sweating freely now and worries he'll get cold once he's stationary in the tree stand. *At least it'll keep me on my toes*, he thinks. It takes two trips to get his equipment up in the stand. It's big as tree stands go and purposely so. He needs ample room to set up the tripod stand for the AR. He'll be making long-distance shots, so a steady rest is imperative.

He makes himself comfortable. He's going to be here for a while. He pops the top on the flask, breathes in the all-too-familiar aroma, and takes a three-second pull. Ah, the burn is spectacular. Immediately, he relaxes and gets in the zone. It's time to get to work.

He takes his high-powered military-issue binoculars and focuses in on Catherine's backyard. He feels as though he could reach out and touch everyone and everything as it comes into focus. To say that all is clear is an understatement.

He focuses first on the car in the street. He has an unobstructed line of shot at the man in the front seat, but the distance and windshield could make it difficult. Next, he finds the man in the tree line along the southwest corner of the fence. He's dressed head to toe in camo. Even his chair is camo. *Definitely private security*, he thinks. *Almost invisible to the untrained eye.*

He scans the rest of the fence line and surrounding areas. It takes him several minutes to pick up the third man on the northwest corner of the fence line. He's hidden way back in the trees. He will be by far the most difficult shot of the three.

He takes several deep breaths before continuing his surveillance and spends almost twenty minutes covering every inch, every nook and cranny, of the backyard. Nothing.

When his focus turns to the pool house, his heart nearly stops. Sitting front and center, visible through a window, is none other than Deke O'Brien. *Shit, how perfect is this?* Deke can watch his whole family perish right before his eyes.

He reaches for the flask and drinks to his good fortune.

CHAPTER 68

Man, I hate surveillance. I'm just not wired right for it.

I've spent the last hour and a half fastidiously glassing the areas abutting Catherine's property. I try to put myself in the killer's shoes, assess strengths and weaknesses of the security landscape, and identify one or more good breach points. I keep coming back to the same conclusion: the northwest side of the property is the best ingress point. The killer will see this too if he's done his homework.

My cell phone vibrates and jumps on the coffee table next to me. It's Donnelley, and I pick up and hit the speaker button.

"Let's have some good news," I say.

"I wish I could provide that," Donnelley says. "We've surrounded the location indicated by GPS. It's a large parking lot adjacent to a shopping mall—but there's no sign of him. We must have seventy-five people on the ground, searching. A handwritten note was found on a piece of cardboard propped up in an empty parking space. It says, 'I'm here. I'm watching you morons as we speak.' We've extended the search area and are bringing in more assistance."

"Keep pounding the sidewalks," D'Antoni says. "It won't matter. It's a diversion."

"Have you shared the make, model, and license plate information of the rental with local law enforcement?" I ask.

"Yes."

"Chevy Chase?"

"Yes."

"He disabled the LoJack," I say. "Probably installed some kind of GPS-jamming device. It's not hard to do with a little research. Keep the updates coming."

The call ends. I get up and refill our coffee cups.

"How you doing, partner?" I say.

"Just dandy. What do you say we switch it up for a bit?"

"Sounds good."

We switch positions.

CHAPTER 69

He's fairly certain he has identified each and every member of the security detail at the back of the house. His plan is to breach on the northwest corner. He'll take out the man in the woods on that side first, and then he'll move on to the guy in camo on the northwest corner. He intends to save the guy in the car for last. He assumes everyone is wearing a vest, so head shots make the most sense. *Easier said than done.*

He takes out the flask and rewards himself with a healthy chug; he feels its impact immediately, and his nerves relax.

Time to have some fun. He takes out the burner phone with which he videotaped last night's adventures. He pulls up the texting function and quickly drafts a message to Deke, attaching the video he made. This is perfect. He should be able to watch Deke's reaction through the binoculars in real time.

He gives the message one last read, hits the Send button, and then reaches for his binoculars and locks his gaze upon the window where he saw Deke minutes beforehand.

Well, well, well. Look what we've got here. An attractive woman has taken Deke's seat. It's D'Antoni—no doubt about it. *Wow, how lucky.*

All the players in the game are now present and accounted for.

CHAPTER 70

The ping of an incoming text jars me back to reality. I put down the binoculars, which are becoming less useful by the minute as the sun begins its descent. *A 617 area code. Oh boy. Here we go.* I jump out of my chair and head over to D'Antoni. I hand her the phone and lean in over her shoulder so we can read the text together. She reads it out loud:

> Hey, Dekey boy. Did you take my advice and get back on Catherine's good side? I hope you got the chance to say goodbye to your kids. Not that Patrick would understand, but at least you would feel better. They're on very borrowed time, my friend.
>
> I threw a little pre-party last night. A warm-up of sorts. I even captured the whole thing for your viewing pleasure. Please don't show this to D'Antoni. I want her to see my junk for the first time up close and personal. Grab some soda and popcorn, and settle in for the show. Enjoy.
>
> Be seeing you soon. The Tysons Corner Ritz is the balls, especially the club floor. MTK

D'Antoni and I glance at each other, our eyes darting with nervousness. Neither of us wants to open the video, but we don't have the luxury of being able to ignore it. D'Antoni hits the Play icon, and I prepare myself for the worst.

The video is a little more than eight minutes long. My stomach churns, and I feel an acidic burn at the back of my throat. I close my eyes for several seconds in a bid to clear the image from my mind. Unfortunately, it'll be with me for a long time.

I quickly forward the text to the entire team, including the forensic techs. Then I call Donnelley on speaker, and I ask him to patch in O'Shaughnessy.

When O'Shaughnessy gets on the line, D'Antoni jumps right in. "We just received a video from Slaughter. Check your phones. We've sent it to the team. He kills a woman in the video. He shows his face, bald head and all—no disguise. Obviously, he knows we're onto him, and he no longer needs to take precautions. As you'll see from the text, he mentions the Ritz Carlton Tysons Corner and the club floor."

"Seventh floor," I say. "You should send a team there. It's too late to save his latest victim, but maybe Slaughter left some clues."

"Don't you guys wanna be on the scene?" O'Shaughnessy asks.

"No time," I say. "He's making his move today. This is a diversion, plain and simple. I wouldn't be surprised if his eyes are on Catherine's house right now. At some point, I think it'd be a good idea to have local law enforcement scour the wooded areas surrounding Catherine's property. I've had the feeling all day that we're being watched. I could have sworn I saw a lens flash in the trees on the far side of Catherine's house about an hour ago, but then it was gone."

I let D'Antoni and O'Shaughnessy talk for a while before joining in the conversation again. "I'm going to play a hunch. I'm pretty sure—almost positive—this freak is watching the house as we speak. I'm going to come busting out of the pool house like I'm on a mission and leaving. Then I'll sneak back onto the property after dark."

"I like it," D'Antoni says. "The quicker we can draw this guy out the better. Are you planning on coming back to the pool house, or are you going to set up inside?"

"I guess I'll leave that up to Catherine. I wanna tell her to pack some bags and leave, but I feel she's safer here than anywhere else."

"Agreed," D'Antoni says.

"Okay," I say. "Game time. Boss, let us know what they find at the crime scene. We'll check back in about an hour."

The call finished, I stand up and stretch. I walk over to the thermos and pour half a cup of coffee, which I chug down. I walk over to D'Antoni and place my hand on her shoulder. "Do me a favor: pay special attention to that wooded area directly across the street. That is where I thought I saw something. I never said anything before because I figured my eyes were playing tricks on me. And be careful. Shoot first. Don't hesitate. He's a born killer. He's probably wearing a vest, so aim high and tight. I'll check in every fifteen minutes."

"Be careful, partner," D'Antoni says.

"Always."

We fist-bump, and I make a production of leaving the pool house with gun and equipment in hand. I run over to the car on the back side of the house. I do not try to make myself a difficult target. I need to sell this to the killer.

Jim is in the driver's seat. I tell him exactly what's going on and what my plan is. We fist-bump, and I jog around to the front of the house, where I catch up with our team. I commandeer their car and rip out of the neighborhood at high speed. I stop about three blocks away and slowly start back.

Now is as good a time as any to call Catherine. I can't just sneak into the house. She picks up on the first ring, her voice tense. "Was that you I saw running around the house?"

"Yes. I should've told you I was here. Things are just crazy. Listen, I'd like to come into the cellar to set up. I have a key to the outside door."

"Why?"

"You and the kids will not even know I'm there. I promise. I won't come upstairs until after they're in bed. It's important, Catherine. Trust me. This is no bullshit. I have reason to believe our guy may be in the area."

"I don't fucking believe this. You mean to tell me your own kids are in danger? How does that make you feel?"

"Horrible. Absolutely horrible. But you guys are safe. I promise. No one is getting anywhere near you. Don't let the kids into the cellar. Everything is gonna be fine."

"Yeah, well, you'd better tell that to Sean. She's insisting on talking to you. Normally, I would stick to my guns, but screw it. She knows something's going on."

"I thought—"

"Hi, Daddy. Are you getting better? Mommy said you've been really, really sick. I miss you. Patrick does too. Mommy said that we have to stay upstairs until a dangerous man is caught. I'm scared, Daddy."

"Hey, cutie. I'm feeling a lot better. I miss you too. Nobody is going to hurt you. Daddy always gets the bad guy. Can you do me a favor?"

"What, Daddy?"

"Can you look after Patrick and Mommy for me? I have to go catch the bad guy."

"Yes, Daddy."

"I love you, partner. Give Patrick a kiss for me."

"Love you too, Daddy."

CHAPTER 71

He takes the long gun out of the bag. The night-vision scope he's purchased is military sniper grade, the best on the market. So is the noise suppressor. It doesn't completely silence a shot, but it does the job. He'll be able to conceal his shooting location and not draw attention to himself.

He sets up the tripod rifle rest next and then plays around with some different shooting positions. When he's finally happy, he settles in and scopes each of his targets. Deke left the pool house more than forty-five minutes ago, leaving D'Antoni all by her lonesome. Unfortunately, he'll have to take her out with the long gun to ensure safe entry to the property. Damn, he had such plans for her too.

He will let it get a little darker before making a move. He drinks deeply from his flask. *Oh, that's better.* A feeling of calm and serenity envelops him.

It's almost game time.

CHAPTER 72

I wait until it's completely dark before I approach the house. I have my night optics on and can see as well as I do in daylight. I spend ten minutes scanning the surrounding areas, looking for anything out of place.

Only when I'm comfortable do I make my move toward the cellar. It takes a couple seconds to work the key in the lock, but then I'm inside. It's pitch black in the stairwell, but I can see just fine. I descend the short flight of stairs and make my way over to a window with a view of the backyard. I need to bring a chair over and stand on it to see clearly. Then I reach for my phone and call D'Antoni.

"Hey, partner," I say. "I'm inside, down in the cellar. You see anything?"

"Nah. At least I don't think so. I've been getting a weird feeling just like you. Probably just nerves."

"You hear from Donnelley or O'Shaughnessy?"

"Yeah. They found the body. No sign of Slaughter and nothing out of the ordinary."

"Be alert, D'Antoni. Tonight's the night. I'm sure of it."

CHAPTER 73

He lets another forty-five minutes go by. *The darker the better.* When night has fallen, he twists his neck from side to side. Now is as good a time as any.

He positions the rifle against the nook of his shoulder; it feels like an extension of his body. He slows his breathing and carefully brings the target into sight. The guy has a hand to his mouth, stifling a yawn. *Don't fret, buddy. Sleep will come soon enough.*

The high-tech night-vision scope lets him know the exact distance: 225 yards. *Piece of cake,* he thinks. He can hit a silver dollar at that distance nine out of ten times if the wind is right. Conditions are ideal tonight; there is hardly a breeze in the air.

The scope tells him exactly how much adjustment is necessary for the distance. He settles on the victim's upper neck. He figures it's still a kill shot, even if he's slightly high or low.

He takes a deep breath and then exhales slowly and squeezes the trigger. *Thwump.*

He watches the body crumple. He stays on the body for a five count and sees no movement.

Quickly, he pivots the rifle to his left and searches for the man at the southwest corner. He's looking at his phone. *Bad boy,* he thinks. *One hundred ninety-two yards.* This time, he focuses on the head, his confidence up. With a deep breath and slow exhalation, he squeezes the trigger. *Thwump.*

Wow, he thinks to himself. *Just like shooting a melon.* The man's head has literally exploded. But there is no time to gloat.

He pivots left again. Windshields can be tricky. This isn't a long shot, however. His practice has shown him that a high-powered rifle shot of less than two hundred yards deflects so little that any deflection can be attributed to shooter error.

He sights in the lower forehead of the driver. *One hundred seventy-four yards. Relax.* He breathes in deeply, exhales slowly once again, and squeezes the trigger. *Thwump.* The driver's body jerks sideways, but he keeps the scope locked on the body for a five count. *Dead for sure.*

Now for the fun part.

He pivots to his right and brings the pool house into focus. This part bothers him. Simply shooting and killing D'Antoni isn't enough. His original plans were much grander than that.

He reaches for the new flask, pops the top, and drinks. *Ah, better.* He finds D'Antoni quickly. She's positioned herself right in front of the window and is now glassing the area with her binoculars. Shit, she seems to be looking right at him. He needs to act fast. At the last second, he decides to try for a nonfatal but disabling shot. This way, he can stick to the plan.

He sights in the portion of D'Antoni's left shoulder not protected by her vest. *Careful.* He squeezes the trigger. *Thwump.* D'Antoni is spun right out of her seat. For ten seconds, he keeps the scope locked on where she was. Nothing.

He leaps out of the chair with catlike agility. He throws on his night optics and his tactical vest, puts the silencer on his nine-millimeter, checks his backpack to make sure he has everything he needs, hoists it over his shoulders, and then starts down the tree as quickly as he can. He leaves the long gun and the carrying case where they lie. Any shooting that takes place from now on will be up close and personal—his city-issued nine-millimeter will have to do.

He's across the street and over the fence in under a minute. *So far so good.* He makes his way to the pool house in a low crouch.

CHAPTER 74

I hear a soft groan in my earpiece. *What the heck was that?* "D'Antoni, you there? D'Antoni, it's Deke."

Nothing.

"D'Antoni?"

Still nothing.

"Joe? Who's out there?"

There is only silence. Dead silence.

I switch over to the FBI channel. "Greg, come in."

"What's up, Deke?"

"I can't get anyone on Joe's team up on the radio, and I can't raise D'Antoni. I heard a weird noise in my earpiece, and I could have sworn I heard glass breaking. I'm headed out for a look. Please send backup, and send another team member inside with my family."

I'm out seconds later. I look left and right as I sprint toward the pool house. I see nothing in front of me and nothing in my peripheral vision. About five yards from the pool house, I come to an abrupt stop. I cannot see anything through the window that now faces me. I crouch down and approach the pool house cautiously.

When I get to the pool house door, I kick it open and quickly get out of the way. Nothing. "D'Antoni! D'Antoni!" I scream.

Nothing.

Fuck this. I execute a dive roll through the door and come up in a kneeling stance with my MP5 at the ready.

A white-hot flash ignites before my eyes, and I'm temporarily blinded. What feels like a burning-hot flame explodes through my left shoulder, knocking me off my feet and onto my back.

I feel as though I've been stabbed in the shoulder with a white-hot poker. In reality, I know I've been shot. I rip the goggles from my eyes with my left hand. My entire left arm is useless.

Gradually, my vision returns.

I look around. The first thing I see is D'Antoni; she's hanging from a beam that runs across the center of the ceiling. Her shirt and bra have been ripped off, and something is written in red ink across her chest. Her face is turning blue before my eyes. Her eyes look as if they will pop out of her head at any minute.

I jump up as quickly as I can—no easy feat with one arm. I rush to my partner and lift the lower half of her body. I scan the room to make sure the killer's not there—I think I heard him run by and out the open door, but everything happened so fast that it's difficult to be sure. Looking up into D'Antoni's face, I can't tell whether she's alive or dead. Spittle drips from her lips, and her entire face is contorted in pain. Several seconds later, a pained cough escapes her mouth, and I thank God.

It takes a couple minutes for me to cut her down while working with one arm, but I manage.

I place her gently on the ground and try to assess her injuries. I jump up, grab her ripped T-shirt from the floor, and quickly cover her as best as I can. She has a nasty bullet wound in her left shoulder, and I'm going to need to check for an exit wound.

I touch the right side of her face and look into her eyes. She can't speak. "You're going to be okay. You're too tough for that moron."

She blinks, opens her mouth, and tries to speak, but her voice fails her. She swallows a couple times and finally forces the words out: "Your family."

"I know, I know. I need to check you first. Honey, I need to see what he wrote on your chest, and I need to see if there's an exit wound."

She blinks again and then removes the shirt with her right hand.

I choke back bile as I read the message. "The little retard is next" is scrawled in red magic marker across her chest. I gently and slowly lift D'Antoni into a sitting position and look behind her for an exit wound. I find one about three inches lower than the entry wound. That makes sense if the shooter was shooting downward at her.

"What's it say?" she says weakly.

"I have to go help my family," I say, my face inches from hers. "You have a clean exit wound. It doesn't look like there's any organ involvement, and no major artery has been hit. Are you gonna be okay?"

"Get outta here," she says. "I'll be fine. How about you? You're hit too."

"No time," I say. "I gotta get back to the house. Can you radio everyone to converge there?"

"Go!" she says.

I jump up and retrieve D'Antoni's gun. I take my jacket off and carefully wrap it around her, buttoning it at the top. Then I put the gun in her right hand, kiss the top of her head, and sprint out the door. I do not slow down as I barrel toward the house.

CHAPTER 75

Fuck, that was close. No sooner did he pull D'Antoni off the ground and tie her to the overhead beam than Deke came busting in. Thankfully, Deke was wearing night optics. All he had to do was flip on the room light to blind him. Then he put a bullet in him. He doesn't think it was a lethal shot. He sure hopes not.

His mouth is killing him. The bitch caught him flush on the chin with a roundhouse kick when he burst through the door. It knocked out one of his front lower teeth and loosened a couple more. It wasn't until he dug his hand into her injured right shoulder that he regained control. *Tough bitch, though.* It was nearly orgasmic, looking her in the eyes while he lifted her off the ground with the rope and noose. The look on her face when she realized how screwed she was will be with him forever.

He opts to go in through the basement door. Two quick silenced shots at the locking mechanism and a well-placed heel kick get him inside. He needs to move fast. He pads up the basement stairs as quietly as possible. He puts his ear to the door. He hears voices—two males speaking at the same time. They seem to be a couple rooms away.

As quietly as he can, he opens the door, leading with the silenced nine-millimeter. He's glad he's wearing a vest; this is likely to get nasty quickly. He makes himself as low as he can and walks forward.

He pokes his head around the foyer into the open living room, where two agents are listening to the chatter coming through their earpieces. Both are wearing vests, so he'll need to make head shots in quick succession.

That shouldn't be an issue.

He assumes a kneeling position and shoots one agent precisely between the eyes just as the other man turns his gaze toward him. He then pivots the gun left and double taps the trigger on the second agent, catching him once in the throat and once in the face. He's up and across the room in a blink and puts the second agent out of his misery with a head shot.

Sirens wail in the distance.

He realizes he must act quickly, not worrying about getting out of the house alive.

There's no way he'll allow himself to be arrested, and there's still much left to do. Any chance of escape is evaporating. *That's all right,* he thinks. Going out in a blaze of glory will merely add to his fame.

He grabs the flask from his pocket and takes a generous gulp. After all, it might be his last.

He turns toward the staircase and looks upward. He sees an agent, who is partway down the stairs, a half second too late, and he takes a shot that hits the center of his chest before he has the gun even halfway up. He stumbles back but has the wherewithal to dive to the left, out of the shooter's line of sight. Even with the vest on, he feels as if he's been slammed in the chest with an aluminum baseball bat. He gasps and chokes for air; the breath has been knocked out of him.

Pointing his gun, he doesn't take his eyes off the area the agent will likely need to cross to get at him. Sure enough, the agent is there a second later.

With another double tap, a pink mist hangs in the air like a cloud where the agent was standing less than a second ago.

Now the wailing sirens sound as if they're right outside the house. He needs to move. He hugs the wall and takes the stairs two at a time. When he reaches the top, he stops to listen. He's been in the house twice before and knows the layout well. The master bedroom is at the far end of the hall. Sean's room is down the hall on the left; Patrick's room is on the right.

He inches forward, listening intently. He hears Catherine's voice coming from Patrick's bedroom. She's saying something he can't make out. He stops right outside Patrick's door, which is closed. He tries to open it, but it's locked, so he puts two shots through the lock and kicks the door open.

No one is in sight. Then he hears whimpering from the closet. He tiptoes over to the closet door and then rips it open.

Doing his best Jack Nicholson impersonation and leering wildly, he says, "Honey, I'm home!"

Catherine has both kids tucked in behind her. *How touching.* She's trying to protect them and make sure they aren't frightened. *Noble, really.* Then she leaps from the ground and is on him in two strides. She's unbelievably strong for her size—but no match for him. He smashes the pistol against the right side of her head, and she crumples, dazed, or maybe even unconscious, to the floor. He decides not to bother with the sux. He could shoot her, but he wants her to witness the death of her children.

He's on the children a second later. They are clearly terrified; their eyes are practically bulging out of their heads. Their expressions are more delicious than the best sex he's ever had.

He picks Sean up by the scruff of the neck and throws her into the wall on the left side of the bed. She hits the wall five feet off the ground with a sickening thud.

He's got to give the little shit credit, though. She's crying, but she's doing it quietly; she's not sobbing and wailing. *Tough little girl. Wow. The kid is actually crawling over to check on her mommy. How touching.*

It's time to get back to the business at hand and destroy Deke's reason to live.

He approaches the little retard with an ear-to-ear grin. Patrick is crying too and shaking all over. *Perfect.* He can't wait to tell Deke that Patrick knew exactly what was going on as he died. He talks to

Patrick in a soothing voice while undoing his belt, trying desperately to contain his bloodlust and only just succeeding.

He finds it easy to secure the belt around Patrick's neck. The boy is crying so loudly now that he's momentarily distracted from the task at hand.

At that moment, Catherine chooses to launch herself at him.

She grabs a vase from the coffee table next to where she has fallen and smashes it into the back of his head a split second before he can react. The belt slips from his hand, and he stumbles backward.

He shakes his head groggily from side to side, trying to regain his bearings. His focus clears just as a searing, ripping pain tears through his upper left shoulder. As he slowly turns his head, he sees that a large shard of the broken vase is sticking out of his flesh. The pain is excruciating, but white-hot anger helps to mask it. He pulls the piece of jagged glass out of his arm with his right hand, badly cutting his palm in the process. His knees buckle with the pain, but he maintains focus—barely.

He feels the warm, wet rush of blood flowing down his chest and back. The wound is bleeding profusely. Did she hit an artery? He pivots toward her, feints left, and lashes out with a vicious right kick that catches Catherine squarely in the sternum. The force of the blow lifts her off her feet and knocks her backward.

He turns his attention back to Patrick. He grabs the belt and lifts the child up into the air as pure rage masks his pain. He walks over to Catherine, smiling with the wide eyes of a demon, showing off his prize.

Catherine struggles to get back to her feet. She can't do it. The kick propelled her into the wall headfirst, and everything is spinning. She can only stare in horror at what unfolds. He stands over her, hoisting Patrick higher and higher. He locks eyes with Catherine, who's sobbing now, pleading.

"Look at your little retard," he says. "I'm doing the world a favor."

CHAPTER 76

I explode into Patrick's room, screaming at the top of my lungs. I don't even know what I'm screaming, but it doesn't matter. I'm not sure how many times I pull the trigger, but Slaughter goes down like a stack of books with a gaping wound in the middle of his face. Blood is everywhere.

Patrick's head hits the floor with a thud when Slaughter drops him.

I sweep Patrick up with my right hand and somehow manage to use my useless left to loosen the belt around his neck. He's gasping and choking. I bury my face in his neck. I kiss him and whisper that everything is okay. "Daddy's here. No one will ever hurt you again."

Gradually, Patrick regains his breath and buries his face in my throbbing shoulder. He cries softly. I cry right along with him and kiss him, telling him how much I love him and how proud I am of him. I don't know how long we stay like that. Catherine eventually pushes me out of the way so she can be with her baby.

Choked coughing comes from my left. I turn toward it and stare into a monster's eyes. He's trying to smile, but the pain must be unbearable. He gasps out something I can barely understand at first.

"He's just a retard. I was doing you a favor, pal."

"Well, you're just a pathetic copycat. You couldn't make it on the ball field, as a cop, with the ladies, or even as a killer. You're an embarrassment, really—a giant failure. No one will even remember you. I've already forgotten you." Then I put a bullet through his forehead.

The room floods with agents and cops. I look to the door, and there's D'Antoni with an ear-to-ear grin. Her left arm is dangling limply, and tears are streaming down her face.

I feel a light tug on my shirt and look down to see my other little miracle staring up at me. She isn't crying—my tough little girl hardly ever cries—but she reaches for me to pick her up. I sweep her up with my good arm and bury my face in her neck. I smell Johnson's baby shampoo and soap. Nothing has ever smelled so good, and I've never felt luckier in my entire life.

Sean looks up at me, her eyes wide with amazement. "You got the bad guy, Daddy. I knew you would."

"I couldn't have done it without your help, princess. I'm so proud of you."

She kisses me wetly on the cheek, and the floodgates open. I'm sobbing now. I bring Sean over to her mommy, who takes her from my arms. Catherine meets my gaze and whispers, "Thank you."

I touch her shoulder. "Let the paramedics get a look at you soon. We can all ride to the hospital together."

My family is safe. That's all that matters.

D'Antoni touches my shoulder with her good hand. I hug her gently and tell her over and over again how sorry I am.

CHAPTER 77

It has been two days since my world almost came crashing down—or, as I prefer to think of it, my new life began. My arm's sore, but it's nothing I can't handle. I refused pain medication at the hospital, or at least anything other than Tylenol. I didn't want to take any chances. I'm in a good spot now. The bullet wound to my upper left arm was a pretty routine through-and-through, with little muscle impairment. I should be back to full health and function in about six weeks. In the meantime, I can enjoy my paid disability leave—and maybe make a dent in the latest installment of the Sean Patrick series.

D'Antoni did not fare quite as well as I did. The high-powered rifle round caused muscle damage to her left shoulder, and while it's too early to tell for sure, there might be some residual nerve damage as well. She underwent fairly major surgery and has a long road of rehabilitation ahead. She's likely to be out of commission for at least ten to twelve weeks, probably longer, according to the doctors. However, they obviously don't know her like I do. She discharged herself from the hospital early and against doctors' orders, forcing me to be complicit in her escape by providing transportation.

I intend to spend a lot of time with D'Antoni in the coming weeks, both in Georgetown and up in Lake Placid. It's already a winter wonderland up in Placid. Getting away for a bit will do both of us a world of good. There's something rejuvenating about the Adirondacks and Lake Placid in particular. As tough as D'Antoni is, I know she's hurting. Anyone would be. She nearly lost her life while protecting my family, and I'm forever in her debt. This beautiful, tough woman, the only partner I intend to ever work with, stuck by me when most would have bailed. Heck, I told her to bail. I'll give her all the time she needs and more to see her through this. I'm just glad I still have her in my life.

Catherine suffered several broken ribs and a concussion. She's already up and running around, acting as though nothing happened. To describe her as tough doesn't do her justice. Patrick and Sean escaped with minor physical injuries, but only time will reveal the mental toll this experience has taken. Time is on their side, though, and I intend to be there with them every step of the way.

I feel blessed that Catherine is the mother of my children, and I hope I can be half the parent she is. My kids deserve it. Shit, I deserve it. Our journey together as husband and wife is over, but our lives are forever entwined through the love of our children.

She's angry—justifiably so—that I once again brought the horrors of my work home.

But hopefully time will heal. I'm living proof that it usually does.

One thing I know for certain is that I will never, ever give up on life again.

How many people get a second chance?

If you enjoyed *Second Chance*, please share your thoughts on Amazon by leaving a review.

For more free and discounted e-books every week, sign up for our newsletter.

Follow us on Twitter, Facebook, and Instagram.

ABOUT THE AUTHOR

Greg Byrne worked as a corporate tax partner for Pricewater-houseCoopers LLP in New York City until 2015 assisting dozens of fortune 500 companies with complex tax issues. He then moved back to his hometowns, Saratoga Spring, NY, and Lake Placid, NY, with his family, to work for himself and pursue his real passion, writing.

Lightning Source UK Ltd.
Milton Keynes UK
UKHW010734110621
385337UK00001B/162